PRAISE FOR THE
USA TODAY BESTSELLING
AMISH QUILT SHOP MYSTERIES

"Isabella Alan captures Holmes County and the Amish life in a mystery that is nothing close to plain and simple, all stitched together with heart."

—Avery Aames, Agatha Award–winning author of the Cheese Shop Mysteries

"Who can best run a quilt shop in Holmes County's Amish country—an *Englisch* outsider or only the Amish themselves? With its vast cast of English and Amish characters in fictional Rolling Brook, Ohio, Isabella Alan's *Murder, Plain and Simple* will be a dead-certain hit with devotees of cozy mysteries."

—P. L. Gaus, author of the Amish-Country Mysteries

"The Amish community and their traditions are nicely portrayed, adding great warmth and authenticity to the novel. . . . Angie's fearless sleuthing keeps the action moving. [Her] relationship and family drama further enhance the plot." —*RT Book Reviews* (4 stars)

"At turns playful and engaging as the well-intentioned *Englischer* strives to rescue her Ohioan Amish friends from a bad fate. . . . A satisfyingly complex cozy."

—*Library Journal*

"This is a community you'd like to visit, a shop where you'd find welcome . . . and people you'd want for [. . .] f interesting information [. . .] rwoven into the story line [. . .] as Angie does."

—Kings River Life Magazine

Also by Isabella Alan

Murder, Handcrafted

AN AMISH QUILT SHOP MYSTERY

Isabella Alan

AN OBSIDIAN MYSTERY

OBSIDIAN
Published by New American Library,
an imprint of Penguin Random House LLC
375 Hudson Street, New York, New York 10014

This book is an original publication of New American Library.

First Printing, June 2016

ISBN 978-0-451-47503-9

Printed in the United States of America
10 9 8 7 6 5 4 3 2

Penguin
Random
House

For the Fisher family
Kathy, Jeff, Becca, and Sam

ACKNOWLEDGMENTS

As always *danki* to my wonderful readers who love the Amish Quilt Shop Mysteries. I love receiving your notes and messages about Angie, Sheriff Mitchell, Oliver, Dodger, and of course, Petunia. It is because of you that I have loved writing this series.

Special thanks to my amazing editor, Laura Fazio, and superagent, Nicole Resciniti, who let me include a Bigfoot subplot to an Amish mystery. I know you were both a little worried about the idea, but with your help, it fits perfectly into the world of Rolling Brook that we have created together.

As always, love and gratitude to my plotter in crime, Mariellyn Grace, and my wonderful beta-reader, Molly Carroll. Thanks too to my feline editors, Reepicheep (Cheeps) and Mr. Tumnus (Tummy) for endless inspiration. Cheeps makes his cover model debut on this book as the inspiration for Dodger.

Thank you to the Grace and Queen families. You are my Bigfoot enthusiasts, and I hope my take on the myth makes you laugh.

Love to my family, Andy, Nicole, Isabella, and

Andrew, for supporting me through an extremely busy year.

Finally, I thank my Heavenly Father, for allowing me to spend so much of my time in a world of laughter and imagination.

Chapter One

The phrase "It looked so easy on YouTube" would go down in infamy in the annals of Braddock family history. It was what my father had said twice after he attempted to demo my mother's kitchen in their new home in Holmes County.

The second phrase would be "You have no idea what your father's been up to."

I held my cell phone away from my ear as my mother screeched that last statement at me.

Mattie Miller, my twenty-two-year-old shop assistant, stocked the needle display in the front corner of the shop and raised her eyebrows at me, and I rolled my eyes in return. It was still morning and Running Stitch, my Amish quilt shop nestled in the center of Sugartree Street in Rolling Brook, Ohio, had just opened for the day. Through the large front window, I saw business on the street was beginning to pick up as early May tourists strolled from shop to shop. As usual, the first stop on any tourist's itinerary was Miller's Amish Bakery across the road from Running Stitch. I could see my best friend and Mattie's sister-in-law, Rachel, doing brisk business. A line of customers extended out of the bakery and curved along the sidewalk.

Oliver, my black-and-white French bulldog, lifted his head from his dog pillow, watching us with his big brown eyes. Dodger, my gray-and-white cat, jumped up onto the cutting table in the middle of the room and pranced back and forth.

"Get down," Mattie hissed at the cat.

Dodger sat in the middle of the cutting table and began giving himself a thorough bath. It was a normal day at Running Stitch, except for my mother's hysterical phone call. Then again, that wasn't that unusual either.

When Mom took a breath, I moved the phone closer to my ear. "What did he do?"

"He threw his back out while removing the kitchen cabinets. I told him over and over to let me call a professional, but no, he insisted he could do it himself. I knew this would be a disaster," she groaned.

"Is he all right?" Worry crept into my voice. Like my mother, I had wanted to discourage my father when he announced that he would be doing the demolition portion of my parents' massive kitchen renovation. As a former corporate executive, Dad was a wiz with numbers, spreadsheets, and board meetings—DIY stuff, not so much. In the end, I said nothing because he had looked so pleased with himself to be taking on this home improvement project. I hadn't had the heart to tell him it was a *really* bad idea. Ever since my father retired, he had been floundering in the search of a purpose. He finally thought he had found it in my mother's kitchen remodel. Who was I to squash that ambition?

"He's in X-ray right now." My mother sounded close to tears, and my mother never cried.

"Oh no," I groaned. "Do you want me to come to the hospital? Is that where you are?"

"No, we're at an X-ray clinic. That's where our doctor sent us when I called and explained what happened. Then, we have an appointment with the doctor. He wanted the X-rays first."

"Is Dad okay?"

"He will be. I'm sure." She paused as if trying to collect herself. "If only that man wasn't so stubborn."

"What do you need me to do?" I asked.

"Go to the house. When your father knocked down the cabinet, he broke the French doors leading into the backyard. I need you to wait there until I can get home and figure out what to do about the doors."

Outside the shop, I saw Jonah, my best childhood friend, riding by in his market wagon. The bed of the wagon was filled with crates of berries, and another Amish man with dark brown hair whom I didn't know sat on one of the crates. Jonah tipped his black Amish hat at some tourists, who snapped a picture at him.

Jonah would know what to do. I had to catch him.

"Mom, I'll be there as soon as I can." I said a quick good-bye and headed for the door. "Mattie, I'll be right back."

"What happened?" Her gray eyes filled with concern as she smoothed her hands over her plain lavender dress and black apron. There wasn't the tiniest wrinkle in the fabric nor was there a loose piece of chestnut hair from her impeccable bun.

I didn't stop to reply because I was hoping to catch Jonah before he disappeared from sight. I ran out of the shop. On the sidewalk, I called Jonah's name.

He pulled back on the reins of his horse and turned in his bench seat to look at me.

I waved. As I ran up the sidewalk toward him, he maneuvered his horse to the side of the road so that the sedan behind him could pass.

"Angie?" Jonah asked with the usual sparkle of humor in his dark eyes. "What's got you all worked up this morning?"

The man in the bed of the wagon shifted his seat on the crate of berries. Now that I was closer to him, I saw that he was much younger than I first thought. He couldn't be more than twenty and was clean-shaven. In the Amish world a beardless face meant that he was unmarried.

I rested my hand on the side of the wagon. "It's my dad. He hurt his back while demolishing their kitchen."

Jonah grimaced and touched his sandy-blond beard that stopped at the second button of his plain navy-colored shirt. "What is your father doing a thing like that for?"

My fingers dug into the side of the wagon. "He thought he could manage it."

Jonah shook his head. He had tried to teach my dad woodworking after Mom and Dad moved back to Ohio.

It had not gone well. It could have been worse, I supposed. Both Dad and Jonah came out of the experience with all their limbs intact.

"Mom said there is a broken door," I said. "I need to go over to their house to see what needs to be done."

"And you want me to come?" He smiled.

"Well, yeah." I smiled.

He laughed. "Not a problem. Let me drop off these berries at the pie factory, and I'll head straight there." He nodded to the young man in the back of the wagon. "Do you mind if Eban comes with me?"

"That's fine as long as you beat my mother there." I nodded to the young man. "I'm Angie Braddock."

"Eban Hoch," he said with smiling light blue eyes. "It is *gut* to meet you. I am new to the county and Jonah is showing me around."

"Oh, where are you from?" I asked.

"A little ways up north in Wayne County."

Jonah held up the reins. "We had better go if we want to beat your mother to the house."

I stepped back from the wagon. "Thanks, Jonah."

He winked and flicked the reins. The wagon and horse clattered down the street. I hurried back to Running Stitch. When I stepped in the shop, I was happy to see Mattie with a customer, who was closely examining my Aunt Eleanor's stitches on a Goosefoot quilt.

I grabbed my hobo bag from the drawer under the sales counter and slipped it over my arm.

Mattie said something to the customer and stepped over to me. "Are you going out?"

I nodded and gave her a brief description of what was going on with my parents.

She covered her mouth. "Is your father okay?"

"I hope so. I don't really know for sure. He was getting X-rays when Mom called." I clicked my tongue. "Come, Oliver," I said to my Frenchie, who was snoozing in his dog bed in the window. "We're going to Grandma and Grandpa's."

The dog jumped to his feet. He loved going to my parents' house. He mostly enjoyed this because my father constantly fed the little black-and-white dog beef jerky while we were there.

"You're leaving Dodger here?" Mattie didn't even bother to hide her distaste. She and my gray-and-white cat had a strained relationship.

"I can't take him to my parents' house," I said. "Remember the last time he was there? He shredded my mom's curtains, and she talked about it for weeks."

Mattie pursed her lips. The cat still sitting on the cutting table cocked his head to one side as if in challenge. Mattie's frown deepened.

Those two would be at each other's throats the moment I stepped out of the shop.

"Dodger will be fine, and you won't even have time to know what he's up to. The street is filling up. I think it's going to be a busy day."

"That's what I'm afraid of. That's when he gets into the most trouble." She eyed the cat with suspicion.

Oliver waited for me by the door.

"I'll be back as soon as I can," I told my assistant. "Just call my cell if you need anything."

"You'll be back by one, won't you?" Mattie asked nervously. "I'm filling in at the pie factory later today, remember?"

"Yes, don't worry. I'll do my best to be back at one. I'll call you if I can't get away."

Mattie chewed on her lip.

I didn't have time to ask her what was wrong. Sometimes I wonder whether things would have gone much differently if I had.

Chapter Two

A half hour later, Oliver and I stood in the middle of my parents' kitchen. I held the Frenchie in my arms, surveying the damage. Half of the upper cabinet hung precariously from what looked like one screw. The rest of it was out on the back deck. The panes of glass in one side of the French doors were shattered. There was glass all over the tiled floor.

I removed my cell phone from my pocket and made a call. Holmes County Sheriff James Mitchell picked up on the first ring.

"It must be a slow crime day," I said.

"That's how I like it," he replied with warmth in his voice.

"I wish I could say it was a slow day for me too."

"What happened?" His voice was immediately tense. I couldn't say I blamed Mitchell. I had a reputation for stumbling into some tight scraps. Being my boyfriend and the county sheriff couldn't be easy.

I gave him the short version of what happened, staring out at the unsalvageable French doors as I spoke.

"Do you want me to come there?" he asked.

"No," I said. "I mean, I would love to see you, but Jonah is on the way. He and I will be able to clean up the mess."

"If you're sure." There was the sound of shuffling papers. "I'm swamped in paperwork at the moment."

In my mind's eye, I could see him sitting at his desk in the sheriff's department with a huge stack of papers in front of him waiting for his signature. "Don't worry about it, Mitchell. I'll call you when everything is settled."

"Good. I wish I could see you tonight, but I have that meeting with the Millersburg police chief."

"I'll be fine."

He laughed. "I have no doubt of that, but I miss you, is all. We've both been so busy. I don't feel like I've seen you in weeks."

I couldn't suppress my smile. "I miss you too, Mitchell."

There was a voice in the background of the other end of the line.

"Angie, I got to go. Call me later. Love you."

He hung up before he heard me say that I loved him too.

I slid my phone in the back pocket of my jeans. As I did, I thought I saw a dark figure moving through the woods at the back of my parents' property. The person moved in the shadows. I couldn't see the person's face. I couldn't even tell if it was a man or woman.

I ran outside. "Hello?" I called to whoever was there.

There was no answer. Far enough away from the broken French doors, I set Oliver on the lawn. At my feet, the Frenchie growled deep in this throat, confirming to me that I hadn't imagined the figure moving through the woods.

I debated calling Mitchell back to tell him about what I'd seen, but thought better of it. He would drop whatever he was doing and rush to my side, and for what? To catch someone cutting through the woods? Most likely it was a hiker out exploring.

Mom and Dad's home stood alone on a hill. The front of the house overlooked a large Amish sheep farm. In the back, there was half an acre of lush green lawn and flower beds. This time of year, the gardens were filled with irises, tulips, bleeding heart, and sweet woodruff. Beyond the lawn there was a tree line that led into the woods. In the time that my parents had lived in the house, I'd never been in the woods. I doubted they had either. Mom and Dad weren't the outdoorsy type.

To my left there was a small silver construction trailer. A large stack of lumber lay next to it under a blue tarp. The trailer was new. I suspected it was another one of my father's ideas. I sighed and was about to call my mother for an update when I heard someone inside the house call my name. "Angie!"

I scooped up Oliver and ran back through the busted French door. I found Jonah and Eban in the kitchen. "You guys got here fast," I said, slightly out of breath.

Jonah smiled. "I told you I'd come as quickly as I could."

Eban stood beside him, holding a red toolbox. "This is quite a house."

I couldn't argue with that statement. The kitchen

was about the same size of the entire first floor of my rental house in Millersburg.

Jonah whistled as he surveyed the damage to the cabinets and the door. "Your father just went for it, didn't he?"

I sighed. "Dad doesn't do anything by halves."

Jonah raised his eyebrows at me. "That reminds me of another Braddock I know."

I held Oliver to my chest. "Can you fix it?"

He nodded. "Not a problem. We'll clean up the glass, board the doors, and finish taking out the cabinet. If we don't, it might just fall on its own accord. We don't want that. How much can we take out?"

"All of it," I said. "The plan was to gut the kitchen."

His eyes widened. "And your father was going to do the demolition?"

I nodded.

He grimaced.

Eban set down the toolbox. "We should get to work then."

"Right," Jonah agreed.

My cell phone rang. I pulled it from my pocket and checked the readout. It was my mother. "We're in the driveway," Mom said. "I need help getting your father into the house."

I told her I would be right there. Jonah and Eban were already sweeping up the broken glass. I took Oliver with me and headed for the front of the house.

When I exited the front door, Mom was setting up a walker in front of my father by the open passenger side door to her car. A thick lock of hair fell out of her sleek blond bob, which illustrated just how upset she was. My mother's hair never disobeyed her. Ever. My wild blond curls, however, did whatever they wanted.

My father took ahold of the walker and winced. My stomach dropped, and I set Oliver on the ground. "Dad, are you okay?"

He half smiled, half grimaced at me. "Oh, I'll be all right, AngieBear. Just as soon as the meds the doc gave me take effect."

Mom took one of his arms, and I took the other. Together we heaved him to his feet and he took a firm grip on the walker. My father is not a small man and had never been thin. At six feet tall, he was over three hundred pounds. I bit the inside of my lip as I watched him move the walker toward the house. His feet shuffled over the cobblestone walk and, for the first time, I saw my larger-than-life father as fragile. It was the first time that I didn't believe he would live forever, and realization smacked me like a sledgehammer to the chest. My breath caught.

"Angela," my mother barked from her spot next to my dad. "Close the car door and help me get him up the steps."

Leave it to my mother to bring me crashing back down to the situation at hand.

I did as I was told and, finally, Mom and I settled Dad on his huge leather recliner in the living room. It was the one piece of furniture in the house that Mom had allowed Dad to pick out.

"What did the doctor say?" I asked.

"Your father has a bulging disc, and because of his weight, it's much worse than it would normally be. He has to go to physical therapy five days a week, starting the day after tomorrow, and we have pain killers."

"Oh, Dad." I squeezed his hand.

"I told you I'll be fine. I might not be wielding a sledgehammer again, but I will be as good as new. You'll see." He smiled at me.

My mother's face was pinched as she fussed with the pillows around my father.

"Was that Jonah's horse I saw outside?" Dad asked.

I nodded. "I asked him to come look at the broken door. He and his friend Eban could finish the whole demo job if you like." I paused. "I think it's a good idea."

Dad frowned.

"Kent, you are in no condition to take on this job. Jonah or someone else can do it." Mom gathered up Dad's favorite Sudoku books and the day's paper and set them on the table beside him. "I told you that from the beginning."

"It looked so easy on YouTube." He sighed so deeply, it was as if the whole of the Internet had failed him.

Mom sniffed. "The Internet makes people overconfident, if you ask me."

He gave me a sheepish face. "Maybe I shouldn't have started right off with the sledgehammer."

Mom pursed her lips and turned to me. "If your father doesn't do well in therapy, he will have to get shots in his back and maybe even surgery."

Dad paled at the mention of the shots. I was sure I did too. We had the same loathing of needles. The last time I had a blood test, I fainted before the nurse even took the plastic wrapper off the syringe.

"I'm sure it won't come to that," I said as cheerfully as possible. "Mom, why don't we let Dad rest, and I can show you what Jonah and Eban are doing in the kitchen?" I pointed at my Frenchie. "Oliver, stay with Grandpa."

Oliver jumped on the ottoman at Dad's feet and sighed contently. I think he wanted to see for himself as much as I had that Dad was okay.

When we entered the kitchen, we found that Jonah and Eban had already cleaned up all the broken glass, removed the high cabinets from the walls, and were in the process of boarding up the broken French door.

Mom blinked. "I can't believe you did this all in such a short amount of time."

Jonah grinned. "It wasn't much trouble."

"Do you think you could finish the job?" Mom asked. "My husband is no condition to do any con-struction. He planned to do everything except the electrical and the plumbing himself. At least he knew he couldn't do those."

Jonah smiled. "We'd be happy to." He nodded to Eban. "This is my friend Eban Hoch, Mrs. Braddock."

"How do you do?" my mother asked formally. "Maybe I should hire a contractor," Mom mused. "It is a very big job."

"Mom," I said. "I've seen Jonah build a barn from the ground up. He's more than up for the task."

"You're right." She plastered on her hostess smile.

"You'll have to excuse my rudeness. I'm so distracted by my husband's injury."

"I understand, Mrs. Braddock," Jonah said. "Is Mr. Braddock okay?"

"He will be. He hurt his back, but as the doctor told us, it could have been so much worse."

"I am glad to hear that. Eban and I will finish boarding up this door, and then you and I can meet and review your blueprints. I want to make sure the door won't let a drop of rain inside. The forecast predicts another storm. Tomorrow morning, Eban and I'll get right to work."

"More rain?" I asked. After a dry April, May was turning out to be a soggy month. I supposed it was trying to make up for the rain we missed earlier in the spring. The spring flowers might like it, but I wish it didn't have to catch up all at once. The Amish farmers murmured about the potential for flooding if the persistent rains kept up.

Flooding would have a devastating effect on many of my Amish friends. I'd learned since moving back to the rural county that many lived or died by the amount of rain they were granted from above. Droughts like those found in Texas were rare in Ohio, but flooding was common, especially in the spring and early summer.

Jonah ignored my outburst. "We'll get right to work. I know several good carpenters and masons who work fast and do excellent work. I can call them in if need be. All will be well."

Mom clasped her hands in front of her freshly pressed linen blouse. She also wore a single string of pearls, which sat perfectly straight on her throat. Mom wasn't one to let her Dallas society style lapse just because she and Dad moved back to Ohio for the warmer months.

"Thank you, Jonah. I know you must be better with your hands than you were as a child when you broke my grandmother's precious lamp," my mother said in the light Southern drawl she had picked up when she, my father, and I moved to Texas when I was ten. Funny, Dad and I never lost our flat Midwestern twang.

Jonah and I shared a look. I bit down hard on my lip to stop myself from bursting into laughter. Jonah didn't appear half as amused as I was.

Mom smiled, but she still looked worried. "The electrician should be here soon. I wanted him to install some recessed lighting over the stove area. He promised to stop by to see the extent of work that needed to be done to accomplish that."

"Your kitchen is large. It should not interfere with what we have to do on this side of the room." Jonah paused. "Who's the electrician?"

"Griffin Bright," Mom said.

Jonah stiffened when he heard the name. I raised my eyebrows at him. Jonah was just about the most outgoing and friendly Amish man—or really any man—in the county. There were very few people who would cause him to flinch like that. Jonah balled his hands at his sides and quickly stretched out his fingers as if he realized he was tensing up. "Perhaps you and I should meet to discuss your plans while Griffin works. I think it would be best if I stayed out of his way."

I gave Jonah a questioning look, but he wouldn't make eye contact. Yep, there was definitely a story there. I would get to the bottom of it. I was nosy like that.

"That sounds like an excellent plan." Mom patted his arm. "The blueprints and everything that you need should be in the trailer in the side yard."

"I was going to ask you about that. What's the trailer for?" I asked.

She sighed. "Your father rented it. He claimed he needed it for the project. I've committed to having it for at least another month, so you might as well use it while you can, Jonah."

"*Danki*," Jonah replied.

She nodded to Jonah. "I should check on Kent. I'll leave you to it. When you're ready to meet with me I'll be in the living room with my husband."

"Since everything is under control now," I said, "I'd better head back to Running Stitch. Mattie will wonder what became of me."

Mom squeezed my hand. "Thank you for coming, Angie."

I smiled. "Of course, Mom. If you call and say Dad's been hurt, Oliver and I will come running."

She sighed and left the kitchen.

After she was gone, I turned to Jonah. "What's the deal?"

"What deal?" Jonah asked as he walked up to the French door and held a piece of measuring tape over the wide opening. "Must you always speak in riddles?"

Eban sent a nail home with the thwack of his hammer. Apparently boarding up doors was old hat for him.

"What's the deal with Griffin Bright?" My eyes narrowed. "I saw how you reacted when Mom mentioned his name."

Jonah pulled me away from Eban to the far corner of the kitchen. There was pain in his eyes, something that I hadn't seen since I told him I was moving away when we were kids. "He killed my cousin."

Chapter Three

"**W**hat?" I yelped.

Jonah sighed. "It was a long time ago."

"But you clearly haven't forgotten." I leaned on my mother's granite kitchen counter. Who knew what she would replace it with? My money was on marble.

He met my eyes. "How could I forget? Kamon was my closest friend," he said in the same hushed tone. "After you stopped visiting your aunt."

I could have been wrong, but I thought I heard a twinge of hurt in his voice.

When I was a child, after moving to Dallas with my parents, I would come spend at least part of my summer with my aunt Eleanor in Ohio. During those summers, I spent much of the time tromping around the countryside with Jonah. Jonah's mother, Anna, who now was a member of my quilting circle at Running Stitch, had been my aunt's closest friend. When I visited I always saw Jonah. Our families were so intertwined. When I would arrive in Holmes County, he and I would fall back into our usual sibling banter.

Since I was an only child, Jonah was the closest thing I had to a brother. We must have looked like an unusual pair: a tall skinny girl with wild blond curls, in shorts and an oversize T-shirt, and a sandy blond boy with a bowl haircut in Amish clothes. Some of my best childhood memories were from those summer days with Jonah and my aunt.

When I reached high school that all changed. I became caught up with friends and life in Dallas. I went to college and met my eventual fiancé, Ryan Dickinson, who swept me into a world of Dallas society, urban life, and a cutthroat career in advertising. I didn't have time for my friends back in Holmes County or my aunt.

Part of me wanted to apologize to Jonah for, in effect, deserting him all those years ago, but I stopped myself. We had both chosen our own paths. Jonah was married now with a working farm and three children, two of whom were the most mischievous twins on planet Earth. I had had a fast-paced career in Dallas until a succession of events occurred: Ryan dumped me right before our big Texas wedding, my aunt Eleanor died of cancer, and I inherited Running Stitch, which brought me back to Ohio. Somehow, we'd ended up back in the same place. We were different people now because of the time we had spent apart, but we had been able to take up a close friendship again much to the disdain of his wife, Miriam. Some would call it fate, but my Amish friends would call it God's providence. I didn't have a word for it myself other than knowing I was happier in Holmes County than I had ever been in Dallas.

Oliver trundled into the kitchen as if he knew I

needed backup for this conversation. No one understood me like my Frenchie, not even my boyfriend, Sheriff James Mitchell.

"What happened? How did your cousin die?"

Jonah groaned and some of the twinkle was back in his eye. "I'm sorry I brought it up. You aren't going to leave me alone until I tell you the whole story, are you?"

"Nope." I grinned.

He glanced at Eban. "I can tell you while I search for some more boards. I don't want your mother to accuse me of slacking off. She's already mentioned the lamp incident once. I'd rather not hear about it again." He walked across the kitchen and opened the working side of the French doors, stepping out onto the deck.

I turned back to the house and surveyed the broken door.

The small construction trailer was back near the woods. It was close enough to the house so that my dad had easy access to it, but far enough away not to bother my mother too much.

I followed Jonah to the trailer, admiring my mother's flowers as I went. I was happy to see so many of the bulbs came up. Zander, Mitchell's nine-year-old son, and I had planted them in the fall. We planted another set around the house he shared with his dad and my little rented house in Millersburg. By the end of it, I was pretty tired of digging in the dirt. Now that I saw the payoff, I forgot how tedious the task had been.

"I should check out the blueprint before I meet with your mom," Jonah said, and started to untie his bootlaces.

"Why are you taking your shoes off?"

"You don't go into a work trailer with muddy boots on," Jonah said. "It's just not done."

He left his boots at the foot of the stairs and went inside. I removed my beloved cowboy boots and did the same. The steps that led into the trailer were metal and hinged and creaked when I stepped on them.

The inside of the trailer was neat. The blueprints for the kitchen sat in the middle of a waist-high island in the middle of the room.

I hadn't seen many blueprints since I was in college. As part of my graphic design degree, I'd taken mechanical drawing as an elective. Even with my rudimentary understanding of how to read a blueprint, I could see the kitchen was in for a major transformation.

Jonah rubbed his beard as he looked over the plans. "It is *gut* for me to see these before I meet with your mother. Now, I have an idea of what her plans are. It's a much bigger job than I expected." He rolled up the blueprint and tucked it under his arm. "I'll take this inside to meet with her."

Outside of the trailer, Jonah laced up his boots, and I slipped on mine again. I was about to ask him again about Kamon, when he handed me the rolled-up blueprint.

Jonah walked over to a pile of lumber, threw back the edge of the tarp, and pointed to a four-by-four piece of plank wood. "That will do nicely. It's not too wet from the rain. There's a tarp under the wood as well, which is a *gut* thing. It'll save me time from going to the lumberyard. All I need to do is cut them down to the right size. It will really only need to be there for about a day. I can install the new door tomorrow."

"Are you going to tell me more about Kamon? You can't just say Griffin Bright murdered him and leave it at that."

He started to move the smaller pieces of wood off the plank. "Kamon was the son of my father's brother. His parents died when he was boy and he lived with his mother's family most of his life. When he was seventeen, he came to live with us. I was fifteen at the time, just started my *rumspringa*, and Kamon"—he paused as if searching for the right word—"he already knew the ways of the *Englisch* world. I admired him. He was trouble and caused trouble. He planned to leave the Amish. At the time, I thought he was what I wanted to be." He wouldn't meet my eyes.

"You wanted to leave the Amish?" I stared at Jonah. Never for a moment had I thought he'd considered leaving the Amish way of life. It was impossible for me to imagine him as anything other than Amish. It was like trying to make Rachel Miller or Jonah's own mother, Anna, non-Amish. It didn't make sense.

"I had my reasons." Jonah started moving pieces of wood again. "My parents took Kamon in because they believed they could keep him on the right path and convince him to stay in our way of life. We'll never know if they might have succeeded. He died a little over a year after moving in with us."

This was all news to me. I had thought that my aunt had kept me in the loop about the happenings with my old friends in Holmes County. Perhaps she didn't tell me about the Grabers' struggles with Kamon and his death because she didn't want to worry me or, more likely, Anna told her not to. The Amish were private people to the core. They wouldn't air their troubles to someone so removed from the community as I had been. I knew I had been only a kid myself at the time and couldn't have done anything to help the Grabers, but guilt washed over me because I had not been there for my friends, not just Jonah but his entire family.

Jonah grabbed the edge of the piece of wood. "Kamon's death put me on the straight and narrow better than anything else could. I gave up my daydreams, was baptized into the Amish church, and started courting Miriam. I chose the life *Gott* wanted for me from the beginning. The life that Kamon told me about was just my imaginings. It was not *Gotte's* will for my life."

"Oh, Jo-Jo," I said, holding the metal handrail that led into the trailer. "I'm so sorry. I never knew about any of this."

He pulled the piece from the woodpile, and I stepped back out of the way. He laid it in the middle of my mother's manicured yard. "You didn't know because you weren't here." His voice was tight.

I blinked at him. Was I talking to my jovial best childhood friend? I couldn't remember a time that Jonah had ever used such a tone with me, even when he was trying to talk me out of investigating a murder, a hobby that I had somehow acquired since moving back to Holmes County.

"Hello?" a deep male voice called from the kitchen. "Jonah Graber, can I speak to you?"

I turned around to see an English man with a broad chest and shoulders and a thick mane of black hair that curled over his ears standing on the deck behind the house. Griffin Bright, I presumed. He was handsome in a gladiator sort of way. Personally not my type, but I bet he had no shortage of admirers.

"Speak of the devil," Jonah muttered and brushed his hands together to remove the sawdust. "Angie, Griffin and I have to discuss your mother's project. Why don't you go back to Running Stitch? Isn't that what you told your mother you planned to do?"

He walked toward Griffin and stepped through the broken French doors. It wasn't until he disappeared into the kitchen that I realized he had never told me how Kamon actually died.

Chapter Four

I stood in my parents' backyard for half a minute, considering all that I had learned about my lifelong friend in the last few minutes.

I wasn't that easily dismissed. Jonah knew me better than most, and he knew this aspect of my personality too. Besides I had his blueprints.

When I stepped into the half-demolished kitchen, I found Griffin and Jonah glaring at each other. Griffin had his arms across his broad chest genie-style, and Jonah had his fists clenched at his sides. Eban had his red toolbox on the kitchen counter and sorted through the tools, but the way he tarried over the task made me think he was really listening to Griffin and Jonah's conversation. Out of the corner of my eye, I spotted Oliver peeking through the threshold that led to my parents' formal dining room.

"Hi!" I said in my best pageant-reject voice, waving the blueprints. "Jonah, you forgot these."

He took them from my hand, and I walked toward

Griffin with my hand outstretched. "I'm Daphne's daughter, Angie."

"It's nice to meet you." Griffin took my hand. His handshake was firm and warm and not a second too long or too short. I'd describe it as professional, clinical even. "Call me Griff. Everyone else does."

"Okay, Griff." I felt Jonah watching me, and I stepped back when Griffin released my hand. "As you can see, my mother brought on Jonah for this job. My dad hurt his back."

Griffin nodded. "I heard. Jonah, I must say I'm surprised to see you here. I didn't know that you were in the contracting business," Griffin said. "I had heard that you were working with goats."

Jonah frowned. "I'm surprised you would know what I was up to, Griffin. I haven't see you in—"

"Gosh, it must be twenty years but, as you know, people in this county talk," he said as if it held a special meaning he knew Jonah would understand.

By Jonah's scowl, I supposed that he did. My head whipped back and forth as I watched the two men. It was like a tennis match. Jonah had said that Griffin murdered his cousin, but that was twenty years ago, and the Amish tendency was to forgive. If Jonah's expression was an indication, he had yet to do that where Griffin was concerned, and I found that the most surprising part of the conversation.

"How is the goat project coming?" Griffin asked.

"It is *gut,*" Jonah said. My friend was always looking for the next big business venture. His most recent attempt had been goat lawn service. With his Nubian goat Petunia as his lead goat, he took a small herd to fields or land that needed to be cleared. The goats ate the vegetation down in a shockingly short period of time and left room for the property owner to turn the land into a grazing pasture or a crop field. Of all of Jonah's business ventures—and there had been many—this was the one that actually seemed to be working.

"I'm still doing that." Jonah's voice still held an unfamiliar tightness to it. "But Mrs. Braddock needed me to come in and take over this project."

Griffin glanced at the broken French door. "Did you do that?"

"*Nee.*"

Griffin frowned as if he didn't believe Jonah. "I have another larger job tomorrow, so I'll be here early around five to sketch out a rough plan for the kitchen. I have already informed Daphne, and she agreed." He pointed to the blueprints in Jonah's hand. "If you could leave those in the trailer, I'd appreciate it."

Jonah nodded. The two men were silent.

I looked from one frowning man to the other and back again. As much as I wanted to stay and see how this played out, I knew I needed to return to the quilt shop and relieve my assistant, Mattie. It was already twelve thirty, and I promised her I would be back by one.

"I'd better get going," I said to no one in particular.

Neither man even acknowledged that I'd said anything.

I tried again. "It was nice to meet you, Griffin."

Slowly Griffin turned his head in my direction and nodded.

"I'll see you later, Jonah."

"Good-bye, Angie," he said to me in such a formal way that it felt like a slight.

"Come on, Oliver," I said to the Frenchie and slapped my thigh.

Reluctantly, he wriggled out from under the table and toddled over to my side. We stopped in the living room to say good-bye to my parents. My mother was in the middle of giving my father a lecture about his diet. He gave me a Help Me look. I promised to check on him the next day.

A red pickup truck I didn't recognize was parked in front of my parents' house. I assumed that it was Griffin's. A sullen-looking woman sat in the passenger seat fiddling with her phone. I smiled at her, but she never looked up from her phone to see me. I shrugged, and continued to my car.

When I reached Running Stitch, Mattie was waiting for me outside the shop. She was sweeping, but I could tell she was mostly fretting over my being late . . . again. I had a reputation in that regard.

She leaned her broom against the olive green brick building that was my beloved quilt shop. "There you are. I have to go straight to the factory."

"I know, and I'm sorry I'm late. The thing at my mother's turned out to be more complicated than I expected it to be."

"How is your father?"

I frowned. "He's using a walker."

"Oh, Angie, I'm so sorry." She clasped her hands in front of her apron. "Is there anything that I can do?"

I shook my head. "But thank you."

"Then, I really must go."

I nodded. "Is everything at the pie factory all right?" I couldn't keep the worry from my voice.

The factory had been open for less than a year and had gotten off to a rocky start with a murder in the factory's parking lot. It wasn't how Aaron or Rachel had wanted to start their new business. Since then, things had been quiet on Sugartree Street, the main road in Rolling Brook and the location where all the local shopkeepers kept their businesses.

"Everything is fine. One of Aaron's workers went to visit family in Indiana. She should be back today, and Aaron will have a full staff again. Then, I'll be here full time again." She smiled at the idea. Before she started working for me Mattie had worked long days at her family's bakery across the street from Running Stitch. She hadn't cared for the job, but she did it because it was expected. When I offered her a job, she jumped at the chance.

Her bonnet sat on the bench. It seemed to me that she had planned to run for the factory as soon as I arrived. She picked it up and put it on her head, tying the long wide black ribbon into a perfect bow. "Anna's inside. She just arrived, and if you hadn't been back in a few minutes, I was just going to leave the store with her."

I smiled. "You could have. Anna knows how to manage Running Stitch better than either one of us do."

She laughed and waved good-bye before heading up the street.

I stepped inside and inhaled the sweet and familiar scent of freshly pressed cotton and linen. The left side of the room was lined with all sorts of fabric, dark and plain options for my Amish customers as well as prints and bright colors for my English ones.

A large cutting table sat in the middle of the room, and several pieces of ribbon sat on top of it in neat piles. I could always count on Mattie to leave everything in perfect order. I typically was the one to walk away in the middle of a project or the one to forget to put supplies away for the night.

Anna Graber sat in my aunt's old rocking chair in the front window and looked like one of the Amish-themed paintings sold in gift shops across the county. Her wire-rimmed glasses perched on the end of her nose and her steel gray hair was pulled back into an Amish bun and covered with a prayer cap as she rocked and pieced a quilt topper that looked like it would be a nine block. Dodger sat at her feet, watching her work. His close proximity to Anna made me think she had some cat treats in her quilting basket. I didn't bother asking. Everyone in my quilting circle had been known to slip my pets extra snacks, despite my protests against it.

"Angie, there you are." Anna pulled her last stitch through the woolen fabric. "Is everything all right at your parents' house?"

"All right as it can be." I told her about the kitchen, my father's injury, and Jonah running to the rescue.

"I'm glad that Jonah can be of some help to your

parents, and maybe this will help him focus his attention on construction and give up the ridiculous goat lawn services idea." She clicked her tongue in a sound of disapproval.

"You're not a fan of the goats?" I couldn't keep the amusement from my voice.

She sniffed. "They are better than the geese." She gave a mock shiver. "Or the turkeys, but they're still a handful, and the noise they make. Sometimes I think the cavalry is coming by the sound of them stomping back and forth on the barn floor. I can hear them all the way in my house."

I chuckled. I was about to ask Anna about her nephew Kamon and electrician Griffin Bright when the shop's door opened and we were descended upon by an entire tour group of shoppers.

The afternoon at the quilt shop was busy. Since it was May, it was just the beginning of the main tourist season in Holmes County. Bus tours and other tourists, who had stayed away through the harsh and unpredictable winter, came back in force just as soon as the tulips bloomed.

When I had a moment of quiet, I had planned to visit Rachel Miller at her bakery, Miller's Amish Bakery, which was directly across the street from my shop. I wanted to ask Rachel about Kamon and Griffin since Jonah had neglected to tell me how his cousin died. After my first inclination to ask Anna about it, I dismissed it. I was afraid it might bring up some painful memories for her just as it had for Jonah. I thought it would be better to gather more information before I broached the topic with Anna.

Rachel was the best person to ask. She would keep my confidence and warn me if there was any reason to drop the subject. I was self-aware enough to know I wouldn't do that on my own. Even though Rachel was almost a decade younger than Jonah and me, I hoped she knew something.

Unfortunately, Rachel had already left the bakery for the day before I had a chance to catch my breath with the many customers who walked through Running Stitch's door. Not that I was complaining. These boom times during the tourist season were what kept all the businesses on Sugartree Street afloat through the winter. No shopkeeper would turn a potential sale away, not even me.

That night, Mitchell had to work late at the sheriff's headquarters, so Oliver, Dodger, and I split a hamburger that I picked up from the Double Dime Diner in Millersburg on the way home from the quilt shop. We ate our dinner in front of the TV and watched *Clueless* for the eight hundredth time. Since it was a modern—okay, modern a few decades ago—adaptation of Jane Austen's *Emma*, I thought it had excellent cultural value for the entire family.

The next morning, I awoke to the incessant ringing of my cell phone. I sat bolt upright and snatched it up, thinking that it had something to do with Mitchell. He had worked the night before, and there was a constant fear that came from being in love with a cop that kept me up until the wee hours many nights. He could be hurt in anything from a confrontation with an angry hunter to a routine traffic stop.

Before I answered, I took a quick glimpse at the cell's screen and flopped back onto my pillow, half out of breath. The number on my cell phone was my parents' house. I groaned. Who knew what kind of decorating emergency my mother had run into now? Was it the countertop? Paint color? Then, I remembered my father's back injury.

"Is Dad all right?" I asked without greeting.

"Angie, I need you to come. Now." The tense voice on the other end of the line wasn't my mother's but Jonah's.

I blinked at my clock on the nightstand. It was six in the morning. "Jonah, what's wrong? Why are you calling me from my parents' phone?"

Dodger, my cat, lay at the bottom of the bed and lifted his head for half a second before he curled into a ball and covered his face with his tail.

"I need you. I need you here at your parents' home."

I sat bolt upright in bed again just as I had when I thought something terrible had befallen Mitchell. "Jonah, what's wrong? Are my parents okay? What's happened?"

"Your parents are fine. It's Griffin Bright." He took in an unsteady breath. "Angie, he's dead."

Chapter Five

Now I was awake. "What? Dead?" I couldn't possibly have heard that right. How could Griffin Bright be dead? I had just seen him the day before, and he had been the picture of health at the time.

"*Ya*, Angie, he's dead. I found him in your parents' backyard. He's outside of the trailer. I—I think he was electrocuted."

"He died in my parents' yard?" I was off my bed like I was the one who had just been zapped with an electrical current. "Where are my parents? Are they okay?"

"They're fine. They're in the house. I asked them to stay inside after I called the police."

"Are you okay?" I was breathless.

"Please come." His voice was tight. "The police are already on the way. I need you."

As if on cue, my phone buzzed, telling me I had another call while I was on the line with Jonah. I glanced at the screen. It was Mitchell. No surprise there.

"Please come," he repeated.

"Of course. I'm on my way," I said without hesitation.

He hung up without saying good-bye. My phone started to ring with the call from Mitchell. I answered.

"Angie, there's been an accident," he said.

I grabbed a pair of jeans hanging over the back of my desk chair and pulled them on. "I know. I just spoke to Jonah. I'm heading to my parents' house right now."

"Wait for me," he said. "I'll drop Zander at his mother's and be at your house to pick you up in ten minutes. My officers are already on the way to the scene. They'll make sure everything is secure."

I rummaged through my clothes basket, the basket that I had yet to fold even though I did laundry well over a week ago, for something to wear. "No way. I'm going now."

My phone began to buzz again. This time the screen told me it was from my mother's cell phone.

"Angie! Wait for me!" Mitchell said in his firmest cop voice. The cop voice worked on suspects, but not on me.

"Not happening. It's my parents, Mitchell. My parents. I'll see you there." I hung up the phone, but not before I heard him growl in frustration.

I dressed, and Oliver and I were out the door within five minutes. The sun was just beginning to break over the horizon as I sped out of my Millersburg neighborhood.

When I reached the county road that led to my parents' large stone house on the top of the hill, I slowed down. Three county sheriff's cars were parked in front of it. There was also an ambulance, and Jonah's horse and wagon loaded with supplies.

I parked on the street and got out. Oliver was on my heels. The front door was open, and Deputy Anderson, a uniformed officer in his mid-twenties, stood underneath my parents' chandelier in the foyer, asking my mother questions and taking copious notes.

My mother glowered at the young deputy. "I already told you. My husband snores, so I use earplugs to sleep. I didn't hear a thing."

"Did your husband hear anything?" the deputy asked.

"You will have to ask him that, won't you?" My mother patted her perfectly-in-place hair. Even when awakened to hear that a man was dead in her back-yard, her hair was perfect. It was mind-boggling. "However, I doubt he heard a thing. Kent slept through a hurricane once when we were vacationing in the Caribbean." Mom pointed at his notepad and corrected something he recorded. "No, that's not what I said. I went to bed a little after eleven not around eleven."

The deputy clutched his pen a little more tightly, but he made the correction.

Mom spotted me in the doorway. "Angie! There you are. I've been trying to call you for the last half hour. Why didn't you answer?" my mother said. "My good-ness, your father and I could have been murdered in our bed, and you wouldn't even know it because you refuse to answer your phone."

I closed my eyes for a moment. "I'm sorry, Mom," I said sincerely. "Jonah called and told me what hap-pened. I wanted to get here as quickly as possible."

"You spoke to Jonah but wouldn't answer your own

mother's call? A man was killed in my house. The least
you could do is answer your phone." She sniffed. I
couldn't tell if it was out of irritation or if she was on
the brink of tears.

"I thought he died in the backyard." I glanced
around the foyer and what I could see of the rest of
the house from where I stood. I was relieved there
wasn't a dead guy in sight.

"It's still my home, Angela." Mom pressed a perfectly folded tissue to the corner of her eye. "Exactly
where in my home is irrelevant."

I raised my hands in surrender. "I know, Mom, and
I'm so glad that you're all right. I've been a mess ever
since Jonah called. I had to come here to see for myself
that you and Dad were okay. How's Dad?"

She nodded as if my worry somehow appeased her.
"He's fine too. The police are questioning him in the
living room. They insisted they couldn't question us
together. It is almost as if they believe"—she paused
to give the deputy a pointed glare—"that we have
made up these events. Is a dead man in my backyard
a lie? You can tell James that I'm not happy about how
I have been treated in my own home. I won't hesitate
to give him a piece of my mind when he arrives."

Poor Mitchell. A suspicious death and a confrontation with my mother in the same morning. He had no
idea what he was stepping into.

"And Jonah?" I asked. "How's Jonah?"

"He's in the backyard being questioned by another
officer," Deputy Anderson answered before my mother
could. "Angie, I'm going to have to ask you to wait in

the dining room. I'll send your mother in there as soon as I'm done questioning her."

"I will," I said. "After I check on Jonah." I started toward the dining room that led into the kitchen.

Deputy Anderson stepped into my path. "You can't go in the backyard. It's a crime scene."

As if the distinction of a place being a crime scene had ever stopped me before. Not to mention, I never listened to Deputy Anderson, and I certainly wasn't going to start now when there was a dead body in my parents' backyard. I stepped around him and hurried through the formal dining room into the kitchen.

The young deputy followed me into the kitchen. "Angie, please. The sheriff wouldn't like it."

Not a great argument with me either. "Anderson, let me worry about the sheriff."

He made a frustrated sound but didn't bother to argue with me anymore. Maybe he was finally realizing that it was waste of time.

Oliver whimpered when we were in the kitchen. I bent over to pick him up. I should have left him at home or at least with my mother in the foyer, but taking Oliver everywhere I went was second nature to me. When I'd left my house in a panic it hadn't occurred to leave him behind. I tucked him under my arm like a football and surveyed the damage in the kitchen.

In actuality it looked much better than it had the day before. The broken French door was boarded up and all the overhead cabinetry had been removed.

A new set of white French doors leaned against the wall.

I stepped through the working side of the French door, which was wide-open.

Outside the activity around the trailer immediately caught my attention. Two crime scene techs walked around the trailer brushing their shoes back and forth over the grass as if looking for something. The coroner, who, in a strange twist of circumstances, I had seen on several occasions since moving back to Ohio, stood at the foot of the trailer writing on a clipboard and shaking his head. I didn't know his name. All I had ever heard Mitchell call him was "Doc." I wondered if it was time we were formally introduced since our paths seemed to always be crossing. Two deputies from Mitchell's department stood on either side of the coroner. All three men were looking down at something on the ground. One of the deputies took pictures of the object with a large and expensive-looking camera. I knew it must be Griffin's body. Despite my unquenchable curiosity, I was glad I couldn't see him.

Petunia, Jonah's one-hundred-plus-pound white, tan, and brown spotted Nubian goat, came up to my side and bumped her head against my hip. According to my Amish friends, she did this because she liked me. I wasn't so sure. It seemed to me that she did this to see how much force it would take to knock me over. She had knocked me to the ground on more than one occasion.

Right now, it wouldn't take much to topple me. The news about Griffin's death still hadn't completely sunk in.

Oliver wriggled in my arms, and I set him on the ground next to the goat. Petunia gently—much more gently than she ever had to me—bumped his head with hers. "What are you doing here, Petunia?" I asked the goat.

She bumped my hip again. This time with a little more force that made me take a step back.

I pointed at the dog and goat. "You two stay away from the crime scene, okay?"

They both stared up at me with soulful eyes as if they understood my every word. I wouldn't doubt it for a moment if they did. This wasn't their first crime scene either.

Jonah stood a few feet away at the edge of my mother's pristine tulip garden with another deputy. Jonah held his black felt hat in his hands and fiddled with the rim. "*Nee.* I told you. I arrived here at six this morning. I wanted to have an early start. The Braddocks were eager to complete the project. I thought if I could do some prep work before the rest of my workmen arrived, we could go straight to work. I was about to start taking out the old French doors when I noticed something unusual near the steps of the trailer. I went to check it out." He gripped his hat a little more tightly. "That's when I found Griffin."

"Did the Braddocks let you in the house? How did you get inside?" The deputy wanted to know.

He swallowed. "No. Mrs. Braddock told me where they kept the spare key in the garden yesterday so that I could come and go as I needed for the job."

"Weren't you afraid of disturbing the Braddocks so early in the morning? Six o'clock seems to be an early time to be on the job."

Jonah folded his arms. "Not if you're Amish. The kitchen is in the back of the house where I wouldn't disturb them. Their bedroom is in the front. As you can see, it's a very large home. Besides, Griffin planned to be here at five, and Mrs. Braddock knew and approved this. I thought me coming at six wouldn't be any more disruptive than Griffin being here."

The deputy arched his brow. "You knew what time Griffin Bright planned to come to the Braddocks this morning?"

Jonah nodded. "He told me yesterday."

In my head, I screamed, "Jonah, stop talking!"

The officer changed his tone to a more conversational one. "Why would Mr. Bright be here so early?"

Jonah's frown deepened. "He said he had another job to do today, so if he was going to do any work for the Braddocks, it had to be at five."

The deputy changed the subject. "What did you see outside of the trailer, in detail?"

"Griffin at the base of the stairs leading to the trailer. His neck was at a peculiar angle. He appeared burnt, at least his hands and feet were. He wasn't wearing any shoes." He spotted me over the deputy's shoulder when he said this. "It looked to me like he was electrocuted. I thought the trailer's generator may have shorted. To be safe, I turned it off before calling the police. I didn't want anyone else to be hurt."

"No shoes? That's strange on a job site, isn't it?" the coroner asked.

Jonah shook his head. "Not when the ground is

muddy like this. It's etiquette. He took off his work boots to avoid tracking mud into the trailer."

"Did you know he would have taken off his shoes?" the deputy asked.

Jonah's brow wrinkled. "Anyone who works on a job like this would have. I took off my boots yesterday anytime I went into the trailer."

"What's your relationship with Griffin Bright?" The deputy asked.

Jonah's eyes flicked in my direction and pleaded with me. I knew what he was asking. He didn't want me to tell the police what he'd told me the day before about Kamon and Griffin. Even though I didn't know the entire story about how Kamon died, I knew that Jonah still felt strongly about Griffin because of Kamon's death, very strongly. But I knew my friend would not feel strongly enough to kill. He was incapable of hurting a soul.

Deputy Anderson appeared at my side. "Angie, please come back into the house."

His comment caught the attention of the deputy questioning Jonah. The older deputy scowled at me.

"Anderson," I began, "I'm just checking on my friend." I turned to Jonah. "You okay?"

He gave me a quick nod just as Sheriff James Mitchell strode into the yard. Deputy Anderson watched in awe as his hero made his entrance.

I might have had a similar expression if I hadn't been so freaked-out about someone dying in my parents' yard and if one of my best friends wasn't potentially the prime suspect for the murder. If it was murder—it hadn't been ruled as such yet.

The officer questioning Jonah looked up from his notebook. "Hello, Sheriff. I was just going over a few things with Mr. Graber here. He's the one who found the victim."

Mitchell nodded, and then he glanced at me with his beautiful aquamarine eyes. Just for a second his cop face softened, and I saw the compassionate man and devoted father I'd fallen in love with. As quickly as the tender expression appeared it hid behind the seasoned cop face again. "Jonah." Mitchell nodded at my friend. "Did you see anything unusual when you approached the trailer? Other than Mr. Bright's body?"

"I—I don't know," Jonah stammered. "It's hard to explain."

"Tell us," Mitchell said.

I was grateful Mitchell hadn't asked me to leave. Maybe he didn't bother because he knew Jonah would tell me everything anyway. I didn't care what his reasons for letting me listen in were as long as he did.

Jonah gripped the rim of his felt hat just a little bit tighter. "When I realized that Griffin was dead, I noticed movement in the woods."

"What was it? A deer?" the other deputy asked.

Jonah paled. "*Nee*. It looked like a wild man."

Chapter Six

There was only one man in Holmes County I knew who resembled a wild man: Nahum Shetler. He was a rogue Amish man, who lived outside of any Amish district. He was also Rachel Miller's estranged father. For nearly a year, I had been hoping father and daughter would reconnect, but Rachel had made it very clear to me that she would deal with her father in her own time. In general, Amish time, especially when it came to relationships, was much slower than English time. The Amish weren't ones to yell and scream in fits of anger, but they could freeze a person out with a frigidity I would have thought impossible if I hadn't seen it myself.

Mitchell glanced over at me. I knew he was thinking Nahum too, but he didn't say the name.

"Was it Nahum?" I asked Jonah.

Jonah shook his head. "*Nee.* The person was too"—he paused as if searching for the right word—"hairy."

Mitchell arched an eyebrow. "Hairy?"

"Like Bigfoot?" Deputy Anderson blurted out.

Mitchell scowled at him, and the young deputy

shrank back. I felt a twinge of sympathy for Anderson. I had been on the receiving end of Mitchell's disapproval more than once, and it wasn't pleasant.

Jonah's brow knit together. "Big? Foot?"

"He talking about a Sasquatch," the other deputy said.

Jonah's frown only deepened. "A what?"

Deputy Anderson attempted to explain who or what Bigfoot was to my Amish friend, but it was clear Jonah didn't comprehend what the deputy was saying. When Anderson went on to tell him about movies depicting Bigfoot, Jonah was completely lost.

Mitchell started toward the trailer where the body lay. I still couldn't see it. He glanced over his shoulder. "Angie, don't follow me."

"I'm not following you," I said sweetly.

"Right." He stood in my path. "Trust me. You don't want to see him." He grimaced. "Electrocution is a gruesome way to die. He will be burnt. I won't go into detail."

I stepped back. In this case, I would take his word for it. I had heard Jonah's description of the scene, and that should be enough.

"Do you think whatever Jonah saw caused Griffin's death? Like startled him to death and caused a heart attack or something?" I was reaching and we both knew it.

Mitchell gave me a sad smile as if he knew what I was up to. He knew me better than most, so I'm sure he did. "Unless Bigfoot knows how to rig an electrical shortage, I think we can assume he's not our guy."

I grimaced. "Maybe it was an accident."

"Not likely. It was intentional." Mitchell said this with such certainty that I shivered.

"How do you know?"

Mitchell sighed. "The live wire was intertwined in the metal stairs with enough voltage from the generator to kill a rhino. Griffin never stood a chance being barefoot, and his feet must have been damp from the rains."

Of all the details I had heard, I was most troubled by the bare feet. If Griffin had been wearing his sturdy boots when he was shocked, he might still be alive. The murder seemed somehow worse because Griffin had been killed with the tools of his own trade, voltage and wire. Was that some sort of message sent by the killer? It seemed like an elaborate and painstaking way to kill someone. How would the murderer know Griffin would be at the trailer at the right time to get the zap? He would if he knew that he was coming to my parents' house at five in the morning, which Jonah had already admitted to the police that he had.

My chest clenched as I remembered Jonah telling the other deputy that he had turned off the generator. That meant his fingerprints were on it. It didn't look good for my friend, but I wasn't going to let Mitchell think that. "In that case, Jonah couldn't possibly be involved. He's Amish. He doesn't work with electricity."

"I know how to use electricity, Angie," Jonah said, who must have overheard and was obviously offended by my comment. "The Amish use generators for work. We need to know how to maintain them."

I could have shaken Jonah just then because his comment was so not helping. However, my annoyance at him fell away when another idea struck me like a four-by-four to the side of the head. "Are you telling me anyone who may have entered that trailer this morning would have been zapped?" I was having trouble breathing as the gravity of the situation hit me. What if Mom or Dad had gone in there? What if Jonah had gone inside before Griffin had? He would have surely taken off his shoes. If Griffin, who was an electrician, hadn't noticed that live wire, Jonah would never have seen it.

Mitchell squeezed my hand. "Angie, are you all right?"

I swallowed and tried to compose myself. Mom, Dad, and Jonah were all alive and well. Poor Griffin Bright was not. I needed to focus on the fact that people I loved were safe, but that also made me feel ill. There must be people who loved Griffin. He wasn't safe. He was dead. "I'm fine," I managed to say after a long second.

Mitchell let go of my hand. He didn't like displays of affection when he was on the job, which made me even more grateful for his touch. He had broken his unwritten rule when I had needed comforting.

Then I asked the question that was bouncing around in my head, even though I didn't want to. "What if the killer hadn't targeted Griffin at all?" I whispered.

"That will have to be a question we'll ask," Mitchell said in an equally low voice. "Now, I have to check out the scene."

I nodded dumbly, still a bit woozy from my morbid thoughts. I had hoped he would have said my idea was impossible, that someone else could have been the intended victim. If it wasn't impossible, my parents were as likely the intended victims as Griffin had been, maybe even more so because this was their house.

"Angie," Mitchell said, "why don't you go inside and check on your parents? My deputies should be done questioning them now."

Since Anderson was one of the questioning officers and was in the backyard, I knew that to be true, but I had one more question. "I think it's safe to say whatever Jonah saw wasn't Bigfoot, but it could have been the killer. Are you going to look for him?"

"Angie," Mitchell said in his most reasonable tone, which I found particularly annoying at the moment, "we'll search the woods. We'll follow every lead. You know that. Now go inside the house. I need to talk to Jonah and my officers alone."

I opened my mouth to protest.

"Please," he said, staring at me with those aquamarine eyes, which always seemed to turn me into a puddle.

I frowned, but I knew I could find out what transpired between Mitchell and Jonah when I had the chance to talk to my friend, and I was concerned about my parents, especially my dad since he had an injured back. However, I wouldn't let Mitchell get off that easily. "Fine," I said, expressing all of my displeasure with my voice.

He sighed.

I looked around for Oliver and found him lying in the grass next to Petunia. The goat, who usually enjoyed crowds, lay on the grass with her head on her front hooves. I knelt beside her. "Are you all right, Petunia?"

Before I knew it, Jonah was kneeling beside me.

"Jonah, I still have some questions for you," Mitchell called, but there was resignation in his voice.

Jonah stood, pulling the large goat up by her lead. Petunia struggled to her feet, but then gave me a strong head butt that sent me reeling back. Luckily Mitchell caught me before I tumbled into the grass.

Mitchell held on to my upper arms until I was solidly upright, and then let me go. I hadn't even known he had crossed the yard to join us.

"Looks like she's fine after all," I muttered.

"Maybe," Mitchell said, "you should put Petunia somewhere else. She tends to be a distraction."

Briefly, I wondered how many county sheriffs had to worry about distracting goats in the middle of their police investigations, not to mention a possible Bigfoot sighting. Mitchell took it all seriously and professionally.

Jonah tried to hand me Petunia's lead. "Can you take her?"

"Me? Take her where?" I squeaked.

"To your shop. I'll come pick her up after the police are through with me."

"Why did you bring her here anyway?" I asked.

His shoulders dropped. "She ate Miriam's favorite apron. I was afraid if I left her on the farm, I'd come home to goat stew."

I grimaced and scratched the goat between the ears. Sure, Petunia was annoying, but I didn't want anything to happen to her. I've seen Miriam when she was mad. It wasn't pretty.

"Do you just want me to drop her off at your farm? It's no trouble. I could put her in the barn with the other goats, so she's out of Miriam's way," I offered. "Maybe that would be better."

"*Nee. Nee*," he said quickly. "Miriam would not like that. It's best if Petunia stays with you, and you both stay away from my farm."

I interpreted that to mean Miriam would not like to see me. Ever since I moved back to Ohio, all I'd received from Jonah's wife was dirty looks and blatant animosity. I wish Miriam was more accepting of me. The Grabers, other than the Millers, were my closest friends in the county. I wish Jonah's wife was open to being my friend or at least tolerating me.

I sighed with resignation, not sounding much different from Mitchell had a moment ago. "Okay, I'll take her. She can hang out in the yard behind Running Stitch until you can come and fetch her."

Jonah let out a sigh. "*Danki*, Angie. I don't want anything to happen to her. I have grown quite fond of her."

Mitchell took a step back in the direction of the crime scene and waited. "Now that the fate of the goat is settled, Jonah, will you join me by the trailer? I would like you to take me through your discovery moment by moment."

Jonah nodded, and two of the men I cared for the most walked away. One was the cop and one was the suspect. Mitchell liked Jonah. The two men were friends, in a way, at least through me. Mitchell would know in his heart that Jonah couldn't have killed anyone, but Mitchell was also a cop. He wouldn't be able to ignore the facts. Jonah had means and opportunity to set the electrified traps for the ill-fated electrician. The only piece Mitchell was missing was Jonah's motive, which I knew about even though Mitchell did not.

"Let's go, guys," I said to Oliver and Petunia. I headed around the side of the house toward the front yard, but two EMTs were coming from that direction with a gurney with an empty black body bag lying on the top of it. I spun around. "I think we should go through the house."

I wanted to leave the yard quickly. The last thing I wanted to see was the EMTs and coroner roll Griffin's body into the waiting bag, especially if he was in as poor condition as Mitchell had described. I had seen that before, and it was never pleasant.

I walked into my mother's house with a goat on a leash and my Frenchie on my heels. We would see how well this would go with my mother. The best course of action would be to move Petunia through the house without being seen. I could tether her to a tree in the front yard before my mother was the wiser.

There were two crime scene techs in the kitchen examining the broken French doors. If the techs thought it was odd that I was walking a French bulldog and a Nubian goat through my mother's half-destroyed kitchen, they didn't let on. Maybe they were immune to my antics at this point. I had been dating their beloved sheriff for well over a year.

Mitchell's men might have ignored my menagerie, but my mother could not.

"Angela Braddock!" my mother screeched the

moment she saw me. "What are you doing with a goat in my house? Is it not enough that your father is injured and a man has died in my backyard? Now you bring a farm animal to tramp through my dining room and mark up my new floors?"

I looked behind me. Sure enough, there was a trail of muddy hoofprints, but I really didn't know what difference that made. There were multiple muddy boot prints all over the floor, crisscrossing the polished hardwood in all directions. I knew better than to say that to my mother.

Mom stared at the floor, placed a hand over her mouth, and burst into tears.

I blinked at her for a moment. I couldn't remember the last time I had seen my mother really cry. Maybe when my aunt Eleanor, her sister, died, but I couldn't actually recall her shedding a tear. My father was the sensitive parent in my family. He had been known to weep at sappy movies and holiday commercials on TV.

Since seeing my mother cry came as such a shock, it took me a second too long to react, and I caught her just as she appeared to be crashing to the muddy hardwood floor under her feet.

"It's all so horrible," she cried into her hands. "That poor man."

I made sympathetic noises and guided my mother toward the living room where Deputy Anderson had said Dad had been questioned by another officer.

Not able to get Petunia outside, I walked her into the living room with her leash in my left hand. My right arm was around my weeping mother.

"AngieBear!" My father waved from his enormous brown leather chair. His walker sat within easy reach. "One of the officers told me that you were here, but then he wouldn't allow me to go into the backyard to see you."

Mom sniffled.

My father's attention turned to her. "Daphne? Are you all right?" Dad sounded worried. I bet he couldn't remember the last time he'd seen my mother cry either. He looked to me. "What's happened?" He struggled as if he was about to get up.

"Please don't stand up, Kent. Your back." My mother sniffled.

"She saw the tracks that the police made on the floor," I said, deciding to leave Petunia out of it, "and lost it."

"Oh, my dear." Dad held out his arms, and my mother perched on his lap. Seeing that they might need a minute, I took it as an opportunity to put Petunia outside. I didn't want her within view when my mother collected herself. I hoped the crying jag would erase my mother's memory of the goat altogether. I didn't hold out much hope of that happening though. I told Oliver to stay in the living room with my parents before slipping out.

In the front yard, I walked Petunia to the one lone tree and wrapped her lead around it. She knocked me with the top of her head, more gently this time.

I scratched her behind her right ear. "I know that you don't like to be away from the action, but you can't go in the backyard and Mom will have a fit if you're inside the house."

She dropped her head and started eating some of my mother's hostas that were circling the tree. I groaned, hoping my mother wouldn't notice. She had bigger problems with the dead body in her backyard, but the munched hostas might just send her over the edge.

Across the street from my parents' stone house, bright white sheep peppered the hillside. South of the sheep farm was a dense wood, much like the one found behind my parents' house. Mom and Dad didn't have any neighbors to speak of. It was the perfect place to commit a murder and not be seen. I wondered what the Amish family living on the sheep farm thought about all the flashing lights and sheriff vehicles coming from the top of the hill.

Across the street there was an enormous oak tree in the middle of the hillside. Usually, the tree was surrounded by sheep enjoying the shade it offered. The sheep were as far away from the oak tree as they could get. It wasn't so much the lack of sheep around the tree that caught my attention, but something half hidden by the tree's trunk. The figure rose and stood. I stared, blinked, and stared.

It looked like—I could hardly even think it—it looked like Bigfoot.

"This has to be someone's idea of a joke," I said.

Chapter Seven

The sound of an oncoming buggy momentarily distracted me from the thing hiding behind the tree. Eban Hoch drove a small pony cart up the steep hill to my parents' home. The closer he drew to the house, the slower he went. He seemed to be taking in the scene slowly. I imagined that the ambulance, police cars, and crime scene vans were not what he expected to find when he left for my parents' house that morning.

I turned back to the tree. The figure was gone, but I suddenly remembered seeing it in the woods behind my parents' house the day before. I hadn't gotten a good look at who or what that had been.

I ran over to Eban as he parked his pony cart behind a police cruiser. "Did you see that?"

Eban climbed out of his cart and tethered his pony's reins to my parent's mailbox post. "What is going on? Where is Jonah?"

I pointed across the street. "Did you see that?"

He pulled down on the reins to make sure they were secure. "Did I see what?"

That was a tough question to answer. "I thought I saw someone behind that tree there." Again, I pointed at the giant oak tree that must have been at least sixty feet tall. The trunk was easily ten feet around.

"*Nee.* I didn't see anyone." He pointed at the house. "Why are the police here?"

I shot one more look at the tree. "I might as well tell you. There's been an accident and the electrician Griffin Bright, who was here yesterday, is dead."

Eban's face paled to a deathly white. "He's dead?"

I nodded.

"What should I do? Should I go home?" he asked.

I shook my head. "The police might want to talk to you."

"Me? Why would they want to talk to me?" He appeared a shade paler.

"You were here yesterday when Griffin was."

He frowned. "Maybe I should go find Jonah and ask him about working today." He took a step in that direction.

"He's in the backyard with the police."

Eban hesitated.

"Jonah would like to see you, I'm sure," I said encouragingly.

Eban nodded and walked around the side of the house.

That left me alone in the front yard with Petunia and whatever I had seen across the street. Part of me wondered if I had imagined it. I mentally cursed Deputy Anderson for putting the Bigfoot idea in my head.

But to be on the safe side, there was no way I was

leaving Petunia outside with a Sasquatch running around. Jonah entrusted her care to me. What would I say to him if I had let an imaginary creature eat his goat for breakfast?

I stared intently at the oak tree, but whatever had been there was gone. Where could it have gone? The tree stood in the middle of a pasture. There was nowhere to hide, and I hadn't seen it run away, but then again, I had been distracted by Eban's arrival. Whatever it had been could have dashed into the woods to the south then.

I still had to tell Mitchell about what I saw. Whoever or whatever it was lurked around my parents' house where a murder had taken place. It might be the killer. The one thing that I knew was that it couldn't have been Nahum Shetler. The thing was too big, and Nahum had never been shy about confronting me before.

I headed back into the house with Petunia lagging behind me eating as many of my mother's flowers she could as she went. At the door, I ran into Deputy Anderson, whose face was still flushed. Part of me felt sorry for the guy. True, he wasn't the most competent deputy in the world, but he idolized Mitchell and wanted only to impress the sheriff. The sad part was he failed at that, repeatedly.

"Anderson," I said, holding on to Petunia's lead, "I just saw something behind that oak tree across the street." I swallowed. "I think it was whatever Jonah saw when he discovered the body. You should go over there and check it out."

Color drained from his cheeks as if I had asked him

to jump from the top of the Empire State Building. "Why didn't you check it out?" he asked.

I scowled. "Me? I'm not a police officer. I shouldn't be running off after potential murderers."

"That never stopped you before," he countered.

He had a point. "I couldn't leave Petunia."

Deputy Anderson stared across the street again at the tree where I had seen the *thing*. I still had no idea where it could have gone. It was hard to guess the size because the tree was so far away.

"Well?" I asked. "Are you going over there?"

He chewed on his lip. "The sheriff sent me out here to get more evidence bags."

"You're wasting time. It might be getting way."

"It?" He swallowed.

I rolled my eyes. "I don't know that it's an it, but it's a something. You need to go check it out."

The young deputy shook his head with the defiance of a toddler. "I can't. The sheriff would wonder what became of me if I didn't return immediately."

"Sure, Mitchell would," I argued. "But once you explain where you were, he'd want you to do this more."

"I'd want Anderson to do what?" Mitchell asked.

I turned to find a tired-looking sheriff standing in my parents' wide front doorway. There were circles under his eyes that I hadn't noticed when he'd first arrived. Maybe they had appeared after seeing Griffin Bright's battered body. I knew every murder that happened in the county sat squarely on his shoulders. He took each death personally and investigated it to the very end. I wondered if the extra weight this time was because the murder involved my parents.

Mom and Dad liked Mitchell and were always kind to him, but Mitchell couldn't forget how far my mother had gone to convince me to take my ex-fiancé, Ryan Dickinson, back. Ryan was a successful corporate law attorney and member of Dallas's high society. Mom thought he was a perfect fit for me and the life she had wanted me to live. Once upon a time, I had too. Then, I met Mitchell. I knew I was misguided in that regard. My mother disagreed with me and went as far as to bring Ryan to Ohio with her and my father my first Christmas back in Holmes County. It had all worked out in the end, but Mitchell had not been amused.

I cleared my throat, and pushed thoughts about that year's super-awkward Christmas to the back of my mind. I had more important things to think about at the moment, such as murder and a Bigfoot on the run. "I thought I saw a person over by the side of that tree. He was watching the house."

"A hiker?" he asked.

"Noooo." I drew out the word. "It sort of looked like a cross between a man and a gorilla."

He gave me a look that said, *Et tu, Angie?*

I waved my hands. "I'm not saying it's Bigfoot, but there was something there. I told Anderson he should check it out."

Mitchell studied me. "Is this a new Angie, one not willing to run headfirst into danger?"

I frowned.

There was a little of the sparkle back in his aqua-marine eyes. "Because if it is, I really like her."

I put my hands on my hips. "I resent that remark."

Mitchell nodded to Deputy Anderson. "Go check it out."

The deputy hesitated.

"Anderson?" Mitchell arched his dark brow.

"Right, sir." He straightened his spine and marched across the street and down the hillside.

Mitchell shook his head and removed his cell phone from his belt. "Send two uniforms across the street to help Anderson search for a suspect matching the description that Jonah Graber gave us at the crime scene . . . Yes, *that* description." He ended the call without saying good-bye.

For a moment, I wondered what it would be like to have the power to bark orders like Mitchell just had and have people snap into action. I had proof that they did because two uniformed officers jogged around the side of the house. Mitchell pointed across the street and they took off down the hill much faster than Deputy Anderson had. I could see all three deputies circling the tree as if playing an odd version of Ring Around the Rosy.

"What's that look on your face for?" he asked.

"I was just thinking that I would like people to hop to when I give the word. Even Mattie questions me when I tell her to do something at the shop, and she's Amish."

His shoulders sagged. "No, you don't. Not really."

I squeezed his upper arm. "Maybe you're right, and it's probably good for the county that I don't have that kind of power. My being a Rolling Brook township trustee is dangerous enough."

He smiled and walked to a squad car in front of the house.

I followed him with Petunia trailing behind me. "Where are you going?"

"I have to get the extra evidence bags while Anderson is Sasquatching."

"Sheriff James Mitchell, are you making a joke while on duty?" I chuckled.

"Don't tell anyone." He opened the trunk of the squad car and removed a box of evidence bags from the empty tire well.

How many did he think he'd needed? The side of the box said it was a hundred count. "You don't think Jonah did it, do you?" I asked. "You know that he couldn't."

Mitchell tucked the box of bags under his arm. "I should have known you weren't really going to stay out of this."

I rolled my eyes. "How can I? We're in my parents' front yard."

Mitchell squinted. "You know Hillary has been complaining to me that Zander has been rolling his eyes a lot lately. You wouldn't know anything about that, would you?"

"Nope," I said a little too quickly before pressing on with my real concern. "Mitchell, I'm serious. Jonah would never hurt anyone. He's the most likable man in the county."

"Gee, thanks." The corner of his mouth quirked up in a half smile. "I was vying for that title."

"You know what I mean. You're going to be hard-pressed to find anyone, Amish or English, who doesn't like Jonah Graber, and equally hard-pressed to find anyone he doesn't like . . ." I trailed off on the last portion of my pronouncement because there was someone Jonah didn't like in the least bit. Now, that one man was dead.

"Angie, do you know something about Jonah's relationship with the deceased that you're not telling me?" His tone was serious. Mitchell didn't miss anything, and much to my chagrin, my face had always reflected every thought passing through my head.

I pushed my long blond curls out of my face. The haphazard knot I had thrown them in that morning as I ran from the house was beginning to unravel. I was stalling. "Not really. I don't know the entire story."

"But there's something that you do know." He wasn't going to let me off the hook that easily.

I didn't answer.

"I thought we agreed we wouldn't keep secrets from each other." His unique blue-green eyes focused on me and did whatever they could to force me to confess. Sometimes—a lot of times—they worked their magic, but not this time. This was Jonah I was protecting. It was going to take a lot more than Mitchell's beautiful eyes to crack me.

I went on the offensive. "You keep secrets from me all the time," I protested.

"I'm the sheriff." He slammed the trunk closed. "I'm obligated to keep secrets from you. It's part of the job."

I folded my arms. "Jonah is one of my best friends, so I'm obligated to keep his confidence."

"Did he tell you not to talk to me about whatever this is?"

"No," I said, because it was true, but then again, I doubted Jonah thought there would be a dead body in my parents' backyard that morning.

"So it is related to Bright."

Drat. I should have just stopped talking altogether. That would have been the safest move. "I can't be forced to speak against my friend."

"That only works for spouses"—he paused—"in court."

"Jonah will have to tell you." I left it at that. "You know he will. He's an honest man. It's his story to tell."

He shook his head. "I need to return to the scene and check in with Anderson by phone. Poor guy looked shaken up by whatever he thinks may be out there."

The officers across the street were still circling the tree. Now it sort of looked like a game of Duck, Duck, Goose. Something had been there—I knew it—but it was just too much to believe it was anything other than a person. Maybe it had been Nahum. Maybe whatever it had been wasn't as large as I first thought.

"Do you really think it's, you know, Bigfoot?" I asked.

"No," was Mitchell's direct answer. "There's no such thing, and even if there was, I doubt it would kill a person with electricity. That is a very human weapon."

He had a point.

He placed his large hand on my cheek for just a moment. "I'll do what I can for Jonah. You know that." With that, he dropped his hand and walked around the side of the house that led to the backyard.

After he was gone, I felt the loss of his brief but warm touch.

Petunia shook me back to reality by biting the head off one of my mother's bright red tulips lining the walk to the front door. A bloodred petal dropped from her lips while she chewed. Not one to miss a snack, Petunia bent her head, scooping it up with her tongue.

I groaned. "Petunia, Mom is going to make goat stew out of you if Miriam doesn't first."

She gave me a mournful sigh and blinked at me.

She always made it so hard to stay mad at her. Dodger had the same talent. Aptly named after Dickens's Artful Dodger, he was twice as destructive as the goat.

"Fine, we'll blame it on a passing deer, but you're going to have to back me up on the story."

She offered me a goaty grin as if she understood. There were plenty of deer in Holmes County to take the fall.

Chapter Eight

I was attempting to pull Petunia away from my mother's tulips when a bright yellow compact car raced up the hill and screeched to a stop in front of my parents' house. The driver parked the car in the middle of the road, and a woman jumped out of the driver's seat. She made a beeline for me, leaving the door of her car wide-open.

Petunia stepped in front of me, and I suddenly felt a lot more grateful for the goat.

The woman was thin and her brown hair was piled on top in an elaborate braided bun that looked painfully tight. There was something about her that was vaguely familiar. "Where is he?" The bangles on her arm rattled together as she yelled the question at me.

Deputy Anderson and the two officers stopped circling the tree and cautiously headed toward us. At least backup was close by.

"Where is who?" I asked.

"Griff! Where is my fiancé?"

I stared at her. "Griffin was your fiancé?"

"Yes," she snapped. "Is he telling people something different? I'll kill him."

Too late for that, I thought.

Anderson spoke in his radio as he approached the woman, and a moment later, Mitchell and another of his deputies came around the side of the house.

"I know he's here," the woman said. "I need to talk to that good-for-nothing scoundrel. If you're not going to tell me where he is, I'll find him myself."

I grimaced. I didn't want to be the one to tell her that her scoundrel fiancé was dead. Thankfully, Mitchell had reached us by that point. "What's going on here?" Mitchell asked.

"I'm looking for my fiancé, Griffin Bright. He should be here working on this house. I told him not to take this small job when he has a big contract in town, but would he listen to me? No. He never listens to me."

"Ms. . . ." Mitchell began.

"Zeff. My name is Mallory Zeff. Now, will you please tell me where Griff is?"

"When was the last time you saw Griffin?" Mitchell asked.

"Two days, when I threw him out of my apartment. He came begging to me to give him more time, but I gave him an ultimatum. The wedding had to happen by the end of this year, or I was leaving him for good."

"Wait," I interrupted. "I thought you said he was your fiancé."

Her dark eyes narrowed. "He *is* my fiancé. We've been together for years. I'm tired of him putting off the wedding. I came here to give him a piece of my

mind. He's not answering any of my calls or texts."
She scowled. "So typical. I don't know why I put up
with him at all."

At that moment, the EMTs pushed the gurney that
held Griffin's body around the side of the house.

The sight of the gurney seemed to shock her, and then
she looked around and seemed to register all the police
officers and their vehicles. "What's going on here?"

"Miss Zeff," Mitchell began. "I need to talk to you
about Griffin."

Understanding dawned on her face. "Griff?" she
whispered. Mallory lunged at the gurney. Mitchell
caught her before she could reach it. Wisely, the EMTs
picked up their pace and transferred Griffin's body to
the ambulance. The tires of the ambulance screeched
as they sped away from the curb.

The woman was crying. "You can't take him. That's
my fiancé. You just can't take him."

"Sheriff," Deputy Anderson said, "I'm sorry to
interrupt, sir, but Mr. and Mrs. Braddock want to talk
to you."

I grimaced. It sounded like Mitchell was being
called to the principal's office, and with my mother,
that was a pretty good comparison.

Mitchell looked heavenward for the briefest of
moments. "Please record Miss Zeff's statement. I will
be right back." He strode to the house.

I watched Mitchell go. I was torn between learning
more of what Mallory Zeff might know about Griffin's
death and shielding Mitchell from a verbal attack from
my mother.

Deputy Anderson made the decision for me. "Angie," he said, "you should probably give Mitchell some backup with your mom and dad." He wrinkled his nose in concern for Mitchell, and I knew he was right.

It wasn't until the deputy led Mallory away that I remembered why she looked so familiar to me. I had seen her before, just a few yards from where Petunia and I stood at that very moment. She was the sullen woman who had been sitting in Griffin's truck yesterday, which meant she had been lying. The last time she had seen him hadn't been two days ago. What else was she lying about?

This knowledge spurred me to find out where Mitchell went. It was even more important than rescuing him from my mother's barrage of reprimands and complaints.

Inside the house, I tied Petunia to the banister in the foyer. Even as I did it, I had a sinking feeling that it was very bad idea. I was about to untie her and take her back outside, when my mother cried, "You can't be serious!"

I abandoned the goat and dashed into the next room. I don't know what I expected to find in my parents' living room, but my mother glaring at my boyfriend was not a welcome sight. She poked her manicured fingernail into his chest. "James Mitchell, I am in the middle of a massive renovation here. I don't have a working kitchen. I need that to be fixed, especially since there is a murderer running loose in this county, and now you say I have to leave my own home. What is Kent supposed to do? He's injured his back. He can't sleep on some hard hotel bed. That will only make his pain worse."

Mitchell almost appeared neutral as my mother poked him, but I saw his right cheek twitch. Ever the gentleman, he would never tell my mother off, even if she might deserve it.

Oliver, who had been seated next to my father's chair doing his best to play the part of guard dog— which was an impossible feat for a funny-face Frenchie— crept over to me at the door.

Dad cleared his throat from his spot on the recliner. "James, as you can see, my wife doesn't want to leave our home." He grimaced. "And I have to agree with her about my back and the hotel bed."

"I'm not saying that you have to leave," Mitchell said in an even voice. "I was only making a suggestion. The investigation in your backyard might go on for some time. We'll move the trailer to the crime lab as soon as possible, but several eyewitnesses saw someone near your property. My first concern is your safety."

Dad reached up and took my mother's hand. "We understand."

Mitchell glanced over at me. I hadn't even known he'd realized that I had entered the room. Not that I should be surprised; Mitchell was always aware of what was going on around him.

"I will not abandon my home," Mom declared.

"I can stay here," I spoke up. "The more people here to keep watch on the house, the better, and with Dad not being able to get around as well as usual, I would like to keep an eye on things. It'll only be for a couple of days. I'm sure Jonah and his men will have the kitchen done as quickly as possible."

Mitchell's head snapped in my direction, and I gave him my most innocent smile. By staying at my parents' home, I might have an opportunity to delve into the murder and clear Jonah's name, and it was true I wanted to keep an eye on my father. His back injury worried me.

Mitchell's eyes narrowed. Sheesh. You'd think that the guy didn't trust my motives.

Mom nodded as if liking the idea. "You can stay in my future grandbaby's room."

Okay, I was already regretting my decision. I dared to peek at Mitchell.

The sheriff's jaw twitched. I didn't know if it was from my obvious scheme to investigate or the mention of grandchildren. Probably both.

I gave Mitchell the best set of puppy-dog eyes I could muster.

He gave a slight shake of his head. The eyes didn't work. They never did. Not with the pageant judges, my parents, or Mitchell. Why then, did I keep trying with the hope of different results?

Dad shifted in his seat and winced. "I hate to ask you to leave your own home, AngieBear. I'm not an invalid." He patted his walker. "With my aluminum steed, I can get around pretty well."

"I want to stay," I said. "I'll feel better if I know you and Mom are safe. If I was at my own house, I would only worry there."

"I think it's a splendid idea, Angie," my mother said

as she gave Mitchell a level stare down. "It will give us a chance to chat about your future."

My future? I would avoid that conversation at all costs, even if it required me to run headlong into Bigfoot's arms. I put a brave face on for Mitchell's sake.

He gave me a steady look. "All right," the sheriff said in resignation. It was almost as if he knew he would never win with a roomful of Braddocks up against him. He was right in that regard. "We still have to process the kitchen," Mitchell said. "Jonah claimed to enter the backyard through the broken French door. We want to make sure his story jibes with the physical evidence. I wouldn't expect any work being done in the kitchen until tomorrow at the earliest."

"That's settled, then," I said and picked up Oliver. "I'll stay. Now, I really have to run. I need to stop at home before opening the shop."

"I'll walk you out," Mitchell said.

In the foyer, we found Petunia still tethered to the banister, munching on a piece of crime scene tape.

Mitchell ran his hand through his dark hair flecked with silver. It definitely had more silver than when I first moved to Holmes County. I refused to make the correlation.

"How in the world did she get ahold of that?" Mitchell asked.

I shrugged, setting Oliver on the floor next to the goat. "Do you think it will make her sick?"

"It's not any worse than most of the stuff that she eats." He paused. "So you just happen to want to stay at your parents' home to protect them?" His voice dripped with doubt.

I put my hands on my hips. "You don't think I'm worried about my own father?"

He held up his hands as if to warn off the barrage of words I was about to throw at him, and I had some doozies in mind too. "I know you're worried about him. You have every right to be. I'm only suggesting that caring for your parents isn't your only motive for wanting to stay here."

My eyes narrowed into slits. "What are you implying, Sheriff?"

He focused his blue-green gaze directly at me. "You want to snoop."

I didn't confirm or deny this.

He rubbed the back of his neck. "This case is going to be a pain. I can already tell. And it's not just because the crime was committed on your parents' property, but that certainly doesn't help."

"Neither does Bigfoot," I reminded him. "That's a new one."

He groaned. "There's no such thing, but there will be some Amish in the county who will be offended just by the rumors of its existence. They aren't much for make-believe, as you know."

I nodded. Martha Yoder immediately came to mind. She would hate the rumor about Bigfoot in the county and would somehow blame me for it. Martha had once worked for my aunt at Running Stitch. She had even taken care of my aunt Eleanor while she was battling cancer.

Because of her loyalty to my aunt during that difficult time, she had expected that she would be the one who would inherit Running Stitch upon my aunt's death. To her surprise, and frankly to mine, Aunt Eleanor left the shop to me. Martha never forgave me for that and, out of spite, opened a rival Amish quilt shop, Authentic Amish Quilts, right next to Running Stitch.

I untied Petunia and led her out the front door. Oliver and Mitchell followed me as I walked the goat to my small SUV parked crookedly on the street. "At least you have a good suspect."

Mitchell arched his brow.

"Mallory, Griffin's fiancée. Something is up with her. She already lied once."

His gaze sharpened. "What do you mean?"

I went on to tell him about seeing Mallory in Griffin's truck the day before.

"Interesting," Mitchell said thoughtfully.

"Can I talk to Jonah before I go?" I asked.

He shook his head. "He's still being questioned. I need to have a little chat with the fiancée." He squeezed my hand. "Don't do anything stupid. Please."

"Me?" I asked. "Do something stupid?"

He shook his head and walked back into my parents' house.

As much as I wanted to stay and support Jonah while he was being questioned, I knew that I could do more good by finding out everything I could about Griffin Bright and those who might want him dead. I also needed to find out how Kamon, Jonah's cousin, died, and why he thought Griffin had been responsible for his death. It would be some time before I could hear the story from Jonah, so I needed to consult another source.

I gave the house one last look and loaded my Frenchie and the goat into my car.

It was still early and the shop didn't open until ten, so I had time to stop at home and shower.

I got home, freshened up, and told Dodger he had to stay home for the day. He was not pleased. But Petunia and Dodger didn't get along, and I couldn't contend with a goat versus cat smackdown on top of everything else.

When I reached the shop, I walked Petunia to the small fenced backyard by way of the narrow alley that divided my shop from Martha Yoder's quilt shop.

"Try not to eat all of the flowers," I said even though I knew the request was pointless.

I was going to be alone in the shop that day. I had given Mattie time off to help at the pie factory. She'd said that Aaron needed her the entire day. The request was unusual. The factory had been open for six months, and this was the first time that Aaron had Mattie fill so many shifts. I hoped that Aaron wasn't trying to take her away from the quilt shop and back into the family business. I didn't know what I would do if I lost her. I'd never find another assistant as good or as flexible with my many ideas.

I glanced at the clock hanging over the sales counter. I still had a half hour before opening. That was plenty of time to check in with Rachel and tell her about the morning's events.

"Oliver, let's hit the bakery."

Oliver perked up at this because he knew visiting Miller's Amish Bakery across the street would mean a sampling of Rachel's homemade dog biscuits.

Through the large window in the front of the bakery, I could see Rachel behind the counter, ringing up an English customer. There weren't any other customers in the bakery, so this would be a good time to catch Rachel before the next rush.

Rachel smiled sweetly at me as I walked through the door. My friend was the epitome of sweetness and what people who know nothing about the Amish conjure in their minds when they imagine the unique culture. She wore a sky blue plain dress and black apron. A white prayer cap was pinned to the top of her chestnut-colored hair that was pulled back to the nape of her neck in a traditional Amish bun. "Angie," Rachel said, "I'm so glad that you stopped by. We've both been so busy these last few days that I feel like I haven't seen you in years."

I laughed. "I feel the same way. We need to make a plan to have coffee at least twice a week even during the busiest times."

"Agreed." Rachel bent over and lifted a jar of dog biscuits from a shelf under the display counter. Oliver's stubby tail jiggled in anticipation. Rachel giggled at his antics and tossed him the biscuit. Oliver caught the biscuit in his mouth and carried it under one of the small round tables in the bakery's small eat-in area to enjoy in peace.

Rachel poured coffee into two plain white mugs.

She handed the mugs to me over the counter. "Doughnuts or muffins?"

I carried them to one of the round tables. "Definitely doughnuts," I said. "Make it a double. It's already been a long morning."

Rachel selected two glazed Amish doughnuts from the display case and stepped around the counter to join me. "What has happened now?"

"You're going to want to sit before I tell you."

Rachel sat, and I relayed the events of the morning. Her mouth fell open as I told her the story.

Rachel's eyes were worried. "Jonah called you to help him?"

I broke off a piece of my doughnut. Before popping it in my mouth, I said, "The incident happened at my parents' house. Why wouldn't he call me?"

"I haven't heard about it before this. Does his family know?" She held her coffee mug by the handle but didn't lift it to her lips.

I swallowed, and the doughnut felt like a pebble lodged in the middle of my throat. "I—I don't know. Maybe not." I slapped my forehead. "I should have stopped at the Graber farm to tell both Miriam and Anna. Maybe I should go now. The shop can be closed for an hour or so."

"*Nee.* I think it's best that Miriam does not hear the news from you," my friend said.

I took a swig of my coffee, hoping that it would wash down the doughnut. All I managed to do was burn my tongue.

Rachel shook her head and stood. She walked into

the kitchen and returned a moment later with a glass of ice water. She placed it on the table in front of me as she sat down.

"Thanks," I said, taking hold of the glass. "Jonah told me about his cousin Kamon. Jonah claimed that Griffin Bright, the man who was killed this morning, murdered Kamon." I sipped my water.

"I haven't heard the name Kamon in a very long time." Her brow furrowed as if my mentioning Kamon made this conversation even more worrisome.

I frowned. "Do you know how Kamon died?"

She nodded. "He was electrocuted."

Chapter Nine

"Electrocuted?" I yelped and nearly knocked over my coffee mug.

Some coffee splashed on the table, but Rachel caught the mug before it could topple over completely. She sopped up the spilled coffee with a paper napkin from the metal dispenser in the middle of the table.

She stacked the wet napkins on my empty plate and switched our two plates, putting her untouched doughnut in front of me.

I broke off a piece of the fresh doughnut. "Tell me."

"I don't know everything," she said. "I was very young. I'm sure Jonah or Anna could tell you all the details." She wrinkled her nose and added, "Or Sarah Leham." Sarah was another member of our quilting circle. She was also a notorious gossip. Rachel and Sarah had settled their differences, but I knew Rachel still didn't approve of Sarah's gossip-mongering.

"All I know," Rachel said, "was that Kamon was going to leave the community. He hadn't before he died. He was working as an apprentice for Griffin Bright and was killed in an accident on a jobsite."

"If it was an accident, why does Jonah claim that Griffin killed him?" I popped another bite of doughnut in my mouth.

She shook her head. "You'll have to ask him that."

I paused before asking her my next question. "Did you know Jonah considered leaving the Amish like Kamon planned to do? He told me as much when he started to tell me about Kamon."

She nodded. "I may have not known about it at the time, but I heard others talking about it years later— about how Jonah had made a rapid turnaround back to the Amish way after Kamon's death. For a while there, everyone thought he would leave the Amish way of life."

I wrapped my hands around my coffee mug as if I needed the warmth. "That just doesn't make any sense to me. My whole life it never occurred to me Jonah could be anything other than Amish. Why would he leave? He loves the Amish life."

"You," was her simple answer.

"What?" I squeaked. At least this time my hands were around the mug, so I didn't flail them about and knock something else over, like the remainder of my doughnut. It would be truly sad to lose a doughnut like that. "What are you talking about?"

She pursed her lips as if carefully considering her words.

"Rachel, tell me what you mean," I pleaded.

"Jonah was sweet on you," she said. "He thought about

leaving the Amish for you. He knew you would never become Amish, so he was willing, at least at that time, to become *Englisch*."

I shook my head, denying it. "He might have had a boyhood crush on me when we were little kids, but it was nothing more than that. A crush is not enough to walk away from your home, your family, or your entire life."

Rachel shook her head. "It was more than a little boy's first crush. I was a child, and even I knew how Jonah felt about the blond *Englisch* girl who visited Eleanor Lapp during the summers. The boys in our district teased him relentlessly about it."

"I didn't know Jonah was teased over our friendship." I frowned. "But I still can't believe he was thinking about leaving his community for *me*."

"Why?" she asked. "Your aunt left her life for your uncle Jacob."

I ran my finger along the mug's rim. "That's different."

"I don't think it is." She took a deep breath as if she needed the extra wind power to say what came next. "Haven't you ever wondered why Miriam doesn't like you?"

"Miriam hates everyone," I said.

She shook her head. "*Nee*, Angie. Only you."

"Ummm . . . ouch." I winced. "So she doesn't like me. Don't tell me it's because Jonah was going to leave the Amish for me."

"It is," she said without an ounce of doubt in her voice.

"That's ridiculous. Even if what you said is true—which I'm not saying that it is—that was twenty years ago." I broke off a larger piece of doughnut.

Rachel shook her head. "*Nee*, it is not. I'm sure Jonah told his wife about his feelings for you, which is why she dislikes you so much. That's the kind of thing an Amish couple would share during courting. Miriam most likely never felt too concerned about it because you were so far away." She paused. "Then you came back."

"He's married," I protested. Miriam couldn't possibly think something between Jonah and me could still happen. The idea made me ill. As Jonah had said, we had each chosen our own paths. He was like a brother to me. "I would never—I could never—even if I wasn't with Mitchell, I would never break up a family! He's my dear friend—but nothing more."

She reached across the table and squeezed my hand. "I know that. I'm sure that in her heart Miriam knows that too, but she can't bring herself to like you because you were Jonah's first love."

This couldn't be true.

She released my hand and was quiet for a moment as if to allow me to absorb this new information.

I tried to imagine what I would do if Jonah had shown up on my Dallas doorstep when I was fifteen, professing his love. I grimaced. It would not have been a pleasant scene. Maybe the Amish, at least some of the Amish, start thinking about courting and marriage at that age, but I hadn't. I still had a mountain of stuffed animals in the corner of my bedroom at the time. Ryan had been my first serious boyfriend, and I'd met him in college years later. We were together seven years before I was ready for marriage, but I was already over thirty at that point. Jonah and I couldn't have been more different in the trajectories of our lives.

Rachel squeezed my hand again. "Did I shock you?"

"Yes," I said honestly.

Rachel laughed. "It was a long time ago. Those old feelings Jonah had for you are gone now, I am sure. He still cares for you, *ya*, but not in the same way. I suppose Griffin's death only reminds him of that time. It must be very painful."

I pushed my coffee mug away. "Rachel, I'm worried."

"About the murder?"

"Yes, but I'm more worried about Jonah. He's the main suspect." I paused, almost afraid to reveal what I was really thinking. "And I'm worried I'll lose him as my friend over all of this. If Miriam hates me as much as you say she does, this could be the event for her to convince Jonah to stay away from me forever. I was the one who asked him to help my parents with the kitchen. I put him at the scene of the crime."

"You won't lose Jonah," Rachel insisted, gripping my hand just a little bit tighter. "You will solve the murder." She smiled. "You always do, and then life will go back to the way it was."

What if this time she was wrong? It was hard to imagine my sibling relationship with Jonah going back to the way it was when I now knew he'd once loved me and had been willing to leave his community for me. I wish I could go back to before I had the knowledge. I wish we could go back to before Griffin died in my parents' backyard.

"Are you all right?" Rachel asked this in her quiet and sweet way, and as she did, it reminded me that Jonah had seen a wild man that morning after finding the body. It hadn't been Nahum if it was the same person or thing that I'd seen. At least, I didn't think so. In any case, I thought better of mentioning it to Rachel just then. She had hit me with an emotional bombshell. I couldn't do the same to her and say something that would bring her father to the forefront of her mind.

"Sure," I said, slightly dazed.

Her large green eyes held understanding. "I guess you will start investigating to find out what happened."

"I will when I can get away from the shop."

She stood and picked up our plates from the table. "Why can't you leave the shop? It's not the middle of the high season. Mattie can take care of the quilt shop for a little while."

"Mattie's not at—" I stopped myself in midsentence. If Rachel thought that Mattie was working at Running Stitch, that could only mean my assistant wasn't helping Aaron at the factory. Rachel would know if Mattie was at the pie factory.

Rachel set out plates on the counter. "Mattie's not what?"

I was saved from answering by the arrival of three elderly men who were morning regulars in the bakery. The men made a beeline for the counter and joked with one another as they picked out their doughnuts.

"I had better let you get back to the counter," I said.

Her brow knit together, but she only nodded as she went to tend to her customers.

As Oliver and I walked back across the street to my shop, my conversation with Rachel haunted me and brought to mind a conversation that I had had with Anna Graber only a few days after I moved back to Holmes County to take over Running Stitch. Anna had said something like, "Jonah moped for days after your family moved to Texas and looked forward to seeing you each summer. It was hard for him when you stopped coming, but it was for the best."

The conversation had stuck with me nearly two years later, and I remember the pang I had felt when Anna had said that to me. How could my staying away from Holmes County been for the best? I had wondered at the time. I hadn't fully understood it, but then again, maybe a small part of me had and I pushed it away. Rachel's revelation confirmed what I might have always known.

And now, I had to worry about Mattie lying to me about working at the pie factory on top of that. I knew that she wasn't working there, because Rachel would definitely know if Aaron had asked Mattie to help out. Oh yeah, and then there was the murder too.

"Angie!" Willow Moon called to me as my foot hit the sidewalk in front of Running Stitch.

I turned to find Willow standing in the doorway of her place of business, The Dutchman's Tea Shop, one of the few truly English businesses in Rolling Brook. No one would confuse Willow for an Amish person. She waved her hand at me, causing the gauzy fabric that made up almost all of her blouses to billow around her face. However, her short spiked purple hair never moved. "Please come over."

"I need to open the shop," I said, fearing that Willow needed a tea taste tester. Been there, done that, and I had barely come away with my life, not to mention my taste buds intact. I didn't know what tealike concoction Willow was brewing up across the street at her tea shop, and I didn't want to know. They were all horrible.

"I'll come to you," she called and made her way across the street to stand next to me on the sidewalk.

I unlocked the front door to Running Stitch and let Oliver and Willow inside before stepping into the shop myself.

"Angie, I'm so glad that I caught you alone," she said as I entered. "We have important township business to discuss."

Willow and I were both Rolling Brook township trustees. I had taken the post in order to represent the interests of the Amish in Rolling Brook. The Amish would not run for political office and depended on their English friends to remember them when making laws and rules in the county. I had found that severely lacking when I first moved back to Holmes County, at least in Rolling Brook, and took up their cause. That didn't mean I enjoyed it. I had found during my time in the positon that most of the work of a township official was boring and tedious. And the long rhetoric-filled meetings were the absolute worst.

Willow and I were usually allies when it came to making decisions for the township. She and I were on one side, and head trustee Caroline Cramer and Jason

Rustle were on the other. Former head trustee—who still acted like and would like everyone to believe he was still in charge—Farley Jung was the tie breaker. It was always a surprise to see on what side of a decision Farley would fall.

"I heard about the accident at your parents' home today," she said without preamble.

I turned on the lights and raised my eyebrows. "How'd you hear about it? I just told Rachel, and she didn't know."

"Farley called," she said, as if that was explanation enough. Actually, it was. It seemed that Farley Jung knew everything that happened in the county. "I heard too that there was a Bigfoot sighting there."

Oh boy. I took a breath and walked over to the cash register. I hit the NO SALE button and the drawer flew open. "Willow, it wasn't Bigfoot. There's no such thing."

"That's not what I heard," she said, and she lowered her voice even though we were the only two—not counting Oliver—in the shop.

I removed my full money drawer from the locked cabinet under the counter and set it into the cash register. "Willow, you can't be serious."

"It was Bigfoot. It's the only explanation." She lowered her voice. "I've seen him myself."

Chapter Ten

I stared at Willow as if she had a unicorn horn growing out of her forehead. Seeing how she was talking about believing in Bigfoot, it was possible that she wouldn't find that thought the least bit strange. "Come again?" I asked.

"Bigfoot! Sasquatch! He's here. There have been a number of sightings in the county over the years. I saw him myself."

"When?"

She tapped her chin with her index finger. "I'd say it was about four years ago. It was definitely before you moved here. Remember the old barn that burned down and where the pie factory is now? Well," she said, warming up to her tall tale, "I was out for a walk one evening. I used to walk to the barn and back to my shop just for a little exercise. I was strolling along and was about to head back to the tea shop when the creature jumped out of a tree on the far side of the barn and ran into the woods. I spun around and ran for my life."

"Was it an animal, like a raccoon?" I asked.

She dropped her hand and her blouse billowed

around her with the movement. "That would have to be a pretty huge raccoon. It was bigger than a man. I knew it was Bigfoot."

"What did you do?" I asked, even though I knew by questioning I was only prolonging the conversation.

"I ran home and called Farley right off." She waited.

I suppressed a sigh and asked, "Then what happened?"

"The sheriff and his deputies came out and checked the scene. They didn't find anything."

"Mitchell was there?"

She nodded. "Oh, yes, I insisted that he come himself."

I frowned. Mitchell hadn't mentioned there had been other Bigfoot sightings in the county. I knew that Willow wasn't the most reliable of witnesses, but I was sure Mitchell remembered the incident.

Willow was still talking. "That was the last time Bigfoot was seen in this county until the sightings around your parents' house this week." She took a breath. "It was also the last time I walked to that old barn by myself at night."

"Willow, you can't really believe that it's anything more than a guy in a suit. Maybe it was someone playing a joke on you."

She folded her arms. "Bigfoots have been reported all over Ohio. If I were a Bigfoot, what better place to hide out than in Amish country? There are plenty of dense forests around here. Plenty to eat and plenty of water."

I couldn't argue with her that Holmes County would be a good place for a Bigfoot to live if there was such a creature, but there wasn't. "Do you know exactly how Farley had heard about the latest sightings? Did he tell you?"

She nodded. "He heard all about it from one of the sheriff's deputies."

Anderson. I'd bet my best quilt frame that it was him. I sighed. The deputy wanted so desperately to impress Mitchell, he should know better than to leak information to a township trustee.

I smoothed the dollar bills in my hands. "Did this deputy say he saw the creature with his own eyes?"

"Nooo," she said slowly. "But he described what Jonah Graber and others on the scene saw."

She made no mention of my eyewitness account, so I thought it was best to keep the tidbit to myself. "Maybe Jonah and the others didn't realize what they were seeing. Maybe it's a bear, or," I added, "a bobcat."

She shook her head, and as usual, her purple spiky hair was perfectly still. "There aren't that many bears around here, and a bobcat isn't big enough."

I was tapped out of my Ohio-wildlife knowledge. "All I do know is it wasn't a Bigfoot."

Willow shook her head sadly. "In any case, the trustees need to meet to see how to handle this."

"Handle what?" I still wasn't following.

Oliver came over and sat at my feet. I appreciated the solidarity. I thought I would need it for whatever Willow had in mind.

"The Bigfoot situation." She threw up her hands.

"What does this have to do with the township trustees? Whoever or whatever it is is Mitchell's problem, not the trustees. It's tied to a murder investigation."

"You can't think Bigfoot did it." She covered her mouth as if in shock.

I sighed. "Since Griffin Bright was electrocuted, no, I don't think Bigfoot did it."

"He was?" She moved her hand over her heart.

Briefly, I covered my eyes with my hand. Mitchell would kill me if he knew I let that little tidbit about the case slip to Willow. Even Anderson knew not to let that slip. I lowered my hand. "Please keep the electrocution piece to yourself."

"Of course." She nodded solemnly. "But the Bigfoot situation is not a problem at all," she said excitedly. "In fact, I think it's a great chance to boost tourism. There are many Bigfoot enthusiasts in the state. We should spread the word that there's been a sighting."

"Why?" I asked.

She threw up her hands as if in exasperation again. "So they can come here and search for the Sasquatch, and while they're at it, they'll visit the county and spend money in our township's businesses. Everyone wins."

I closed the cash drawer and stepped around the counter. I leaned against it. "The sheriff won't like a bunch of people coming into the county and tramping through the woods when he's trying to find a killer. I know your intentions are good, Willow, but it could undermine his investigation into who killed Griffin Bright."

Willow bit her lip. "I hadn't thought about that," she said.

"What's that face for?" I asked suspiciously.

She squinted at me. "I might have already spread the word."

I covered my eyes with my hand. When I lowered my hand, I found Oliver at my feet doing the same thing. "What do you mean by spread the word?"

Willow had the grace to appear a little bit sheepish. "There is a Bigfoot Ohio group online. I go in there on occasion for updates because I'm a Bigfoot believer."

Of course she did. "Oh-kay . . ."

"And I posted the sighting information on the group's message board." She scrunched up her face as if afraid of what my reaction to that announcement might be.

I felt a headache form right between the eyes. "When you posted on the message board, did you say where the last sighting was?" I had a sinking feeling.

She nodded. "Sure. I gave them the address, so they would know right where to go."

I gripped the counter for support. "That's my parents' house! Are you telling me Bigfoot enthusiasts are en route, en masse, to my parents' house?"

"Oh, I hadn't thought about that either." She placed her heavily ringed finger to her cheek.

"Willow!" I yelped. "What if a bunch of Bigfoot fanatics show up on my mother's doorstep?"

She was thoughtful. "I can't see Daphne being happy about that."

"Neither can I, and in this case, I wouldn't blame her."

Willow hurried to the door. "I'll get online right now and delete the message."

I groaned. "Hopefully it's not too late."

She ran out the door. Oliver and I watched her skip across the street and into the tea shop. This was going to end badly. Of that I was sure.

Chapter Eleven

After Willow disappeared into the tea shop on her important errand, I turned to Oliver, who sat at the front window. "I have a bad feeling about this, Ollie, a really bad feeling."

He gave me a sympathetic look.

For the moment, I tried to push thoughts of Bigfoot and murder from my mind and concentrate on opening the shop. As the morning went on, a few tourists came and went. When it was quiet, I fielded phone calls from my mother about what was happening at their house. The last I heard, Mitchell and his officers were still there, so was Jonah. Poor Jonah. I couldn't get what Rachel had revealed to me just that morning out of my head.

At midday, Mattie ran breathlessly into the store. "Angie, I heard about Griffin Bright." Some of her hair had slipped out of the bun on the back of her head. "I came as soon as I heard the news. Are you all right? Are your parents all right?"

I nodded yes to both of those questions. "Everyone is fine. At least everyone except for Griffin. He will never be fine again." My face fell when I thought of the vibrant man I had met the day before.

Mattie shivered. "How horrible. I heard he was electrocuted."

I nodded. "It was nice of you to come from the pie factory to check on me."

Her smooth brow knit together. "The factory?" she asked.

"Yes," I said, watching her closely. "Your brother's pie factory. That's why you asked for the day off from the shop, so that you can help your brother." I frowned. After my conversation that morning with Rachel, I hoped that Mattie would tell me what she was up to on her own.

Her face turned a blazing shade of red. "Oh yes, the factory. That's where I was. I thought I would come here and see if you needed any help." She wouldn't look at me. Mattie wasn't much of a liar.

I was about to ask her where she had really been that morning when an enormous tour bus parked just outside of Running Stitch, and soon we were descended upon by two dozen tourists. That left no time to talk.

After the group left, Mattie grabbed her basket and was out of the door like her skirts were on fire. "Sorry to run, Angie, but I'm needed at the factory."

"Mattie," I started, but I was talking to the closed door.

Oliver looked up at me and tilted his head to the right, his ears pointed to the door.

"She's up to something," I told him.

Oliver remained silent.

I chewed my lip. It was approaching lunchtime, and

I still hadn't heard from Jonah about picking up Petunia. The last time my mother called, she said he left over an hour ago. Perhaps he wanted to break the news to Miriam without the goat in tow. Miriam liked Petunia just as much as she liked me.

I wish that Mattie was here, so I could ask her questions about Griffin Bright and his life. Did he work alone? Did he have a business partner? Was he ever married? Did he have children? I knew next to nothing about him. I had done a quick Internet search on his business but came up with nothing. It wasn't unusual for small businesses in Holmes County, even the English ones, not to have a Web site. Running Stitch hadn't had one until I took it over. The most common way people learned about services in the county was by word of mouth or an occasional ad in the newspaper.

I called my mother. "Mom?" I said when she picked up on the first ring.

"Angie, thank goodness. The police finally left. James said that Jonah can begin construction on the kitchen tomorrow afternoon."

"That's good news," I agreed. "How did you pick Griffin as your electrician?"

"That seems like an odd question," she said.

"Please just answer it."

Mom was quiet for a moment as she thought. "Actually, I believe it was the lady at the diner that you go to all the time. Your father and I were there." She sighed. "You know he likes that greasy food even though the doctor says it's not good for him. We were talking about plans for the kitchen and the need for a good electrician.

Your friend overheard and suggested Double Bright Electric and said it was a two-brother team."

"Linda at the Double Dime Diner recommended him?" I asked as if there was another possibility. There wasn't. The Double Dime was just about the only place I ate out. I went there so often, I was considering notifying the post office it was my new address.

"Yes."

"You said it was a two-brother team," I said. "But Griffin was there alone yesterday."

"I never saw the other brother. When Griffin came to do the estimate, he came alone."

"What was the brother's name?"

"Griffin never mentioned it. He said that he could handle the kitchen job himself, so I never asked for his brother's name," Mom said, sounding a little miffed.

"That makes sense," I said, backing off. I told my mother good-bye and ended the call deep in thought. Yesterday, Griffin had been alone when I met him in my mother's kitchen, but that didn't mean he had been alone this morning. What if his brother had come with him to help with the job? And what if that brother had killed him? I shivered. I had to learn more about Griffin and his unnamed brother.

I needed to talk to Linda at the diner, the sooner, the better. My stomach rumbled in agreement, giving me another reason to stop by.

If I left that early in the day, I would have to close the shop early. It wasn't something I usually did, but there was no one there to ask to watch my business. In this case, it was more important to help Jonah than to sell a quilt.

Besides, I had had a good day with that last bus tour earlier. I found myself feeling frustrated at Mattie for taking the day off. Not that she wasn't entitled to a day off. She deserved it, and she'd said it was to help her family. But was it really? I knew there was something that she was keeping from me, and that didn't sit well with me.

I went into the backyard to check on Petunia. The goat was snoozing in the shade. She sniffed the air when I stepped outside but didn't open her eyes. She would be all right for a little while longer.

Back in the shop, I gathered up my ever-present hobo bag and started to remove money from the cash drawer in preparation to close up when the door to Running Stitch opened. I should have locked that first. The last thing I wanted to do was kick a customer out; that would be worse than being closed when she came to the door.

To my relief, the Amish woman who came through the door wasn't a customer, but Sarah Leham. Sarah was a thin Amish woman who wore wire-rimmed glasses low on her long nose. It made her appear as if she always had a secret or was on the lookout for one, which was an accurate description of her personality.

"Sarah, what are you doing here?" I asked. "I was just about to close up the shop."

"Close up the shop? Whatever for?" She removed her navy shawl and hung it on one of the wooden pegs along the wall.

"I assume you heard about Griffin Bright," I said.

"'Course I have. That's why I'm here. I came as quickly as I could. One of the children stayed home from school ill today or I would have been here sooner."

"Is she all right?" I asked.

"It's nothing. Just a little head cold." She waved away my concern. "She's up now playing with her toys. Jeremiah can't work in the field until they dry out some from all the rains, so he's home keeping an eye on her."

"I'm glad to hear that." I propped my elbows on the counter.

"It's good for my husband to take care of the children now and again. It makes him appreciate me more. Besides, he told me to go ahead. He remembers what a help you were to his brother when he was in trouble last year. When I told him that you had to help Jonah with a similar issue, he told me I had to go so you could investigate. You know everyone loves Jonah Graber. There isn't a person in the county who doesn't know him and like him."

Last year, Sarah's brother-in-law Levi had been a murder suspect when the bishop from his conservative district had been killed. For a moment, I wondered if Sarah knew about Jonah's history with Kamon and wanting to leave the Amish. I stopped myself from asking her. It wasn't a conversation I wanted to have with Sarah. It would be halfway around the county by the end of the day if I did. Sarah didn't need a telephone to spread news. It was quite impressive, actually.

She held up her quilting basket. "I thought that you would have some investigating to do on Jonah's behalf, so I'm here to mind the store for you."

I beamed. "Sarah, you're a godsend. That's why I was closing. I'm headed to the Double Dime Diner to talk to Linda about Griffin. She was the one who suggested my mother hire him as the electrician for a kitchen remodel. She might know more about him."

She smiled. "Great minds think alike. You run along. I'll take care of the shop, and if you're not back by closing time, I'll lock up."

I hugged her. "Thank you, Sarah."

"Any word from Anna?" she asked.

I shook my head as I walked back around the counter and returned the money I had removed back to the cash register. "No, I'm sure I'll hear from her soon." I couldn't keep the worry from my voice.

It was odd that I hadn't heard from Anna about what happened that morning. Usually my aunt's closest friend was the first to run to my side when I got tangled up in a murder investigation, which seemed to happen to me a fair amount. I tried not to worry what her absence might mean. Maybe Anna was staying close to home to help Miriam deal with all that had happened. Whatever happened to Jonah would ultimately impact the entire family.

If Sarah noticed my concern, she made no comment on it. Instead, she made plans. "The quilting circle needs to meet about all of this. I'll contact the other ladies while you're out, and we can plan to meet here after supper. We need to have a meeting as it is. We haven't worked on the quilt in a week or so. I know my own stitches start to get lazy when I don't practice." She pointed at the queen-size Goosefoot quilt tethered to the large quilt frame in the back of the shop.

"That sounds like a great idea, Sarah. I hope everyone can come." I bit the inside of my lip. Both Mattie and Anna were acting strangely. I tried not to let it bother me, but it did. At least I could depend on Sarah to be consistent in her nosiness.

"One more thing. Petunia is here," I said.

"Petunia?" Sarah asked.

I nodded. "She's in the backyard. I just checked on her, and she's fine. My garden, on the other hand, is doomed."

She blinked at me. "Petunia's fine?"

I smiled. "Can you check on her from time to time? And make sure she doesn't eat my fence."

Sarah's eyes doubled in size behind her glasses. "I didn't sign up to goat-sit."

I grabbed my hobo bag from the counter and my jacket from the peg on the wall. "She'll be fine. She's low maintenance."

Even to my own ears that last statement rang as false, but Oliver and I were out the door before Sarah had a chance to respond.

Ten minutes later, when I parked my small SUV on the street next to the Holmes County Courthouse, which dominated downtown Millersburg, and glanced across the street to the Double Dime Diner, I knew something was wrong. The inside of the diner was dark. I jumped out of the car and scooped up Oliver. After pausing briefly for a minivan and an Amish buggy to pass, I ran across Jackson Street.

When I hit the curb, I stared at the CLOSED sign on the Double Dime Diner's glass door. The Double Dime was never closed during the day, not even on Christmas. Worry creeped up my back. Something was very, very wrong.

Chapter Twelve

In my arms, Oliver whined. He sensed something was wrong too, and I knew it wasn't just because he was disappointed over the bacon Linda would have snuck to him had she been there—although I was sure that was part of it.

I set Oliver on the sidewalk and stepped closer to the door. I leaned forward and cupped my hands around my eyes as I took a good look inside. Everything seemed to be in order. The barstools were turned upside down on the counter. The pass-through between the kitchen and dining room was closed. Nothing was disturbed. The place was just closed. That was the disturbing part. I stepped back.

"You look like you lost your puppy," my friend Jessica Nicolson said as she walked up the sidewalk toward me. "But I see he's standing right there next to you."

Oliver went over to greet our friend. She bent down to scratch him between the ears, and as she did, her red hair fell over her face. Oliver always liked Jessica because she was the reason we have Dodger. Her cat,

Cherry Cat, was Dodger's biological mother. Oliver was grateful to Jessica and Cherry Cat for letting us take in the once tiny ball of gray-and-white fluff. Now Dodger was a hefty twelve pounds of feline muscle and sass. Cherry Cat was solid gray and didn't have any of the white markings that Dodger had, but she certainly had sass to spare. That should have been a warning to me.

"Do you know why the Double Dime is closed?" I asked.

She examined my face. "Do you want something to eat? I think I might have some peanut butter crackers back at my shop."

My stomach growled in response. "I'm starving, but I wanted to talk to Linda more than grab a bite of lunch. What happened? Why is the diner closed?"

She brushed her hair over her shoulder. Jessica had the coloring of a true Irish lass with pale skin and blue eyes to go with her red hair. "I saw everything. I was sweeping my walk. The police came. They were there for about a half hour, and then Linda kicked everyone out and closed up. I think it's the first time I'd ever seen the place closed in the middle of the day." She frowned. "You wouldn't happen to know anything about why the police were here, would you?"

I wrinkled my nose.

"Oh boy," she said. "Spill."

I gave her a condensed version of that morning's events. I left out my conversation with Rachel, but I included Willow and the descending Bigfoot lovers.

She tried unsuccessfully to stifle a laugh. "When are they coming?"

I grimaced. "I hope never." I prayed Willow took her post on the message board down in time.

"How are your parents?" Her tone turned concerned.

"Mom's fit to be tied, and Dad hurt his back trying to demo the kitchen himself. That's how I pulled Jonah into this mess to begin with, because I needed his help to take over the kitchen remodel since Dad threw out his back."

She winced. "I'm so sorry your father was hurt."

"Thanks." I smiled.

"But I'm really glad your mom is all right; she's one of my best customers. I'd hate anything to impair her remodel project." She grinned. "I'm kidding."

Jessica owned Out of Time, an antiques shop just down the street from the diner. She had been helping my mother find unique furnishings for her new home. In that regard, Jessica is the daughter that my mother wished she'd had.

"How do I find Linda? In all the time I've known her, I don't think we've had two conversations about her life." I frowned, feeling terrible. I ate at the Double Dime Diner at least twice a week. Linda owned the diner, but she was also the one and only waitress, and she knew so much about my life and the investigations that I had been involved in. What did I know about her other than she worked in the diner and liked her hair fashioned in a 1960s-style beehive?

"I guess you could try her home," Jessica said matter-of-factly. "That would be a good place to start."

"Do you know where she lives?" I asked.

She nodded. "Actually, I do. I gave her a lift home

once when her car was in the shop. It's in that small trailer park on Wells Road. I can't remember the trailer number, but I'll recognize it when I see it. Let's go."

"What about your shop?" I asked.

She smiled. "I was thinking about cutting out early today anyway. Let me just go close up, and we can hit the road."

Within twenty minutes, Jessica, Oliver, and I were turning into Strawberry Way Trailer Park. The sign that welcomed us to the park was shaped like a strawberry. There were at least two dozen trailers in the park, and they were all well kept. The tiny lawns surrounding them were mowed. Spring flowers bloomed in flower boxes, and brightly colored wind chimes glittered and played in the light spring breeze. Elderly homeowners sat on the wide porches attached to their trailers, sipped iced tea, and waved to us as we drove by.

The only eyesore in the entire park was the road. The road through the trailer park wasn't paved but composed of loose gravel. Although it wasn't raining at present, all the rain that we'd had in the last couple of days left the road and the parking lot a muddy mess.

I parked the car and could feel my car's tires sink into the mud as the car came to a complete stop.

"Are you sure you want to walk through this with your boots?" Jessica asked.

I looked down at my feet. I was wearing my beloved cowboy boots. They were a one-of-a-kind, custom-made pair that I'd found and fallen in love with in Dallas over a decade ago. They were aged brown leather with hand-stitched blue flowers running up the sides. I loved my boots, and I always wore them when I needed a little extra boost of courage, like this morning when a dead guy was found in my parents' backyard. "I'll be careful," I said.

Jessica grinned and got out of the car. Gingerly, I did the same. I lifted Oliver out of the backseat, opting to carry the Frenchie rather than let him sink into mud.

"That's Linda's trailer there," Jessica said, pointing at a butter yellow trailer with navy blue shutters. A hanging basket of purple pansies dangled from the porch's eaves.

I was grateful that trailer wasn't far. As we walked across the parking lot, I took care to avoid the worst of the mud, picking my way there on my tiptoes.

We reached the edge of the trailer, and a short paved walk led to Linda's porch steps. Jessica and I did our best to scrape the mud from our shoes before we walked up the whitewashed steps that led to the equally white porch.

The front door was open. Only a screen door separated us from the trailer's interior. The inside of the trailer was neat and tidy like the rest of the trailer park. I caught sight of a rose-printed sofa, blue carpet, and wallpapered walls before Jessica stepped forward and rang the doorbell.

Less than a minute later, Linda was at the screen door. "Angie? Jessica? What are you two doing way out here?"

I wouldn't call the trailer park "way out," as it was less than ten minutes from the Double Dime Diner, but I knew our arrival must have come as a surprise.

Linda pushed open the screen door and stepped out onto the porch. She wore a purple sweat suit and her normally high and beehived hair was wet and plastered to her head. It was the first time I had seen Linda outside of her 1950s waitressing uniform and her hair below the stratosphere.

Linda must have realized that too because she patted her head. "I wasn't expecting company. I just finished washing out my hair. I must look a fright."

"You look fine," I insisted. "We're so sorry to bother you, Linda, but I was wondering if I could talk to you. I went to the Double Dime first . . ." I trailed off.

She interrupted me. "It's about Griffin, isn't it?"

I nodded.

"Thought so," she said. She might have been surprised by our arrival, but she didn't seem the least bit taken aback by the reason for our visit. "You all have a seat on the porch while I do something with my hair." The screen door closed after her. Jessica and I sat in two white resin patio chairs across from a vinyl-covered glider that reminded me of the one my grandmother Braddock had on her patio when I was a small child. All of my grandparents had died before I was an adult, and I felt a surprising pang of loss for missing out on having my grandparents longer. In many ways, my Amish aunt Eleanor, who was ten years older than my mother, had filled that gap in my life.

The porch's floorboards were cleaner than my kitchen floor. I winced at our muddy shoe prints marring the pristine surface. Before I could stop him,

Oliver walked through my boot prints and tracked mud across the porch. "Ollie," I complained.

Jessica opened her purse and rummaged through it. "I might have something in here." A second later she came up with a wad of fast-food napkins. She handed them to me, and I knelt on the porch beside Oliver and started cleaning his paws.

Oliver didn't like it and kept pulling his paws away. I think anytime I touched his feet he thought I might put his red boots on him that I made him wear in the snow during the winter. He hated those boots. "Ollie, you're making this more difficult than it has to be."

I was still kneeling on the porch arguing with my dog when Linda reappeared in the doorway. She had a pink turban wrapped around her head, which resembled the beehive look that she was known for, and carried a tray of lemonade.

Jessica jumped out of her chair and held the door open so that Linda could walk out onto the porch. The tray of lemonade smelled like bacon. Then I noticed there was a dessert plate of bacon in the corner.

Oliver caught a whiff of it too and stood at attention. His stubby tail wiggled in anticipation. It seemed he was horribly spoiled by every person in the county.

"I'm sorry Oliver made such a mess," I said from the place I knelt. "If you have a bucket and scrub brush, I can clean it up in no time." I grabbed Oliver around the middle and he wiggled in my arms as all of his focus was on the little plate of bacon on the tray.

She smiled. "It's no matter. I can spray it down with

the hose after you leave. There's no harm done. Now, get off the floor and take a seat. Poor Oliver looks like you are torturing him. The poor soul."

I let Oliver go.

"Here you go, you poor dear," Linda cooed, and set the dessert plate of bacon at Oliver's feet. I gave it a forlorn look. Since I still hadn't eaten lunch, I could have gone for my own little dessert plate of bacon to stop the gnawing feeling in my stomach. Before I could stand, Oliver already had his pushed-in nose buried in the dish.

I resisted the urge to take the plate from him. There were four large pieces of bacon on his plate, which were much more than he needed to have in a week, not to mention in a day. Oliver would not be getting any of his doggie treats that night. That was for sure.

I scrambled to my feet and sat back on the resin chair, and Linda set the tray of lemonade on the metal coffee table between the chairs and the glider. "It's real nice of you to come by." She nodded to Jessica, including her in the comment.

"Your home is adorable," I said, meaning it. "I wish our visit was for a happier reason."

She nodded and picked up the pitcher of lemonade. "I've been meaning to invite you by, but it's not often I'm away from the diner. I'm there much more than I'm ever here in the trailer."

"Why is the diner closed?" I asked.

She froze as she poured lemonade into the glass. I thought the glass would overflow, but she seemed to snap out of it just before the lemonade crested the rim of the glass. She set the pitcher down, picked up the overfilled glass, and handed it to me. "Careful there," she said. "I might have put a bit too much in."

I thanked her and sipped from the glass until it was at a level I was comfortable with holding. After I did this, I slid back into my seat and waited for the answer to my question.

Before she answered she poured another glass, not nearly as full as mine, for Jessica and a third for herself. She leaned back into the glider's floral vinyl seat and kicked off the floorboard with her stocking-clad toes. The glider gently rocked back and forth, falling into a drowsy rhythm. "I just couldn't go on working after the sheriff and his men stopped by to tell me . . ." She looked down at her hands and closed her eyes as if holding back tears. When she looked up again, I saw there were tears in her eyes. "I had to close the diner after he told me about Griff. I couldn't stay there and make idle chitchat with diners when I knew Griff was dead, lying in the county morgue."

"Did you know him well?" I asked. "Was he a customer?"

She shook her head.

I leaned forward and took her hand with my free hand. "Linda, I'm so sorry. I can tell you cared about him."

She squeezed my hand back. "Not as sorry as I am, and I did care about him, more than I can say. It's my fault he's dead."

I let go of her hand. "How can you say that?"

She picked up a glass of lemonade from the tray. "I was the one who told your mother about Griff's electrician business. If I hadn't done that, she would have found someone else for the job and he would still be alive."

"You can't know that," I protested.

She placed her glass of lemonade back on the tray without tasting it, as if she couldn't stomach it. "I've been expecting you to come." She touched her pink turban as if to check that it sat in the correct position on her head. "Maybe not so soon, but I knew you would want to get to the bottom of what happened. I want you to do that. It's important to me to know how Griff died and who killed him."

"What was your relationship with Griffin?" Jessica asked.

Linda looked us both in the eye in turn. "He was my son."

Chapter Thirteen

"**Y**our son?" I asked. That was the last thing I had expected her to say.

She nodded. "He was my foster son actually. I was the closest thing to a stable family he and his brother ever had. I never had the opportunity to adopt them. I would have if I had been able to." A sadness washed her face. "I never could, but I still thought of the boys as my children. I tried to do my best for them."

There was another kernel of information. "What is his brother's name?"

She nodded. "Blane. He's two years younger than Griff. I always considered both of them my family even if we weren't flesh and blood. Those boys—men now, since they are a couple of decades older than you, Angie—are the only family that I have. That I have ever had really. I was as much an orphan as they were."

Before I could ask another question, Linda went on unprompted. "I never married. Never had the inkling to, but I do love children. Back in those days, they were reluctant to let a single woman take care of foster

children, especially two boys. There was all this gib-
berish that a child needed two parents to be brought
up right. That's the ideal," she said, "but it's not the
only way. By the time Griffin and Blane came to live
with me, they had been in nine homes. The boys were
eleven and nine. They stayed with me all the way
through high school."

"Did the boys get along?" Jessica asked.

"Those two boys have been at each other's throats
since the day I first knew them. According to their
foster information, no one wanted them, but I took
them on. I knew what it was like to grow up without
parents. Those two only lashed out at each other because they were hurting and angry at the world. They
didn't mean it. I did what I could to keep the peace
between them. Sometimes tragedy brings two people
together. Sometimes it rips them apart."

"Did Griffin and Blane tolerate each other better as
adults?" I asked.

Linda sighed. "They don't hit and kick anymore like
they did when they were boys, but they still weren't
close, even though they worked together."

"They disliked each other, but still worked together?"
Jessica asked.

"Blane is an electrician too. Together, the boys were
co-owners of Double Bright Electric." She smiled. "I
always thought they got the 'Double' in their name
from my diner."

I looked up from my own glass. Griffin had made
no mention of a business partner when I met him the

day before in my mother's kitchen. "How long have Blane and Griffin been in business together?"

She sighed. "Must be ten years, I would guess, but they used to be. They weren't by the time that Griffin died."

"What happened?" Jessica asked.

"Griffin told me that they had officially dissolved their partnership when he visited me on Mother's Day. So that was what . . . a couple of weeks ago? He said he bought out Blane's half, but even though it was more than fair, Blane was not happy with the settlement."

If there was a lightbulb hovering over my head, it would have started glowing at that moment. Blane was a strong suspect. But why didn't I feel more excited by the prospect?

"Why did they argue about it?" Jessica asked. "What caused them to dissolve their partnership?"

"Griffin didn't say, and I didn't push for the information. I was just happy he was telling me anything about his life at all. I take what I can get with those boys." Tears sprang to her eyes. "I suppose I'll take what I can get with Blane now. He's the only one I have left. Not that I've seen him in a very long time. He's not as good about coming around as his brother was."

"Did you know about any of Griffin's other jobs? Aside from the job at my parents'? He mentioned yesterday that he would have to be at my parents' house early because he had another larger job he was working on."

She stared at me. "You spoke to him yesterday?"

I nodded.

"How did he seem? Was he happy?" She smiled and

pointed at the hanging basket of pansies. "He brought those to me for Mother's Day. Aren't they beautiful? He brings me pansies every year. I love them so. Did you know that pansies signify remembrance? I don't know if that's why Griff chooses those flowers for me. I like to think that it is." She leaned forward as if eager for a report of her foster son.

I set my lemonade glass on the tray. "He seemed fine. Happy, I would say. I didn't have the impression that anything was bothering him. But then again I only met him in passing. He was there to look over the electrical work in my mother's kitchen." I didn't add that Jonah had been there too. I wondered if Linda knew Jonah had been the one to discover Griffin's body. I wasn't going to be the one to tell her. I didn't want her to suspect Jonah in any way. I knew he couldn't have killed Griffin. There was no way.

"You asked if I knew of any other jobs that Griffin was working on." She thought for a moment. "He had just signed a big contract with Eby Amish Mercantile. It seems the owner wanted to increase its electrical capacity and bring the wiring that was already there up to code. I got the impression that the wiring in the building was very old."

"The mercantile in Rolling Brook?" I asked, as if it could be anywhere else. Second only to the Millers' pie factory, Eby Amish Mercantile was the largest business on Sugartree Street and always a popular stop for the Amish tour buses that made their way through town as they ventured through the county.

She nodded. "Griff said it was under new ownership,

and the new owner was the one who wanted all of these improvements. I took that to mean that he was doing more than just updating the outlets."

I had heard that someone new was planning to buy the mercantile, but I had known it hadn't happened yet because the sign over the building still read EBY AMISH MERCANTILE. I had assumed that the new owner would have wanted to rename the business. Perhaps I was wrong.

"Was this job at the mercantile before or after the brothers' partnership broke up?" I asked.

She thought about my question. "I'm not certain, but by the way that Griff had been talking, it all happened around the same time."

Could have been a coincidence, but I highly doubted that it was.

"Do you know the name of the man Griffin was working for?" I asked.

She shook her head.

Oliver licked his empty bacon plate for every last morsel. A power washer couldn't have done a better job at cleaning that plate.

I wasn't worried that Linda didn't know the name of the new owner of the mercantile. The mercantile was one block from Running Stitch; I could go down there and introduce myself. It was a neighborly thing to welcome a new business owner to the neighborhood and my duty as a township trustee. If I happened to ask a few questions about Griffin while I was at it, there was no harm in that.

"What about Griffin's fiancée, Mallory Zeff? What can you tell me about her?"

She wrinkled her nose. "I never knew what Griff saw in the woman. At least he had the good sense never to marry her."

Jessica and I shared a look. Linda's entire demeanor changed at the mention of Griffin's fiancée.

"You don't like her," Jessica said. It was a statement, not a question.

"I don't. I always thought she was with Griff for his money. As far as I can tell, she spent more of her time asking him to buy things than anything else."

"A gold digger?" Jessica arched an eyebrow.

Linda shrugged. "If the shoe fits."

"If Griffin never married, who gets his business?"

Linda shrugged. "Blane is his only living relative, so I would assume him." She stared at her hands.

"But . . ." I trailed off.

She met my gaze. "But the last time Griff was here, he told me that he planned to go to a lawyer to write his will. He said he should have done it years ago. In the will, he planned to name me his sole heir." She blinked back tears. "I thought it was a sweet gesture, and to be honest, I didn't think any more of it until this moment. I never expected to outlive him. That's not supposed to happen." A tear rolled down her weathered cheek.

That made Blane a suspect. I swallowed hard. Because it made Linda a perfect suspect too.

Chapter Fourteen

I picked up my almost full lemonade glass again. I hadn't drunk from it since the initial swig to prevent it from spilling. Wanting to be polite, I took another sip. My stomach churned as the acidy liquid sloshed around in my empty stomach.

"I'm sorry I'm not good company for you today," Linda said. The creases in the skin of her face seemed to deepen, and she drooped with fatigue.

I set my glass back on the tray. We had overstayed and worn Linda out. I knew from my own losses that grief was one of the most exhausting conditions in the world. It felt as if you'd just run a marathon and not moved for days all in the same moment.

I stood. "We should go so you can rest."

"Don't you worry." She smiled but didn't get up from her seat. "I'll be right as rain tomorrow, and the Double Dime will be open bright and early, ready for business. You come in and bring that sheriff of yours with you, and I will feed you proper." She narrowed her eyes. "Have you eaten today?"

I could have asked her the same question. "I had a couple of doughnuts for breakfast—and coffee." I added the coffee because it sounded healthy—sort of, I guessed, in comparison to doughnuts.

She sniffed. "Sugar like that isn't going to get you through your day, no way. You need a hearty bowl of stew and some crusty bread."

Linda's meal prescription sounded right on the mark. She always knew what folks needed to eat when they entered the diner. It was her gift.

I leaned forward and kissed her on the cheek. "I'll be in tomorrow for that stew. I bet Oliver will be hoping for more bacon too. You spoil him."

She blushed at my kiss but seemed pleased by it too. "Everyone can use a little spoiling now and again."

Back in the car, I was quiet as I thought over everything that Jessica and I had learned from Linda during our short visit. As always, Linda proved to be an excellent source of county information, but this time the information she held was her personal story.

Jessica leaned back in her seat. "If Blane is an electrician too, he would know how to electrify those stairs, and he would know his brother would remove his muddy boots before going into the trailer."

I nodded slowly.

Jessica eyed me. "I thought you'd be more excited that you have a prime suspect that's not Jonah. Wasn't that the purpose of coming out here?"

"It was." I paused. "But if Blane killed his brother and goes to prison because of it, who will Linda have left as far as family goes?"

"It didn't sound like Blane was much family to her," Jessica said.

"True," I said. "But it still might break her heart."

Jessica didn't have an answer for my question.

After I dropped Jessica off at Out of Time, I drove back to Running Stitch. It was after four by the time I got there, and as promised, Sarah had locked the shop up tight. I went out back to check on Petunia.

The goat galloped to me when I stepped into the tiny backyard. "Baaa!" she complained and butted my hip with her head.

I stumbled back but managed to stay upright. You would think that as many times as Petunia had tried to and succeeded to knock me over, I would've come to expect it.

"Baaa!" she cried again.

I sighed. "I know you aren't used to being left alone all day, but I couldn't have taken you to Linda's trailer. You would have eaten all her neighbor's flowers—"

"Angie Braddock," a clear strong voice rang out. "Are you talking to a goat?"

I glanced over the white picket fence that separated my tiny backyard from the alley and small patio behind Authentic Amish Quilts. "Hello, Martha," I said, ignoring her question. I wasn't ashamed to be having a conversation with Petunia. I talked to Oliver and Dodger all the time, but Martha just wouldn't understand.

"Sarah Leham closed up for you again," she said bitterly. "It must be nice to have people willing to fill in for you so much, so you can run around the county and stick your nose in places where it doesn't belong."

I walked over to the fence and held on to the top of one of the posts. "What do you mean by that, Martha?"

"Only that everyone in the county has heard by now about the *Englischer* dying in your parents' home. I imagine you'll pry into that investigation as you have so many others . . ."

I held on to the post a little more tightly. The wood dug into my fingers. "What difference does it make to you what I do?"

She jerked her neck back as if I had smacked her, and I immediately regretted my sharp tone. For the last year and a half I had been trying to make peace with this woman, and I certainly wasn't going to win her over by questioning her.

She sniffed. "I hope you will leave the Amish community out of it this time. You have made enough trouble for us, as is."

My guard went up. Any investigating I'd done since moving to the county had been to protect the Amish community or individual members of it.

Before I could think of a comeback, Martha went on. "I do have a concern, which I'll share with you since you are a township *trustee*." She said "trustee" as if my status as such was in question.

"I'm happy to share whatever concern you might have with the rest of the trustees," I said smoothly.

At my feet, I felt Oliver lean against my leg in a show of support. Petunia came to my other side and did the same.

"I heard a wild man was spotted outside your

parents' house this morning. You know the Amish in the county will not receive any fanciful tales like this."

I swallowed. This wasn't good if the Amish community was hearing the Bigfoot rumors too. I silently hoped Willow had gotten that post down in time. Maybe she had. It had been nearly six hours since I'd told her to take it down, and I hadn't heard another peep about it.

I forced a laugh. "Oh, you know how rumors like that can be exaggerated, especially in a township as small as Rolling Brook."

"So you are saying this is not true?"

"I'm saying that it is nothing to worry about."

She stared over the top of her wire-rimmed glasses at me. "We will see about that." And with that, she spun around and marched back into her quilt shop.

Slowly, I let go of the top of the fence. My knuckles cracked with the effort.

Petunia gave me a pitiful look.

I glanced over at Martha's back patio. I really didn't want to leave the goat there with Martha keeping watch. I removed Oliver's leash and clicked it on her collar. "All right. You can tag along with Oliver and me."

Both animals grinned.

I looked from one to the other. "But you both have to be on your best behavior."

They blinked at me with solemn faces.

Instead of going back inside of Running Stitch, I walked with Oliver and Petunia down the narrow alley between the two quilt shops and out onto the sidewalk.

On the sidewalk, I turned in front of Authentic Amish Quilts and headed in the direction of the mercantile. Petunia pranced ahead of me on the leash with her head held high and eyes bright as if she were leading some sort of parade. Oliver walked briskly beside her. His legs were much shorter than the goat's, and he had to take three steps to her one.

The mercantile looked like a general store that was reminiscent of those found in the Western television shows of my parents' youth. Like all the businesses on Sugartree Street, the Eby Amish Mercantile closed at four, but I was hoping someone who knew about Griffin Bright would still be in the building.

As we drew closer to the mercantile, I noticed it was under construction as Linda had said, but the construction was much more extensive than I had first assumed. Large wooden crates were piled up against the side of the large clapboard building. Above the crates, the siding had three shades of beige paint lined up together as if someone was trying to choose a color. Each shade was slightly darker than the last. I was surprised this was the first time I'd noticed the work being done on the mercantile. Every day, I parked in the community lot across from the Amish store before walking to Running Stitch. I wasn't as observant as I thought I was.

When I was a child, the mercantile had been a regular stop for Jonah and me. We purchased penny candy with the money that we had scrimped and saved or with the coins that had fallen out of my father's pockets that I would dig out of the couch cushions. In the time I had owned my quilt shop, I hadn't been in the mercantile nearly as often. The Ebys and I were civil to one another but, in general, the family and their slew of relatives ignored me. The February before my aunt died, I had visited Holmes County because she was feeling poorly. Her cancer had gotten worse. While I was in the township, I happened to solve a decades-old murder with the help of my aunt and the ladies in the quilting circle that put a member of the Eby family in prison. It goes without saying they weren't my biggest fans.

I stopped in front of the door, and Petunia licked the clapboard siding as if she was giving it a taste test.

I narrowed my eyes. "Don't eat anything."

She had the grace to appear sheepish.

I stood in front of the door a little longer, considering my next move. Oliver cocked his head as if to ask me if I was going to knock. His one black ear dipped lower than his white one.

I tried the door to the mercantile. To my surprise, it was unlocked even though the CLOSED sign was flipped outward. I peeked inside. "Hello?"

There was no answer.

Before stepping into the shop, I tied Petunia's leash to a bench outside. "Stay here. Oliver and I'll be back."

Her ears drooped into a pout. Taking Petunia inside of the mercantile with all those Amish delicacies was just too much of a risk.

Inside of the shop, boxes were piled up to my waist, blocking the door from opening the entire way. As carefully as possible, I stepped around them. Oliver wriggled inside around my feet.

Overhead, many of the drop ceiling's panels were removed, exposing the beams and electrical wires. A stepladder was in the middle of the room in front of the empty sales counter, and electrical wire dangled above the top of the ladder. An open toolbox sat at the foot of the ladder. It was as if whoever was working in that spot had stepped away for a moment with every intention of returning. I couldn't help thinking that the man who had stepped away might have been Griffin, and those tools waiting for their owner to return had been his as well.

"Hello?" I called out again. "Anyone here?"

Still no answer. Oliver nosed the floorboards around the ladder. He whimpered.

I placed my hands on my hips. "If you're trying to tell me there's a dead body in here, I'm out. One a day is my limit."

There was a shuffling sound in the back of the store that attracted both Oliver's and my attention. A rack of hand-carved wooden canes stood by the cash register. I grabbed one of the canes and choked up on it as if it were a baseball bat. "Stay behind me," I told my dog.

Oliver shuffled backward as I stepped around the ladder.

The shuffling sound came again. It sounded as if someone was moving boxes. I lowered the cane. Moving things around would be expected if the mercantile was in the middle of a major renovation.

I inched down the aisle only faintly aware of Oliver belly-crawling behind me. He stopped crawling, stood at attention, and took off down the aisle with his tongue hanging out.

"Oliver!" I cried. I skidded to a stop at the back of the store. To my right, there was a small office and a man and woman in Amish dress stood in the doorway. Oliver danced around their feet and appeared to be very pleased with his discovery. I dropped the cane on the floor. The man I had never seen before, but the woman I knew. "Mattie?"

Chapter Fifteen

Mattie jumped away from the man as if she had been burned. "Angie! What are you doing here?"

"I could ask you the same thing," I said. "I thought you were at the pie factory."

The man stepped forward and extended his hand. "Angie Braddock, I take it. I have seen you in town, but we haven't formally met."

I stared at his hand. "No. We haven't."

With his hand still extended, he said, "Mattie speaks highly of you. I'm Liam Coblentz. I recently bought the mercantile from the Eby family. I'm new to Rolling Brook, but not to the county. I live over in Berlin."

"I've heard nothing about you." I gave Mattie a pointed look as I shook his proffered hand. Even though the man was in Amish clothing, the handshake was decidedly English. Typically, Amish men didn't shake hands with women, especially not with English women they didn't know.

As I shook his hand, I took time to study him. He was handsome and clean-shaven. His lack of facial hair told me he wasn't married. A good detail to note since Mattie had been looking deeply into his eyes when I first spied them. He wore plain dress, but his dark hair wasn't cut exactly in the traditional Amish bowl cut. It was a little longer than the hair of most of the Amish men I knew and curled around his ears. His hazel eyes were kind. I guessed he was around thirty.

I arched my brow at her. "Mattie, can I talk to you a moment? Alone?"

Liam smiled. "I need to move some boxes in the office." Liam got the hint. That was one point in his favor, but the man was working off a deficit in my book.

Even after Liam was gone, I led Mattie away from the back of the store. We stood in an aisle lined with dried Amish noodles of every shape and size on one side and jars of canned goods, from pickled beets to sliced peaches, on the other. "Is he the reason you've suddenly had to fill in at the pie factory so often in the last few days?" I hissed.

She stared at her hands.

"Rachel didn't seem to know that you were working at the factory today. Now I know why— because you hadn't been working there."

"I'm so sorry for lying to you, Angie. I know I should have told you the truth, but I just could not bring myself to do it. I will understand if you fire me."

I took a breath. "No one is getting fired, least of all you. I don't think that Running Stitch could survive without you."

"Danki." Her blue eyes filled with tears. "Did you tell Rachel that I lied to you about working in the factory?"

I shook my head. "No, I didn't."

She gave a sign of relief. *"Danki*, Angie. *Danki* for covering for me. I know that I don't deserve it. Lying is wrong—I know this—but there wasn't any other way that I could . . ." She didn't finish her thought.

"See Liam?" I asked.

She nodded.

"Mattie, what are you doing sneaking out of work to see a guy? I've never known you to behave like this." As soon as I said that, I realized that I was wrong. Mattie had snuck out to see her previous beau in secret on a number of occasions because Aaron and Rachel had not approved of him. Did that mean there was a reason for them to disapprove of Liam too?

"You make it sound so scandalous," she said. "We've done nothing wrong. We talked and went for a ride. That was all."

"Does your brother or Rachel know about him?"

"Nee, and please don't tell them. Liam is only my friend, nothing more. You know how people talk. If I am friends with a man, they will automatically assume that there is something more to our relationship." She took an unsteady breath. "There is not."

That might be true on Mattie's end, but I saw how Liam looked at her. He definitely cared about her.

Oliver whimpered at my feet.

"Can you see why I haven't told my brother or Rachel or anyone? If you question me about Liam, how much worse do you think Aaron will be?"

My shoulders drooped. "Much worse. Look, I think we still need to finish this conversation, but right now, I need to talk to Liam about Griffin Bright."

She sighed. "I knew you would find out that Griffin had been working for Liam. I warned him of this. He said that the sheriff was here this afternoon asking him about Griffin."

As usual, Mitchell was two steps ahead of me. He was the sheriff and had all the resources of his department behind him, but it didn't irk me any less.

"Does Mitchell know you're friends with Liam?" I asked.

"Nee. Nee." She shook her head. "You're the first to know. I should have been honest with you instead of making up that story about the pie factory. I was just afraid."

"Afraid of what?" My brow knit together. "Mattie, I don't care who you date. I'm happy if you finally found a good guy, but you can't lie to me about it. Why would you? You know I would support you. I want you to be happy."

"I wasn't worried about you, but Rachel is your *gut* friend. What if you told her? It would be a disaster, even if you only told her by accident."

"I would never tell anyone anything that you told me in confidence," I said, unable to keep the hurt from my voice.

She hung her head. "I know that."

I sighed. "I still need to talk to him," I said after Mattie's silence stretched into a long minute. I could never keep quiet like the Amish did. I have to fill the empty space with words.

Her shoulders drooped. "Why? Why does it matter that Griffin was his electrician? Griffin had a popular business. He must have had many jobs throughout the county. Will you visit every last one of them?"

"I'm here because this job was the one that was the breaking point between Griffin and his brother," I said. "It might be significant to the case."

"You mean Blane," Liam said behind me.

I jumped.

Liam held up his hand. "I'm sorry to interrupt, but I was finished with everything I could do in the back room. If I moved any more boxes while I waited for the two of you to reappear, I'd just make a bigger mess." He smiled. "Mattie told me you might drop by with questions. I'm happy to help in any way that I can. I was so very sorry to hear about Griffin's passing. He was a good electrician and was enthusiastic about the work."

"What about his brother, Blane?" I asked.

He nodded. "He was with Griffin when they made a bid on the work, but then when the project began Griffin told me that the two of them had parted ways."

"When did they make the bid?" I asked.

Liam rubbed his clean-shaven chin and thought about that for a moment. "I'd say it was about two months ago when I first took over the mercantile. I asked the Bright brothers and another electrician to come in and give me an estimate. They were the higher of the two bids and so my second choice."

"Your second choice?" I asked.

"There was another man I hired first." He pointed toward the front of the store. "He left that mess you saw when you first came into the mercantile. I was sorely disappointed. He had promised me a quick and professional job, and it was anything but. I need the work to be done quickly. I can't run a business with wires hanging all over the place."

"What was his name? The other electrician?"

"Rex Flagg," he said. "He works out of Millersburg. He seemed to be a nice enough guy," Liam said as if he felt obligated to compliment the first electrician in some way. "But he was unbearably lazy."

I tucked the name into the back of my mind to look into later. "When he fell through, you hired the Bright brothers."

He nodded. "In hindsight, I should have hired them right off and the job would be done by now."

"When was the last time that you spoke to Blane?" I asked.

"Actually," Liam said, "I just got off the phone with him while the two of you were out here talking. I called to ask if he would take over the job."

I frowned.

He grimaced. "I know it must seem callous to you that I'd be calling for a replacement for Griffin so soon, especially his brother, but you've seen the condition of the mercantile. I've already been closed for two whole days because of the mess. I can't be closed much longer and hope to come out ahead this month."

Of all people, I could certainly understand concern for one's business, but I still thought that it was cold of Liam to call Blane on the day his brother died to take the job. In my estimation, Liam had just lost the one point that he had earned with me. I glanced at Mattie, and she twisted the edge of her apron in her hands.

"What kind of work are you having done?" I asked. "I know it's electrical, but the job looks more extensive than a repair job."

"I'm upping the number of wires and outlets in the building. At the same time, I'm having the Internet installed and making general improvements. I thought it was best to get the entire job done at one time. Now that everything is held up with Griffin's death, I'm no longer so sure of that."

I frowned. "The Internet?" This announcement was a surprise for an Amish businessman. When I first moved to Holmes County, one the first things I did was increase the electrical capacity of the shop and install Wi-Fi, but I was English and needed those things for my business. Did Liam need them too? That didn't seem like a very Amish necessity to me. Then again, he was from Berlin. Maybe he was from an even more liberal New Order district than the Grabers and Millers were a part of. It wasn't uncommon for Amish bishops to make exceptions to their limited technology rules if their members were using that technology for business.

He nodded. "The mercantile needs to join the twenty-first century, and that transition includes a Web site. Since I'll be here all day, I need to be able to work on the Web site while I'm at the mercantile. Eventually, I hope to sell items through an online store."

"You know how to build a Web site?" I couldn't keep the doubt from my voice.

"Angie," Mattie interrupted, "I don't know what the Internet has to do with Griffin Bright."

I didn't either, but I knew the average Amish man didn't know HTML. I pressed on. "Won't Blane feel odd working on his brother's jobsite?"

Liam frowned. "I suppose that's possible, but he didn't hesitate to take the job. He starts tomorrow and said that he should finish in a couple of days. I'm glad for that."

"According to one of Blane and Griffin's family members," I said, deciding to leave Linda's name out of our conversation, "their partnership broke up around the time Griffin took this job."

"That must be why Blane was only with Griffin on that first day. I don't know anything about any sort of disagreement that they had. Griffin only told me that he was going to do this job alone. I had already signed the work agreement for the contract, so I wasn't in a place to argue. As long as he delivered, I didn't care."

"And was he delivering?" I asked.

He nodded. "Until today."

Until today because he was murdered that morning. Liam didn't need to add that last part. We all knew it.

Liam cleared his throat. "It's time I head home. It has been a very long day. You look quite tired yourself."

He didn't know the half of it, and I still had Petunia

to contend with. I couldn't take the goat back to my parents' house, where I had promised to spend the night. By now, Mom must have noticed the decapitated tulips that Petunia had left in her wake.

I still had one more question. "Tomorrow, when Blane is here working on your store, I would like to drop in and talk to him about his brother."

He nodded. "I don't see any harm in that. I will see you both tomorrow then."

Mattie nodded and whispered good-bye in Pennsylvania Dutch.

He smiled in return, and I had the sneaking suspicion that my shop assistant's life was just about to become a lot more complicated.

Chapter Sixteen

As soon as we got outside of the mercantile, Mattie dashed down the sidewalk, saying she had to make it home in time for supper and would see me at Running Stitch later for the quilting circle meeting.

"Why do I think she doesn't want to talk to us about Liam?" I asked the dog and goat.

Petunia head butted me in the hip, which caused me to fall against the mercantile. I grunted and rubbed my shoulder. "I think it's high time we got you home."

"Baa!" Petunia said.

I shepherded the Frenchie and goat to my car and headed for the Graber farm.

Anna, Jonah's mother, must have heard my car approach because she stood on the front porch of her *daddihaus* and waited for me. Anna's husband had built the *daddihaus* for himself and Anna to retire to when he turned the family farm over to his only son, Jonah. Jonah, Miriam, and their three children lived in the big house where Jonah grew up.

I climbed out of the car and opened the door to the

SUV's backseat. The goat jumped out first as if glad to be home. I didn't blame her. The vast Graber farm must have been a relief after being stuck in the tiny garden behind the quilt shop all day.

Oliver exited the car with more care. He scanned the area before jumping out of the car. He always approached the Grabers' farm with some wariness. Jonah had gone through a string of attempts to farm fowl. At first it was geese, which turned out to be a disaster and almost impossible to sell. After the geese he made an even more ill-advised decision to farm turkeys. The turkeys had been worse, a lot worse. The big tom in the flock had had murder in his eyes.

Somehow over the winter, Jonah had managed to unload the turkeys too. I suspected that he sold them at a loss. Until Jonah had taken the construction job at my parents' house, he had been concentrating on his new business venture of goat land clearing. Petunia would naturally be the lead goat. No one would ever question that.

I frowned as a dark thought hit me. I knew Jonah was helping me and my family when he took the job at my parents' house, but he must have also taken it for the extra money. I had always worried about Jonah and his tendency to bounce from idea to idea to make the farm viable. He didn't have the steady temperament of many Amish men, such as Aaron Miller, who was as consistent as bedrock. Everything Aaron did was thorough and measured. Thinking of Aaron brought to mind Mattie and her new friend.

Anna came down the three steps from her wide

porch. "I'm glad you've come. I was hoping you would. I almost walked to the shed phone to call you."

"Anna, I'm so sorry about everything. How are you? How is Miriam?" I clasped her hands in my own. They were surprisingly cold. Whenever I thought of Anna, I thought of warmth, so I found it disconcerting that her hands would be chilled.

She gave me a sad smile. "*Gott* will set it to rights. We will get through this trial as we have so many others."

I was about to say something more when the front door to the main farmhouse smacked against the house's wooden siding with a resounding bang, and Jonah's nine-year-old twins, Ezra and Ethan, dashed down the steps. Their eleven-year-old sister, Emma, moved down the steps at a much slower pace. Miriam was a few steps behind her daughter. Miriam was a beautiful tall woman with fine features and pale skin. Her dark blond hair was pulled back in the standard Amish bun and covered by a prayer cap, but on her, it appeared elegant, almost like a crown, as she held herself perfectly erect.

Rarely did Miriam come out to meet me when I visited the Graber farm. Even when I was a visitor in her house, she barely acknowledged me. Now I knew why. Seeing her stony glare made me realize everything that Rachel had told me about Jonah and his feelings for me when we were children were true, and Miriam would never forgive me for it. I swallowed back an apology that bubbled in the back of my throat. I had nothing to apologize for, I reminded myself, but like always my natural inclination was to fix the situation. I might have apologized to Miriam for something, if I thought it would help, but I knew it wouldn't. I couldn't even guess how many times Jonah must have tried.

Miriam came into the yard and stopped ten feet from me. Her lovely face was drawn and she gripped her hands in front of her apron.

"Miriam, how are you?" I asked. "I'm so—"

"What are you doing here?" Jonah's wife wanted to know. "Where's Jonah? Have you brought him?"

I looked at Anna. "Jonah's not here?"

"Nee," Miriam snapped. "Your sheriff came by an hour ago and took my husband to the police station."

"Did he arrest him?" I yelped. I should have come sooner. How could Mitchell arrest Jonah without letting me know? I would have thought that my boyfriend would have the courtesy to tell me when he was about to arrest one of my best friends.

"Nee, Angie," Anna said. "He only wanted to talk to him."

"Why didn't someone call me?" I asked. "I would have come and asked Mitchell what was going on. I could have helped."

Miriam pursed her lips, and Anna gave me a warning look.

"Helped? You? When have you ever helped our family?" Miriam gripped the sides of her apron as if attempting to steady herself. "We do not need your help. My husband would not be in this situation if it hadn't been for you."

My mouth fell open. I had already thought the same

thing, of course, but it didn't hurt any less hearing it from Jonah's wife. I tried to remind myself how upset Miriam must feel, how upset I would feel if something like this happened to Mitchell.

When I didn't say anything, she asked, "You're the one who asked him to go to your mother's house. Is that not true?"

"That's true, but—"

"But nothing," she snapped. "You caused all of this."

"I understand why you are upset, but I didn't cause anything." I concentrated on keeping my voice even. "Whoever murdered Griffin Bright was the one who caused the trouble, not me."

"How do we know it wasn't you?" Miriam asked.

"Miriam," Anna said in a warning voice, "you know that isn't fair."

"What's not fair is my husband sitting in a jail cell because of her," Miriam said.

I looked to Anna. "You said he wasn't arrested."

"He wasn't," Anna reassured me.

"Maybe he wasn't arrested yet, but he will be. I know it in my heart, just as I knew you coming back to Holmes County would ruin my family."

"Miriam, I—I—"

"I don't want to hear what you have to say." She glared at me. It was as if Miriam was finally releasing all the anger and jealousy she'd stored up against me for the last twenty years. "And he saw Griffin, a man who hurt my husband so deeply when he was young, who killed his closest friend and cousin. You should have known better. You should be ashamed."

"I—I didn't know about Griffin when I asked Jonah for help. I didn't know my mother had hired him, and even if I had, I didn't know his past with Jonah or anything about Kamon. I heard of Kamon for the first time yesterday."

She snorted. "I'm surprised Jonah didn't tell you every last detail before now. You're the one who he runs to when he needs help."

My brow furrowed in confusion. "What do you mean?"

"You know exactly what I mean," she spat. "My husband made a horrific discovery this morning, and did he come to me for comfort? *Nee*, he called you. He always thinks of you first. He always has and always will."

"Miriam, you're wrong." I took a breath. "Jonah only called me first because I have a phone. I'm much easier to reach, and Griffin died at my parents' house. Those are both logical reasons as to why he would call me."

"Those are not the reasons, and you and I both know it. He should have done everything in his power to let me know what happened. Instead I have to hear it from Sarah Leham shouting the news to me from a passing buggy. I'm sure she enjoyed breaking the news as she was rushing to your side. They all do. *Englisch* and Amish, everyone in the county is under your spell." Her hazel eyes narrowed. "But I am not."

I almost laughed at how untrue that last statement was. Martha Yoder wasn't under my spell and neither were others, many others. Instead, I said, "Jonah didn't want to worry you. I'm sure that was it."

"Did he say that? Did he say anything about me at all?" She choked back tears on the last word.

I tried to remember if Jonah had said anything about his wife that morning. Nothing came to mind, but that wasn't fair. Mitchell and his deputies hardly let me speak to Jonah. Other than asking me to take care of Petunia, he'd barely said a word to me directly.

A single tear rolled down Miriam's cheek, and I wanted to comfort her. I knew she wouldn't let me.

"I see." Her words were heavy and resigned. "Your silence is my answer."

"Miriam, please, take care." Anna took a step toward her daughter-in-law. "None of this is Angie's fault." Anna's voice had its normal even tone, but there was a wariness there that I didn't recognize.

Her daughter-in-law glared at her. "You always take her side. Both you and Jonah always do."

Take my side? Take my side in what?

Anna opened her mouth, but Miriam was faster. "Did you want your son to marry her? An *Englischer*? Did you want your son to be an *Englischer*?"

"*Nee.* Of course not. That would have never happened," Anna said firmly.

"I'm your daughter-in-law, your family; therefore you should take my side over hers." She gestured at me. "Always. But you and Jonah never do. Angie this, and Angie that. 'Did you hear what Angie did?' That's all I ever hear." She spun on her heels and ran back to the big farmhouse.

The door slammed closed behind her. Emma stood at

the corner of the house, clutching her ever-present book to her chest. There was no telling where the twins were. Emma caught my gaze and turned away. I bit the inside of my lip. I had always felt a kinship with the bookish girl. Would that be ruined because of what she overheard her mother say? I couldn't blame Miriam. My heart hurt for her and I sympathized with her feelings.

Anna touched my arm. "Don't mind Miriam. She's been so upset since the police arrived."

"Anyone would be," I said, barely above a whisper.

Anna clasped her hands in front of her. "She doesn't understand why Jonah still wants to be your friend. It is not common for an Amish man to be such close friends with an *Englisch* woman."

"Anna, I would never . . ." I couldn't even finish the sentence.

She rubbed my arm. "I know, child, and I know that the same is true for my son. However, Miriam has lived over half her life hearing Angie Braddock stories, and here you are in person, taking her husband's time and attention away from her. That is not easy for her. It would not be easy for any woman. You have to understand that."

"I would never take Jonah away from his family, and I asked him to help with the construction job at Mom and Dad's house because I trust him and can count on him as my friend, nothing more. I knew it would be a good job for him too. My parents pay well, and I know Jonah is doing everything he can to keep your family farm afloat. I thought the extra cash flow would be welcome."

Anna nodded. "This is true. Sometimes he doesn't have the best ideas about how to go about it." She chuckled. "Especially after his failure with the geese and turkeys. Don't let Miriam confuse you; she was glad when Jonah took the job at your parents' home. It gave her a reprieve, however short, from Jonah's constant talk about the goats and the need to buy more to increase their speed for clearing land. I think she was afraid he might come home one evening with a full herd of goats. I was too."

"Are they okay financially?" I asked.

"*Gott* will provide. He always does." She said the words with complete confidence, a confidence I envied.

But I couldn't help but think that her answer was the same as a no. I cleared my throat. "I'm going to the sheriff's department to see if I can find out what's happening. I have to know for myself Jonah wasn't arrested."

I thought about calling Mitchell to ask him what was going on, but thought better of it. I didn't want to give the sheriff any warning that I knew about Jonah's being taken to the police station. Mitchell knew me well and would assume I would head straight to the sheriff's department to confront him. He would be right, and the last thing I wanted was for him to try to stop me.

"Miriam doesn't want your help," Anna said. "She wouldn't like it if she knew that you were headed to the sheriff's department. It would only make her angrier than she already is."

"What about you?" I searched her kind face.

She laughed. "Oh, I say go, and find out as much as you can. Sarah Leham stopped by a little while ago and we discussed the quilting circle meeting we are having tonight at your shop. I think that's for the best, and I would like you to come to it with a full report."

"You'll be at the meeting?" I asked.

She straightened her shoulders. "Of course. When have I ever missed a quilting circle meeting? Besides, it's *my* son who we have to save from going to prison this time."

I smiled. "I'm glad." I squeezed her hand. "I think I will need your ladies' help to get to the bottom of this. Whoever killed Griffin had put an incredible amount of thought into it. So many details had to fall perfectly in place. Even if Griffin left his boots on, he probably would still be alive."

"That says to me whoever killed him knew him and knew how he would behave," Anna said with as much confidence as Miss Marple pointing out the killer over some light dinner conversation. I'd created an Amish grandma crime solver. Great.

Chapter Seventeen

The sheriff's department was a large octagonal-shaped building set off by itself on a lonely county road within the village of Holmesville. I stepped into the main lobby and found Mitchell's grumpy clerk Nadine sitting at the desk. Terrific. In this case, I would have much rather been greeted by Deputy Anderson. I would have been able to pry more information out of the young deputy. Nadine was as immovable as Stonewall Jackson.

Before I could say anything, she clicked her tongue. "Sheriff's occupied right now. You'll have to come back for a social call." Her voice was heavy with disapproval. She hadn't liked me from the first moment we'd met years ago when I had been in this sheriff's department to be fingerprinted because I was a murder suspect. Being a murder suspect was an unconventional way to meet my future boyfriend, to say the least. From her death glare, I could guess what Nadine thought of it. Although Nadine would never utter a disapproving word against the sheriff.

"I'm not here for a social call," I said in my most businesslike voice, doing my best to sound like the township trustee that I was. "I want to talk to the sheriff about a case, the Griffin Bright case, to be exact."

She sniffed and didn't appear impressed. "I'm *sure* he doesn't want to see you about it."

I stuck my hands on my hips. "Is he with Jonah Graber right now? Is that what has him so occupied?"

She pointed the eraser end of her pencil at me. "I can't tell you that. That's police business, not yours. You're in no position to stick your nose into it."

Now, I was annoyed. "I understand if you can't give me any more information without Mitchell's approval, but Jonah Graber is my friend. I have a right to see him."

She pursed her lips. "Only his legal counsel can see him at the moment."

"Does he have a lawyer? Is the lawyer in there with him?" I asked. I should have thought about finding Jonah a lawyer before this. I had been so intent on finding out all I could about Griffin and the people in his life that it hadn't occurred to me until Nadine brought it up.

"I can't answer that," she said primly.

"But—"

I was interrupted when the door between the reception area and the rest of the station opened. Mitchell and Jonah stepped out, followed by Deputy Anderson. Anderson looked mildly alarmed when he saw me. On the other hand, Mitchell didn't appear the least bit surprised or concerned that I was there.

"Jonah, you're free to go," Mitchell said in his most

official voice. "Please stay in the county until I say you are free to leave."

"Stay in the county?" Jonah asked, honestly confused. "Where else would I go?"

I glared at Mitchell. "What's going on?" I asked. "Why did you take Jonah from his house tonight?"

Mitchell sighed, and I felt a little bad about the glare. I knew he was only doing his job, but I still wanted answers.

"We only needed to clear up a few details about his statement this morning," Mitchell said.

"Was his lawyer present? Did you offer him a lawyer?" I asked.

"I didn't ask for a lawyer, Angie. I have nothing to hide," Jonah said, sounding incredibly tired. "Not anymore."

I wanted to ask him what he meant by that but thought it would be best to wait until Jonah and I were alone. I touched Jonah's arm. "I can take you home."

He nodded dumbly. There was no more fight left in him. "*Danki*, Angie." He stumbled toward the door. My heart broke. I had never seen my jovial friend so defeated.

Before I left the station, Mitchell called out, "Angie?"

I turned. The sheriff's expression softened, and he appeared just as tired as Jonah was. This wasn't easy on him either, and I wasn't helping. I smiled at him. I wanted him to know that I understood, but I couldn't say anything with Nadine looking on. "I'll call you later," I finally managed.

Mitchell nodded.

I guided Jonah out the door.

In the car, Jonah buckled his seat belt and stared out the front window of my car. He didn't say anything.

I knew I needed to say something to break the ice. Clearly Jonah wasn't going to start the conversation. I cleared my throat. "I took Petunia back to your farm earlier this evening." I figured goat talk was a safe starting point.

Jonah covered his face with his callused hands. "Angie, you should not have done that. I asked you not to go to the farm."

Apparently, I was wrong about the goat talk being safe. "Petunia was going stir-crazy in the tiny yard behind Running Stitch. When you didn't come by closing time, I knew I had to take her home. She couldn't spend the entire night behind the shop, and I can't take her to my mother's."

He dropped his hands. "Your mother's? Why would you take Petunia there?"

"I'm spending the night at my parents' house to keep an eye on things. Mom's shaken up over everything, and Dad's in poor health. I thought I could help out."

He snorted. "You want to snoop. Does the sheriff know this? He's going to see right through your story about protecting your parents."

I didn't say that Mitchell knew about my intention to snoop the moment I offered to spend the night at my parents'.

He pulled on his sandy blond beard. "I told you I would come and collect Petunia when I could. You shouldn't have gone to the farm. It will only make matters worse." His tone was morose again.

I glanced at him as I rolled to a stop at a traffic light in Millersburg, one of the few in the county. "When you didn't come and collect her by the time the shop closed, I knew something must have happened. I was worried. And when I hadn't heard anything from Anna either, I was extra worried. It's not like her not to tell me what's going on."

He lifted his head. "I know," he said sadly. "I asked her not to speak to you until I knew what I was going to do."

I frowned. "Why?"

His gaze was still fixed straight ahead. "I shouldn't have asked you to help me this morning. It has made a difficult situation worse."

"How?" I asked. I thought it was a fair question.

He didn't answer.

"Well, Jo-Jo," I said. "You did ask for my help, so I'm in now. I'm not giving up until whoever killed Griffin is safely behind bars. I have to find out what happened to Griffin for your sake, for my parents' peace of mind, and for Linda's too."

He looked up from his lap. "Linda?"

I nodded. "From the Double Dime Diner. She was Griffin's foster mother. She is heartbroken over his death. The Double Dime was closed today."

He gasped. "Closed? It never closes."

My grip tightened on the steering wheel. "I know."

"I did not know this about Griffin's past." His voice was thoughtful.

"Griffin was quite a bit older than us. He would have been a foster child before we were even born. Both Griffin and his younger brother, Blane, lived with Linda from a young age all the way through high school, although she never officially adopted them. So, you see, Jonah, I can't give up trying to find out what happened to Griffin. This is bigger than you just being a suspect now."

"I know that you won't." Resigned, he asked, "What else did you learn?"

I smiled a little, happy to hear some of Jonah's natural curiosity had returned to his voice.

I told him about my visit to the mercantile and how Griffin and his brother dissolved their partnership over the project there. I bit my lip, stopping myself just in time before I let it slip that I had seen Mattie at the mercantile.

"I wouldn't be surprised if Blane might be behind it." Jonah's voice was thoughtful. "Until yesterday in your mother's kitchen I hadn't seen Griffin in many years, but I'd seen Blane often around the county. He always looked sour, as if he sucked a lemon for half the day."

That was interesting. The way Blane was described to me was very different from the perception that I had gotten of his brother during our brief meeting. Maybe that was why the two couldn't work together. They were opposites, and got along like oil and water. There was another thing about my brief visit to the sheriff's station that bothered me. We were only a few minutes from the Graber farm, so if I wanted Jonah to answer, I would have to ask him now.

"What did you mean when you said you didn't have anything to hide anymore after leaving the sheriff's department?"

He was quiet for a long moment, and I thought he wasn't going to answer until he finally said, "I meant I no longer have to hide Griffin's tie to my cousin Kamon's death."

"I didn't tell Mitchell," I said.

"I know that." He removed his felt hat and played with the brim in his lap. "The sheriff found it in an old police report when he was looking for information about Griffin."

"Was Griffin arrested when Kamon died?"

Jonah shook his head. "*Nee.* He was never arrested or charged, but Mitchell said that he was listed as a person of interest in that case. Since I had been too, he knew there was a connection. That's what he wanted to talk to me about tonight. He would have spoken to me at the farm, but I thought it was best to have the conversation away from Miriam and the children. I volunteered to go to the station with him. It was my idea."

"Oh," I said, slightly relieved. "That's good news. Miriam gave me the impression that you were arrested."

He sighed. "I'm sure that's what she believes. I tried to explain to her why I had to go, but she wouldn't listen. I do love her so, but . . ." He trailed off.

I was glad that he didn't complete his thought.

Considering how Miriam felt about me; I knew it was best if Jonah didn't confide in me about any marital problems he might have with his wife.

"How did Kamon die? I know he was electrocuted. Rachel told me. But why do you feel Griffin was responsible?" I asked, changing the subject back to murder.

Jonah sighed. "It was very cold and rainy that May. Now that I think about it, it is amazing to me how similar this spring has been to the one when Kamon died. Kamon was apprenticing with Griffin. Of course my parents didn't approve because Kamon was learning to be an electrician and that was a very *Englisch* job. It still is. However, my parents didn't forbid him from working for Griffin. They believed if they had, Kamon would have finally left the community forever. Sometimes I think it would have been better if they had. Then, he would have headed out to Colorado like he always said that he would." He swallowed. "And he would still be alive, an *Englischer*, but alive." He took a breath. "I knew it was more than their fear of losing Kamon that stopped them. My parents were afraid that I would go with him. I might have. I was angry at my parents for not letting me work with Griffin. Instead, I was tethered to the farm with my father. I was not happy about that. They were right to make me work on the farm, of course. I was the only son in the family. The farm would be mine someday and I needed to know how to run it. However, that's hard to recognize at a young age when there is so much more you want out of life." His voice sounded wistful.

"Why did you want to work with Griffin? Did you have an interest in electricity?"

"In electricity?" He shook his head. "*Nee*, no, not really, but I wanted to work for Griffin mostly to be like Kamon, who I looked up to so much. At the same time I wanted to do it because it was forbidden. Maybe I was a bit rebellious." He laughed. "You know how teenagers are. I'll have a time of it when the twins reach that age." He gave a mock shudder and some of the humor was back in his voice.

I smiled, happy to hear a little bit of the Jonah I knew so well, but I needed to steer the conversation back on track. We were on the county road that led to Jonah's farm. I needed my answers before we reached the Graber farm. "Kamon died in the spring," I said.

Jonah sighed, and again the humor left him. "That's right. Griffin and Kamon where working at a factory. There was something wrong with one of their machines in the assembly line. The factory is gone now. The company moved away to another part of the country where manufacturing is cheaper, and the building they owned has since been torn down."

So much for checking out the scene of Kamon's death, I thought. Although there probably wasn't much I could have learned from it after twenty years.

"Kamon was electrocuted while trying to fix one of the machines. The company's investigator determined that it was an accident. Kamon shouldn't have crossed the wires like he had without cutting the power first. It was a stupid mistake and something that could've been easily avoided if Kamon had received the proper training."

"Why then do you think Griffin was responsible?" I asked. "Because of Kamon's lack of training?"

"Because Griffin should have been there!" Jonah cried. "If he had been there, he would have stopped my cousin from making such a stupid mistake and Kamon would still be alive." He turned toward the window. He was done talking, at least for the night.

I shifted in my seat. I'd never felt awkward around Jonah before. He was my oldest friend. He knew me better than almost anyone, but Rachel's revelation proved that perhaps I hadn't known him at all. That made me saddest of all.

I turned into the Grabers' long driveway. The sun was low behind the Grabers' large barn, but it wouldn't set for another hour. Miriam stood in front of the house with her arms wrapped around her waist.

The twins whooped as they chased Petunia around the yard. I didn't see Emma. Again, I wondered if the young girl's opinion of me had changed after witnessing the argument between her mother and me earlier that evening. Anna was missing too. I frowned.

One of the towheaded twins broke off from the running trio and skipped to the car. I lowered my window.

"*Grossmammi* told me to tell you that she has already gone to the quilt shop for the meeting tonight," Ethan—or was it Ezra, I could never tell the twins apart—said to me through the open window.

"Thank you," I said with a smile. At least that explained where Anna was. It made me feel a touch better.

The boy bolted back to his brother and the goat.

Jonah unbuckled his seat belt. "Angie, it is all right you brought Petunia home. I'm sorry that I snapped at you earlier over it. That wasn't fair."

"You don't need to apologize, Jonah." I stared through the windshield. Miriam still made no move to approach the car. "I wish Miriam could see that I'm trying to help too. When I showed up, I wasn't sure if she was more upset by seeing Petunia or me."

"It's probably a tie. She likes you both just about the same." The light teasing sound that was so familiar was back in his voice. He opened the car door, said good night, and walked toward the house. Before he reached her, Miriam turned her back on him and stormed inside.

Even from where I was in my car, I could see Jonah's shoulders fall dejectedly. My heart ached for my friend, but this time I knew better than to fix this situation. In the case of Jonah and Miriam's marriage, the only way I made any difference was by making it worse.

As I drove back to Running Stitch, I blew out a breath that I hadn't realized I had been holding. I knew in my heart that Jonah and I would survive this. Someday soon, things would go back to the way they were. I just had to solve a murder to make sure that they did, and the sooner, the better.

Chapter Eighteen

Back on Sugartree Street, I parked my SUV in the diagonal parking space in front of Running Stitch and next to Anna's buggy and her horse, Maggie. As I turned off the ignition, in my rearview mirror I saw a large man lumber out of the Dutchman's Tea Shop. Willow had an eclectic crowd who partook of her tea concoctions at the shop, but I had never seen this man before. I wouldn't have thought anything of it if I hadn't gotten a good view of his T-shirt, which read, BIGFOOT IS REAL.

I groaned. Apparently, Willow hadn't taken the posting on the message board down fast enough. I knew all along that it had been wishful thinking on my part that she had gotten it down in time. Nothing posted online really goes away.

I took a deep breath, debating if I should approach him. Maybe he could tell me if there were any others like him in the county.

Before I could make my decision, Anna threw open

the front door to Running Stitch and frantically waved for me to come inside.

Oliver and I headed for the shop. As I expected, all the members of my quilting circle—Anna, Rachel, Sarah, and Mattie—had beat me there. The quilt frame with the large red, yellow, and white Goosefoot quilt stretched across it was pulled into the middle of the room and, except for Anna, the other members of my quilting circle sat around it, each in their usual spots. The quilting for the night was already well under way.

Anna closed the door after me and locked it. "I told them that you went to the sheriff's department to find out what was going on with Jonah, so you might be late. What did you learn? How's Jonah? Where is he?" Anna asked her questions in rapid succession, which was out of character for her. Typically, she was much calmer and more thoughtful when she spoke. Then again, this was the first time her son was a prime suspect for murder.

I slung my hobo bag on the sales counter. "Jonah is back home. I was only at the sheriff's department for a few minutes before Mitchell had finished questioning him and Jonah was free to go."

Anna let out a sigh. "That means the sheriff doesn't think Jonah is a suspect."

I gave her a sympathetic look. "I wouldn't say that. I know Mitchell, and I know that he doesn't believe that Jonah could have killed Griffin Bright. At the same time, he won't completely rule Jonah out as a suspect until he has the proof to back it up. I'm sure when he does, he happily will."

Anna frowned, and the wrinkles that I had never noticed before deepened around her mouth.

"Angie," Sarah said. "There's a plate of food for you there on the cutting table."

As soon as she spoke, my nose caught a whiff of a lovely scent that made my stomach grumble. It must have had the same effect on Oliver because he waddled over to the cutting table and braced his paws on one of the table's legs.

I clapped my hands. "Down, Oliver."

He gave me a forlorn expression that would have put Oliver Twist, the orphan he'd been named for, to shame.

Sarah chuckled and took up her needle again. "I figured that you hadn't eaten much of anything today with the Double Dime Diner closed."

I removed the aluminum foil from the top of the plate. It was still warm. The heavenly smell of roasted chicken and mashed potatoes with gravy washed over me. It took everything I had to stop myself from devouring it on the spot.

Thankfully, I remembered my manners in time and carried the plate over to the quilting circle. As I took my seat, taking care to keep my plate far back from the beautiful quilt that we had been hand quilting for an English client. Anna settled in her seat and began to thread a needle.

I set a napkin on the floor and placed a piece of chicken on it for Oliver. I knew that he had had bacon at Linda's trailer, but it had been a very long day and he deserved a snack.

I dug my fork into the potatoes. They literally melted in my mouth.

"Angie," Rachel said. "How can we prove to the sheriff that Jonah had nothing to do with the murder?"

I swallowed. "If he had an alibi, that would work," I said. "Griffin died sometime between five and six this morning." I glanced at Anna. "Can anyone at home vouch for Jonah being home at that time?"

Anna frowned. "I cannot. I saw him leave the farm in the wagon at four this morning."

"At four?" I blinked at her over my piece of chicken. "What was he doing leaving the farm at four? He couldn't have planned to work on my parents' kitchen at that hour."

She buried her quilter's knot deep into the center of the quilt where it would never be seen. I had seen her do this hundreds of times, and every time I wondered how she did it so effortlessly and without even looking at the quilt as she concealed the knot. Anna pursed her lips. "I don't know."

"Does Jonah usually leave the farm at that time?" Sarah asked, leaning toward Anna. "Does he have some work to do that he had to leave so early for it?"

Anna stared down at the quilt for a moment as if taking the time to consider her answer. *"Nee,"* she said finally. "I wake up every morning at a quarter to four. I could sleep in as late as I wanted to, but I just can't seem to do it after all those years being married to a farmer. I had to get up with Jonah's father every day.

By four, I'm up and in my kitchen making my coffee."
She paused. "I have never seen Jonah leave the farm
at that time," Anna added.

I lowered my fork. That wasn't the answer that I had
wanted to hear. Clearly, I needed to have a conversation with Jonah about why he was leaving his farm so
early in the morning and where he might have gone.
I supposed it was possible that he'd gone to work at
my parents' house, but I had trouble believing that.

"Do you have suspects, Angie?" Sarah asked, shaking me from my dark thoughts.

I scooped up another forkful of mashed potatoes and
held it while I answered. "Actually, I do. That's what I
have been doing ever since I left my parents' house this
morning. I have a few good ones." I went on to tell them
about my visit with Linda from the Double Dime Diner
and Liam from the mercantile. "So just from today's
search we have three viable suspects: the brother, Blane
Bright, and the rival electrician who lost the mercantile
job, Rex Flagg, and the angry fiancée."

Rachel made six tiny stitches on her portion of the quilt
before pulling the needle through. "Could Liam Coblentz
have something to do with it? I do not know him."

I understood Rachel's need to blame an outsider,
any outsider, to Rolling Brook. I took care not to look
at Mattie when Liam Coblentz's name was mentioned.
"I don't see what motive he might have."

"But he is still a suspect," Rachel persisted. "Just
like Jonah is. We have to believe, like the sheriff does,
that everyone is a suspect until proven otherwise,
don't we?"

I could feel Mattie stiffen next to me in her seat.

"Angie?" Mattie asked. Her voice was strained, but I could tell she was doing her best to mask it. "Who was that man walking outside back and forth in front of the Dutchman's Tea Shop when you first arrived?"

Rachel nodded, unwittingly, taking the bait to change the subject. "He was outside of the bakery when I was locking up before coming over here. He asked me if I had seen *him*, but I had no idea who *him* was. I didn't answer and ran over here as quick as I could."

I covered my face with my hands. "I think *him* is Bigfoot."

The women stared at me as if I had just told them that the "him" was a Martian.

I went on to tell them about the supposed Bigfoot sighting that morning, and Willow's ill-placed post on the Internet about it. When I lowered my hand, I found all four of them were staring at me open-mouthed.

Sarah sat back from the quilt frame. "Why, I've never heard of such a thing."

"The Amish don't share silly stories about make-believe creatures like that," Anna said with a shake of her head. "I will never fully understand *Englischers*."

I forced cheerfulness into my voice. "The man might have been the only one to see the message online. I'm sure he'll leave in a day or so when he discovers there is nothing like that lurking in the woods of Holmes County."

"Of course there's not," Rachel said with a slight quaver to her voice.

The tone of her voice made me wonder if she was

thinking about her father, Nahum, who lived in the forest. Was she worried the wild man that Jonah and I saw was actually Nahum, like I first thought? Or was she worried that her father might be in danger because there was a Sasquatch loose in the woods?

Sarah adjusted her glasses on the bridge of her thin nose. "What is your next move, Angie?"

"Tomorrow, I plan to talk to Blane and Rex, so that's a start. I also want to see if there are any other viable suspects. The more we have, the better it is for Jonah."

Anna rested her hand on the edge of the quilting frame. "How can we help?"

"I might need help covering the shop while I investigate," I said.

Sarah's eyes flitted in Mattie's direction. "We're all willing to pitch in, Angie, and mind the shop, but won't Mattie be here to do that?"

Rachel's forehead furrowed ever so slightly, and I knew she must be remembering our conversation that morning when I had almost told her that Mattie hadn't been working in the shop that day. To my relief, she didn't say anything, but that didn't mean it wouldn't come up later.

I opened my mouth to say something, but Mattie cut me off. Maybe she had seen Rachel's expression too. "You don't have to worry about the shop, Angie," Mattie said. "I'll be here every day just as I have been since the day that you hired me."

Sarah cocked her head and gave Mattie a quizzical look. The curious Amish woman was picking up the clues that something was up with Mattie.

I gave Oliver one final piece of chicken and finished my plate of food, not leaving a scrap behind. "Thank you for dinner, Sarah. And thank you all for coming out tonight to talk all of this over, but I think it's best that we call it a night. You need to be with your families, and I need to get to my parents' house. I'll be spending the night there."

"Whatever for?" Sarah asked.

"To keep an eye on my father and help my mother," I said.

"And to snoop," Anna said as she jabbed her needle into her apple-shaped pincushion.

I sighed. Was I really that obvious? "Maybe a little."

The women chuckled and began packing up their needles and thread to leave. I was happy the tense meeting was ending on an amusing note for them.

Mattie stood. "Angie, don't forget that we have our quilting class tomorrow at nine in the morning."

I rubbed my forehead. As usual, I had forgotten the class. Again, I wondered how I would be able to operate Running Stitch without Mattie there to remind me about everything that the shop had going on, which actually was quite a bit for such a small business. Our quilting classes were popular. We upped our offerings to three times per week and even had a waiting list for the Saturday class, which was the most popular day of the week for our classes. Next door, Authentic Amish Quilts also offered quilting classes, but from what I heard, they weren't half as popular as those offered at Running Stitch. A tiny part of me reveled in that knowledge.

"We're making the quilted pot holders," Mattie said as if to jar my memory.

I smiled as I got up from my chair. "That's right. I love that pattern you came up with, and the ladies of the class will too," I said as if I hadn't forgotten.

At the door, I said good-bye to the ladies and watched them ride away in their buggies. Oliver and I went back inside to make sure the shop was secure for the night. It was well after dark by the time I closed and locked Running Stitch's front door. I was just turning the key in the lock when a man's voice said behind me. "Nice night for a walk."

I jumped and dropped my keys on the sidewalk.

Chapter Nineteen

Mitchell scooped my keys up off the sidewalk and balanced them in his palm. "Angie, are you all right? Did I scare you?"

I placed a hand over my heart. "Yes, you scared me. You can't come up to people like that!"

"I'm sorry," he said, sounding as if he meant it. "I would never set out to frighten you, especially after the day you've had."

In the gas-lit street outside of my quilt shop, I could see Mitchell clearly. His face was a mask of concern. He held a leash in his hand. His precocious Boston terrier, Tux, was at the end of that leash. Oliver and Tux were the best of friends and the two small dogs touched their pushed-in noses and sniffed each other.

"What are you doing here?" I asked. "How did you know I'd be here?"

"I'm a good investigator." He grinned. "I swung by your house and when you weren't there, Tux and I decided to stop by here and see if we could catch you."

"You could have just called," I said.

His face softened and he leaned forward, kissing me. When he stepped back he said, "I can't do that over the phone."

I intertwined my fingers with his. "I guess not."

He grinned. "And I wanted to see you, to make sure we were okay. You looked pretty mad at me when you were at the station earlier this evening."

I looked up at him. "You'd taken one of my best friends to the sheriff's department for questioning," I said. "I think that is more than enough reason to be irritated with you."

"I was willing to talk to Jonah at his home, but he wanted to discuss the case at the station."

"I know," I said. "Jonah told me that. Stop staring at me with those beautiful blue-green eyes of yours. I can never stay mad at you when you look at me like that."

He grinned. "I know."

"Where's Zander?" I asked, glancing up and down the street for Mitchell's nine-year-old son.

"He's with Hillary tonight," he said. "She and I both agreed it would be best if Zander stayed with her as long as the homicide investigation is going on. My hours will be erratic for the next few days."

I straightened the strap of my hobo bag on my shoulder. "Only for the next few days? You think the case will be wrapped up that soon?"

He sighed. "Nice try, Angie." It was amazing that he could express so much frustration in one utterance of my name.

I held up my free hand. The other was still holding Mitchell's. Despite my annoyance at him, I couldn't make myself pull it from his light grasp. "I get it. You can't tell me."

"But you can tell me what you've learned," he said.

I frowned, but rather than argue, I quickly related everything that I had learned that day with the exception of finding Mattie with the mercantile owner and the fact that Jonah had considered in his youth to leave the Amish church for me. He wasn't the only one who could hold back information. In my case, my reserve was to protect my friends' feelings. For Mitchell, it was all business.

"I know all that," he said.

"Why don't you just rub it in," I said irritably, finally pulling my hand away from him.

"I didn't mean to." He ran his hand through his salt-and-pepper hair. "I'm only trying to make a point that I don't need your help to solve this case."

"I have to help Jonah."

"I can't argue with you when you dig your heels in like this." He loosened his grasp on Tux's leash. "Are you still going to be at your parents' tonight?"

"Yep," I said, trying to sound as innocent as possible. I didn't want to give Mitchell any ideas as to what my plans were for that night. At the same time, he knew who he was talking to.

"Angie." There was a lot of weight in the way that Mitchell could say my name at times.

"Mitchell, don't worry." I smiled brightly.

He groaned. "Of course I worry.

"There's something else that I need to talk to you about," Mitchell began.

"Does it have to do with the murder?" I asked.

"No," he said slowly.

I yawned. "Is it pressing?"

"No." He studied my face.

"Then can it wait until morning? I'm exhausted. I'm not used to getting up so early, and I have been on the run all day long."

"You know, in all the time that it took you to ask all those questions, I could have told you what I needed to say, but I think you need all your working faculties to have this conversation. It's best if I wait."

I nodded automatically. "I should head over to my parents' house before I keel over. I know if I check my phone I will have about fifteen hundred messages from my mother asking me where I am, and I need to swing by my house to pick up my overnight bag and Dodger."

"You're taking Dodger to your parents' house?" His voice held an air of disbelief.

"He's been home alone all day. I can't leave him alone all night. First of all, Oliver would miss him."

My Frenchie made a snuffling sound as if in agreement.

"And second of all, he'll tear my house to shreds."

"So you are going to let him tear your mother's house to shreds instead?" He shook his head. "I wouldn't want to be you tomorrow morning when your mother finds her favorite throw pillow in pieces."

I grimaced because throw pillow destruction was a distinct possibility where Dodger was concerned.

He leaned forward and kissed me again. "I wish I could come over to your parents' house and stay with you. That's really the only way to keep you out of trouble."

I frowned. "Mitchell, that would never work."

"I know. I love you, but unfortunately, I can't trust you when it comes to situations like this." His face broke into a smile. "So I have Deputy Anderson parked in front of your parents' house keeping an eye on the crime scene and you."

I scowled. "You don't trust me?"

"Nope." The smile widened.

I was about to argue the point when he stopped me with another kiss, one that was much more satisfactory this time around and woke me right up.

After Mitchell and I finally said good-bye, I did exactly what I had told him that I would do. I swung the SUV by my house, threw together an overnight bag, picked up Dodger, and headed to my parents' house.

Sadly, when my SUV crested the hill and their large stone home came into view, I knew I wasn't going to bed anytime soon.

Chapter Twenty

Three cars with out-of-state plates were parked along the road. This wasn't good. This wasn't good at all. I parked at the end of my parents' driveway.

Willow and my father, who had a firm hold on the arms of his walker, spoke to three unknown men, one of whom was the large man with the Bigfoot T-shirt I had seen in Rolling Brook earlier that evening. The group stood under a light post in front of my parents' home.

Across the street, Deputy Anderson sat in his cruiser watching them with a worried expression on his face. I wasn't sure if he was more worried for himself or for what the Bigfoot enthusiasts would do to the crime scene.

With Oliver and Dodger in the backseat of my car, I removed my cell phone from my hobo bag and speed dialed Mitchell.

"Miss me already?" Mitchell asked with a teasing sound in his voice.

"Always," I said. "But that's not why I called. I just arrived at my parents' house."

"What's going on?" His voice was sharp and in an instant morphed from boyfriend mode to sheriff mode.

I glanced at Deputy Anderson in the cruiser. He still made no move to exit the car, and I didn't know how long he had been sitting there. "Has Anderson reported back about what's going on here?"

"No. Should he have?" He groaned as if he had been anticipating a call like this one.

"You might want to call him."

"Angie, what do you mean?" Mitchell asked.

On the other end of the line, I heard shuffling as if Mitchell was moving around the house. He was probably trying to find his badge and gun. Poor guy never really got a break from the job.

"Just give Anderson a call," I said. "He can explain. I need to check on my parents."

"Angie," Mitchell protested.

"Call Anderson," I said, and ended the call.

I opened my car door and allowed Oliver to jump out while I toted Dodger in his cat carrier.

I glanced over to Deputy Anderson's cruiser and saw him holding a phone away from his ear. I couldn't hear his voice, but I knew Mitchell must be on the other end of the line and he wasn't happy.

Willow waved at me, beaming from ear to ear. At least someone was pleased with this situation. That someone was decidedly not my mother.

Before I could reach the small group under the

streetlamp, Mom came flying out of the house. "Angie, what on Earth is going on here?" She wagged her finger at me. "First a man is killed in my backyard, and now I have strange men loitering in my front yard. How much more will I have to take?"

Willow inched her way toward us, and her smile wavered as she overheard my mother's complaints. Mom and Willow had been allies when they had planned a library book sale together the previous fall. It appeared all the goodwill Willow had garnered with my mother during that time had been canceled out with the unannounced arrival of the Bigfoot people.

"Now, Daphne"—Willow wrapped her heavy paisley shawl more closely around her shoulders—"I can explain. There's been a little mix-up."

I assumed that the "little mix-up" was posting my parents' address on the message board for the entire world to see on the Internet. Willow was the queen of the understatement.

"A little mix-up?" my mother asked. "A man was killed in my backyard and now strange men are knocking on my door asking me if I've seen Bigfoot. Bigfoot! Why on Earth would anyone ask me that?" She directed that last question at me.

"How would I know?" I asked. With my mother, playing dumb was a recommended diversionary tactic.

Sadly, it didn't work this time because Dodger spat and hissed in his carrier.

Mom pointed at the carrier. "You brought *him*?"

"I couldn't leave him home alone." I stepped back, holding Dodger's carrier away from her, just in case.

She'd had a rough day. I wasn't sure what she might be capable of as she was teetering on the edge.

Dad shuffled forward on his walker, and the three men inched behind him.

Willow smiled. "Angie, this is Ray, Anthony, and Ken. They're members of the same Bigfoot enthusiasts' group as I am. They wanted to come and check out the scene. I came along with them because I thought it would make your parents more comfortable . . ." She trailed off because clearly that had not been the case.

"So they aren't here because of the posting online?" I asked.

"What posting online?" Mom asked. She didn't miss anything.

Willow chuckled. "It's nothing." She raised her eyebrows at me in attempt to be subtle. Willow was a lot of things. Subtle was not one of them. "I'm glad you're here, Angie," Willow said with her eyebrows still elevated. She turned to her friends. "Angie is one of the eyewitnesses."

I frowned. How did Willow know that? I purposely hadn't told her about what I saw behind the giant oak tree this morning. Was it only this morning? It seemed as though I'd lived a week in that time.

Dodger hissed inside his carrier again. If I didn't get him settled in the house soon, no one would get any sleep tonight.

Movement in the deputy's cruiser caught my eye. He slunk low in his seat. Ahh, there was my answer. Deputy Anderson told Willow about my Bigfoot encounter. I should have known.

The three men examined me as if I were a mythical creature living in the woods. It wasn't a great feeling. I scowled in return.

The shortest of the three men stepped forward and extended his hand. "Raymond Sacks, president of the Central Ohio Bigfooter Society. I'm so very pleased to meet you."

I shook his hand. He was the shortest by far, maybe just over five feet tall. His wire-rimmed glasses slipped down his nose and he pushed them back into place with his index finger in a habitual move. He released my hand. "Can you tell us what you saw? No detail is too minor. We want to know everything."

"Yes," Anthony, a tall wiry man, agreed. "We want to know everything. You have been witness to something that we have all dreamed of, but not lucky enough to have experienced ourselves."

"Speak for yourself," Raymond said. "I have seen the Sasquatch on at least two occasions."

Anthony snorted. "Both of those were proven to be impostors. You should not claim them as true sightings; you're only embarrassing yourself."

Raymond's face flushed to a deep red. "I know what I saw." He forced a smile. "Jealousy does not become you, my friend."

Anthony's face turned an odd shade of purple and he balled his fists at his sides.

"Gentlemen," I said, not really in the mood to break off a fight between two grown men over the existence of Bigfoot. It had been a long day and, like my mother, there was only so much I could take. "I really don't think you should be here. The police declared my parents' backyard as a crime scene."

"How tall was the creature?" Ken asked, ignoring my suggestion. He was over six feet and wore bright white sneakers on his feet that appeared to be so new they came straight from the box. The shoes wouldn't last three seconds in the muddy woods.

"I don't know," I said. "He was far away."

"Where was he?" the short man asked.

Before I could answer, the sheriff's SUV came charging up the hill and rolled to a stop behind my car. Mitchell jumped out of the SUV and marched straight for us.

Willow made a little *eep* noise. I couldn't say I blamed her. Mitchell looked as if he was ready and willing to toss someone into the county jail and throw away the key.

On the street, Deputy Anderson also slipped from his car and ran over to the sheriff. He tried to say something to Mitchell, but Mitchell waved him away. The deputy slunk back.

"James!" my mother cried. "Thank goodness you're here. Can you please ask these men to leave?"

"That's what I came to do." His mouth was in a firm line. "Since my deputy seems to be incapable of doing it himself."

I winced on Anderson's behalf.

"You can't make us leave," Raymond said. "We have a right to be here."

"No," Mitchell said. "You don't. This is private property that belongs to the Braddock family, who have asked you to leave. The farm across the way is also private property owned by an Amish family. I know for a fact that they would not want you walking through their land in the middle of the night."

"We came a long way to see Bigfoot," Ken, who was the largest of the men and the one I had seen in Rolling Brook earlier that evening, said. "We're researchers."

"Researchers?" my father asked. "Bigfoot researchers? Are there such things?" My father looked intrigued by this new information.

If we weren't careful, my father could have another ill-advised hobby. This one would probably go as well as the kitchen remodel.

"Please leave quietly, or I will have to write you a citation for insubordination." Mitchell's tone meant business. I certainly wouldn't hang around if he spoke like that to me.

"This is the most inhospitable place that I have ever been," Anthony said.

"This is not open for debate. The Braddocks have asked you to leave and so have I." Mitchell's voice held a hard edge.

Willow smiled. "Why don't we all head to my tea shop for a little refreshment? We can regroup and find other places for you to search for Bigfoot. He's out there," she said, like a true believer. "But with all the commotion around the Braddocks' home, why would he stay around here where he could be seen by so many people?"

"You have a point," Ray said slowly.

After more muttering to themselves, the three men and Willow went to their respective cars. I took the opportunity to deposit Dodger inside my mother's house while she was giving Mitchell a piece of her mind. I knew that might take a while.

When I got back outside, Willow and her pals were gone, and Mom and Dad were making their way toward the house. They moved much slower than normal with Dad using the walker. I frowned. My father was supposed to begin physical therapy the next day. I hoped that it would help. He put on a brave face, but I knew he must be in a lot of pain. Oliver followed behind them, keeping a worried eye on my father. He loved his grandpa almost as much as I did.

I started to walk over to Mitchell and his young deputy but stopped in the middle of the yard when it was clear the two officers were in a heated conversation. Not that they kept their voices down. I could hear everything that was said from where I stood.

"Anderson, go home. I have another deputy on his way here, and he'll guard the crime scene tonight." Mitchell's voice was heavy with disappointment.

"But, sir, I had everything under control," Deputy Anderson protested. "Willow and those men never left the front of the house. They never went around back toward the crime scene. I wouldn't have allowed them to do that."

"Go home. That's a direct order." He folded his arms. "We'll talk about this in the morning in my office."

"Yes, sir." Anderson's voice quavered.

A small part of me felt bad for the deputy. Sure, he wasn't the best at his job, but the guy meant well. He'd skated along in Mitchell's department for years, but maybe his incompetence was finally catching up with him. I would hate it if Anderson were to be fired; I liked the guy. Not to mention, if Mitchell hired a new and more reliable deputy, I might not be able to get away with as much in the county, as far as my snooping went.

Like a dog with his tail between his legs, Deputy Anderson bowed his head as he climbed into his cruiser.

Oliver whimpered at my feet. "I feel bad for him too, Ollie."

Oliver and I were always emotionally in sync.

Mitchell strolled over to me stone-faced. "Willow told me that you knew about this Bigfoot club or whatever it was coming to Rolling Brook."

"I don't think it was actually a club."

He stared at me.

"Sorry. Just thought it would be best to clarify." I paused. "Yes, I knew about the Bigfoot people, but I hoped I wouldn't have to tell you because they wouldn't show up. When Willow posted my parents' address on that message board for Bigfoot superfans, I was as upset as you are now."

"She put it on the Internet?" He ran a hand down the side of his face.

"Yes." I winced. "I told her to take it down. She did right away. I guess these guys saw it before she could remove the posting."

"Do you think others will show up?" His hand was still over his face so his voice was muffled.

"That's a better question for Willow. I don't even know where she went online to post the news." I studied his weary face. "According to Willow, this isn't the first time you have had a Bigfoot encounter as the sheriff."

He groaned. "If you are talking about Willow's close encounter with Bigfoot on Sugartree Street a few years back, then yes, this isn't my first rodeo."

"What happened then?"

"Well, there wasn't a murder involved. Willow made a fuss for a few days, and I had my deputies search the woods and general area. They came up with a whole lot of nothing. We finally ruled that it must have been a figment of Willow's overactive imagination. Most likely it was an animal and she mistook it for Bigfoot."

"And do you think these sightings are figments of imagination too? Both Jonah and I saw—"

"No, I don't, but I don't believe it's Bigfoot either. Most likely someone playing a prank, which is a complication I don't need with this murder." He rubbed his eyes. "I guess it was right to send Zander to Hillary's for the night."

I touched his arm. I knew how much he hated to give up time with his son. "You know I would normally offer to watch him for you, but since I'm staying with my parents tonight, I don't think you want him here."

"No, I don't. If Zander knew about this Bigfoot thing, I would never hear the end of it. He loves those Bigfoot-hunter specials on television." He shivered. "And if he did hear about it, Hillary would blame me."

That I didn't doubt. Mitchell had a fairly good relationship with his ex-wife, Hillary, but their marriage ended over his strange hours and police work. Hillary was hypersensitive about Zander's being affected by any of Mitchell's cases. The last thing in the world that

she wanted was their son to follow in his father's foot-
steps and become a cop.

"Bigfoot aside, do you have any leads other than
what you learned from Jonah?"

He chuckled. "You never stop."

"It never hurts to ask, right?"

He shook his head.

A new cruiser drove up, and Deputy Riley exited
the car. Riley was much older than Anderson and had
been on the force longer than Mitchell had been sheriff.
If he was unhappy about having to stay up all night
to guard the crime scene, he didn't show it.

Mitchell quickly pecked me on the cheek, something that he would not normally do in front of one of
his officers. "I need to talk to my deputy and head back
to the station. I want to look into this Bigfoot thing.
Please stay inside the house tonight."

"I will," I promised. I meant it too. Had Anderson
been the deputy on watch I might have been able to
slip out of the house to take a peek at the crime scene,
but I wouldn't have a chance with Riley on the job.

Oliver and I headed toward the house and Mitchell
and his deputy spoke in low voices beside Mitchell's
car. As I shut the front door to my parents' house, I
focused on the large oak tree across the street where
I had seen the person or thing or who knew what. I
could barely make out the trunk in the dark. Whatever
I had seen beside the trunk this morning might just
be the key to solving this murder.

Chapter Twenty-one

I woke up the next morning in a bright yellow room with cramped toes because I'd knocked them on the poles at the end of the daybed all night long. Daybeds are not for tall people. I would have been better off if I had slept on the floor.

I blinked at the yellowness of the room. I would call the color goldenrod. All the furniture was white, polished to a high sheen, and adorable. It was a baby's room or, at least, my mother wished it was a baby's room. My parents' large house had five bedrooms, and she reserved this one for her unfulfilled dream of being a grandmother. There wasn't a crib in the room—she hadn't gone that far—but a giant giraffe mocked me from the corner. I covered my face with my pillow so that I wouldn't have to make eye contact with it.

On the floor, Oliver whimpered his sympathy, and I had to wonder why it wasn't enough that my mother had a granddog and grandcat. It wasn't that I was opposed to the idea of children. I loved Mitchell's son, Zander, but—a thought made me sit straight up in bed.

What *had* Mitchell wanted to talk to me about the day before?

The giraffe watched me with shiny glass eyes. The brute.

Had he wanted to talk about this room? Well, not this specifically, but marriage and babies and the future? I smacked my head with the heel of my hand. How could I be so stupid not to think of this before? What else could it be? Didn't Mitchell say he wanted me to have all my "working faculties" for the conversation? I wanted to marry Mitchell, didn't I? I knew in my heart that I did. The problem was I didn't have the best track record as far as successful engagements went. Okay, my track record was terrible. I slid back down under the blankets and covered my face with the pillow.

Oliver whined and placed his paws on the side of the daybed.

"You little mongrel!"

My muddied thoughts were interrupted by shouts from the other side of the bedroom door. I threw the covers back and ran into the hallway just in time to see Dodger streaking down the grand staircase. I may have been mistaken, but it looked to me as if he was grinning. Bringing him to my parents' home had been a very bad idea.

Mom pointed to me. "Your cat climbed up my curtains."

She pointed to the curtains that covered the window at the end of the hallway. Sure enough, the gauzy fabric was decorated with tiny little pinpricks that I knew all too well. I had given up having curtains in my own house after Dodger had scaled them half a dozen times.

"I'm sorry, Mom," I said groggily, trying to hide a yawn. "I can make you some new ones. We still have the same fabric at the shop."

"That cat is a terror." Even though it was only seven in the morning, she was dressed and in full makeup. I didn't look that put together at noon.

"He's not so bad," I said automatically, coming to Dodger's defense.

My mother plucked an invisible piece of lint from the sleeve of her thin cashmere sweater. "Jonah and his helper are already here setting to work." She pointed to me. "You need to make sure that cat stays out of their way." She made her way to the stairs.

I groaned and headed back to my room to dress for the day. Dodger would be going with me to Running Stitch, and on a day that I had a quilting class. I hoped Mattie would understand.

Twenty minutes later, I reemerged from the yellow room more awake. The first order of business was to find Dodger and make sure he wasn't disemboweling one of my mother's throw pillows like Mitchell predicted that he would.

"Ollie," I said to the Frenchie at the top of the grand staircase. "Go find your brother."

Immediately, the black-and-white Frenchie trundled down the stairs in a half run/half tumble. It was adorable. I took care not to laugh. Oliver could be sensitive about his stocky build.

At the bottom of the stairs, I watched as Oliver

headed through the formal dining room into the kitchen. That figured. Dodger would want to be in the center of the action.

In the kitchen, I found Jonah and Eban in the process of tearing out the countertop and lower counter.

"Mrs. Braddock said we can take all the counters and cabinetry we remove, so take care when removing the granite. I would like to keep it in one piece," Jonah told the younger man.

I wasn't surprised by Jonah's comment. The Amish didn't let anything go to waste. They were the ultimate recyclers. It was common in the county to see them in flea markets and school rummage sales looking for something that the English had cast aside for something newer, bigger, and better.

Dodger was perched on the counter opposite the broken French doors. His tail swished back and forth across the granite. My mother would never tolerate a cat on any counter. He purred as I approached. I wagged my finger at him. "It's not even eight in the morning and you've already upset Grandma."

His white whiskers curled upward.

I put my hands on my hips. "Furthermore, if she knew you were on the counter, she would flip her lid."

The coy feline's smile was back. He was hopeless.

I turned to find Jonah and Eban staring at me.

I gave them an innocent look. "What?"

Eban laughed. "Do you always talk to your animals?"

I grinned back. "Yep."

This only made the young Amish man grin more broadly. "Then, I guess everything Jonah has told me about you is true."

I narrowed my eyes at Jonah. "Are you spreading rumors about me?"

He placed a hand innocently to his chest. "Me?"

I rolled my eyes, glad that Mitchell wasn't there to see it. Then he would know where Zander got the habit from for sure. "What did he tell you?"

Eban's eye twinkled. "That you are quirky and high-strung." He paused. "Oh, and that you solve murders in your spare time."

I arched my brow a Jonah, who was smiling. "Quirky and high-strung? Here I am trying to keep you from going to jail and you're telling Eban I'm a nut," I said, but I couldn't help but smile. I was so relieved that Jonah seemed to have recovered from his dark mood from the night before. I wouldn't have cared if he had told Eban I had escaped from the circus.

"I never called you a nut," Jonah teased.

"Good to know." I tried to hide my smile.

Still laughing, Eban knelt in front of the lower kitchen cabinets to the left of the French doors and began removing the hardware with a screwdriver. I was happy that Eban was there. He seemed to be able to keep Jonah's mind off the murder.

"I'm glad to see you here today, Jonah," I said. "I wasn't sure you would be able to come, considering . . ."

He tucked a flat carpentry pencil behind his ear. "If you think that Miriam wouldn't want me to come, you're right." He sighed. "But she knows that this job pays well, and we could use the money."

I bit the inside of my cheek, physically holding back the question on the tip of my tongue about the Grabers' financial situation. The Amish didn't like to talk about their personal affairs, and I didn't know anyone who enjoyed talking about their finances, even with a close friend.

On the floor, Eban carefully placed each handle pull and all the screws from the cabinetry into a small cardboard box that he pulled along beside himself as he made his way down the long stretch of cabinetry. His movements were controlled as he paid close attention to details. I had no doubt his work would be meticulous. I was relieved that Jonah had found someone whom he could count on for this job. My mother would accept nothing less than perfection.

I picked Dodger up off the counter and cradled him in my arms.

Jonah nodded at the cat. "I'm glad you are here to collect him. He's been eyeing the French doors. I think he was in the process of planning an escape."

Dodger began to purr. The cat had no shame.

I tucked the cat under my chin. "Will you finish taking the kitchen apart today?" I asked.

He nodded. "And we will begin installing the hardwood floor. It should be delivered by ten this morning. Once the floor is down, the job will go swiftly. The cabinets are already made and waiting at a local warehouse."

"Who is taking over the electrician work now that . . ." I trailed off.

"Now that Griffin is dead? That I don't know. You will have to ask your mother."

I smiled. "Maybe I'll wait a little bit on that. She's not in the best mood after Dodger's antics."

He laughed. "I think Eban and I are on her trouble-maker list too. She wasn't happy when we tracked mud into the house from the backyard."

I shook my head. "Don't worry. Her bark is worse than her bite."

"Reminds me of another person I know," Jonah muttered.

I grunted.

Jonah made a face. "Angie, should you be looking into the murder? One man is dead. It could be dangerous."

"Jonah, we already went over that yesterday. I'm not backing down now."

He sighed. "Maybe I should come with you."

"And abandon my mother's kitchen remodel? No way," I said. "Mom would never let me hear the end of it." I took a breath. "But I have a question."

He stroked his beard again. "I have a feeling that I'm not going to like this question."

I shifted Dodger in my arms so that his forepaws hung over my right shoulder. The cat made no move to jump from my arms. I knew I should be concerned about his extra affection. When it came to Dodger, that could only mean he was plotting something. "Yesterday morning, you left your farm at four a.m. But you told the police that you didn't arrive here until six. Where were you during that time?"

He frowned. "How do you know when I left the farm?"

I scratched Dodger between the ears. "Anna saw you leave."

He didn't say anything.

"Jonah, are you going to tell me? It's important."

"It is personal. I would rather not speak of it." He wouldn't meet my eyes.

I stepped back. "What did you tell the police about your whereabouts that morning? I know they must have asked."

"They did several times."

"What did you tell them?" Dodger was beginning to grow heavy in my arms. He wasn't a small cat, but I was reluctant to put him down because he might make a beeline for the French doors.

"I told them the same thing that I have just told you. That I would rather not speak of it."

My brow knit together. "And Mitchell was okay with that?"

He opened and rooted through a toolbox that was sitting on a card table in the corner of the room. "He was not pleased, but I am not obligated to tell him where I was."

"Jonah," I said in exasperation. "You're a prime suspect for murder. If someone can provide you an alibi, tell the police. That's your best chance of being cleared."

"I was alone. There is no one who can give me an alibi, so where I was is irrelevant. I told the sheriff that."

I felt my eye begin to twitch. I was shocked that Mitchell had allowed Jonah to leave the sheriff's station last night with how uncooperative he was being. I knew Mitchell must have let him go as a favor to me, which made me only more determined to find out who the real killer was.

"Jonah, you have to tell the police. Maybe someone saw you wherever you were and can provide your alibi."

He removed a small crowbar from the toolbox. "I already told you I was alone."

I felt my heart sink. "Jonah, this is important."

"I know this," he said. The good humor that had been in his voice when he and Eban had been teasing me just a few minutes ago was gone. "I should get to work and you should go to your shop. I don't have an alibi. That is final." He turned away from me and began speaking to Eban in Pennsylvania Dutch and pointing at the countertop.

As I stared at his back, my shoulders slumped. Dodger pressed his nose against my cheek as if to comfort me. Like Oliver, he knew when I needed to be consoled.

"AngieBear!" My father's voice boomed through the house.

I ran to my father with Dodger hissing in my arms.

Chapter Twenty-two

I skidded to a stop in the living room and placed a hand on my chest. "Dad, are you okay? I thought something happened."

Dad sat in his enormous leather chair. Oliver was sitting at his feet and from the empty plate on the side table it appeared that the pair had shared a morning muffin. "I'm so sorry, my girl." His eyebrows pinched together in regret. "I just wanted to make sure you would stop and see your dear old dad before you left for the day."

"You know I wouldn't leave without saying good-bye."

He nodded. "I do, but not being able to see my favorite child to the door because of this silly back injury drives me crazy. Your mother would chain me to this chair if she could."

I kissed him on the forehead. I was still carrying Dodger. "I'm your only child," I said.

"It is a good thing because I can't imagine loving another one as much as I love you."

I grinned. This was an old conversation that I had had with my father for as long as I could remember, and I never tired of it. From the smile on his face, he never did either. "When is your physical therapy appointment?"

He groaned. "Your mother is taking me to the torture chamber in a few minutes." He shivered and gestured to his clothes. "She made me put this on this morning."

Dad was wearing bright blue sweats. Dad dressed much more casually since he left his high-powered corporate job in Dallas, but he still wasn't a sweats kind of guy. I tried to remember if I had ever seen him in sweatpants before. Nothing came to mind.

"You look cute," I said.

He wrinkled his nose. "You know that girl who turns into a blueberry in *Charlie and the Chocolate Factory*?"

I nodded.

His mustache drooped. "Well, now, I know what she felt like."

"Dad," I chuckled, "you don't look like a blueberry, and I'm sure if you even hint to Mom that you would like some other workout clothes, she would run to the store. You know she loves any excuse to shop."

He sighed.

"Promise me you will do the exercises the therapist asks of you," I said in a much more serious tone of voice.

He made a face. "'Exercise' is a dirty word in my book, only to be surpassed by 'diet.' I loathe both of them."

"Dad," I said in exasperation, knowing that I sounded much like my mother. "Do it for me?" I asked. "It really scared me when Mom told me you were hurt." Without warning my eyes filled with tears.

He held out his hand to me. "Oh, AngieBear, I would do anything for you."

I smiled and squeezed his hand. "Good. Mom will be glad to hear that too."

He sighed again. "I suppose it won't be so bad if I can get some better threads. A man can only stand to be a blueberry for one day."

I laughed. "Can you watch Dodger for a bit?" I asked. "Mom's not too happy with him at the moment."

"Sure thing." Dad patted his lap.

I settled Dodger in my father's chair, and Dad stroked the large cat's silver back. Dodger began to purr. Looking at the pair sitting contently together, I wondered how I hadn't realized it before. My father, who had been looking for something to keep him occupied ever since he retired, didn't need a new hobby. He needed a pet. An idea tickled the back of my brain, but I would have to discuss it with my mother before I acted. If I showed up at their house with a puppy or kitten without her knowledge, the repercussions would be epic.

I went out the front door and found that Oliver had come outside with me. I stared down at him. "You decided to join me because Dad's out of snacks?"

He cocked his head.

"All right." I laughed. "I'm going to check the perimeter. You can come too, but if we see any Bigfoot-sized anything, we're out of there."

He glanced around the yard as if to make sure the area was secure. I didn't see anything and headed around the side of the house.

I stepped through the gate that led into the backyard. The small construction trailer that had been there the day before was gone. I knew it sat in Mitchell's impound. There were muddy ruts in the lawn where the tires for the trailer had once been. I grimaced. My mother wouldn't be happy with the mess that trailer had left behind when she saw it.

Other than the marks in the grass, there was no indication that a murder had happened the day before. I didn't know if that made me feel sad or relieved, because it was as if the tragedy of Griffin Bright's death never was.

From the spot where the trailer had been, I stared into the woods. This was the place where Jonah had seen the "wild man." The woods were still at the moment. Oliver sniffed a nearby flower bed. Since the Frenchie was calm, I thought that whatever Jonah saw must not have been close by.

I clapped my hands. "Oliver, it's time to go."

Before leaving the backyard I glanced at the back of the house. Jonah set one of the two broken doors gingerly on the deck. He gave me a half smile. I felt a pang in my heart. In the lapse of one day, our easy friendship had become a complicated mess.

In the end, I was the one who looked away first. I cleared my throat. "Come, Oliver."

The Frenchie lifted his head out of my mother's garden. His muzzle was covered with dirt.

"It's time to collect your brother and head to the shop," I told my dog.

As I left the yard, I turned back to the deck where Jonah had been standing one last time. He was no longer there. I would prove his innocence. I silently promised that to us both.

Chapter Twenty-three

By the time I reached Running Stitch, Mattie was already there and had everything set up for our nine a.m. quilting class. The class was held an hour before the quilt shop actually opened. Since the classes had grown so much in the last year, we'd discovered that it was better to hold the quilting classes outside of the shop's regular hours because it was just too crowded inside the small shop to allow any shoppers to view the merchandise.

A few days before, Mattie had made up small kits of fabric and batting to make tulip-shaped pot holders for everyone in our Friday morning class. Each kit included fabric cut to the correct size and shape, thread, needles, a tiny pair of scissors, and a small pincushion to keep track of the needles.

Oliver followed me into the shop, and I set Dodger's carrier on the floor. When I opened the cat carrier's door, Mattie didn't make her typical sarcastic comment about the cat's arrival.

I studied her. "What's wrong?"

Dodger bounded out of the carrier and scaled the shelves of fabric.

Mattie set a quilting kit on the last folding chair in the circle. "Wrong? There's nothing wrong." She looked around the room. "Do you see something amiss for today's class?"

"No," I said. "Everything is perfect as far as your setup goes. You're a pro at this, Mattie. I'm asking what's wrong because you didn't say anything when I let Dodger loose in the shop."

"I don't have anything against Dodger. He's a beautiful cat." She wouldn't meet my gaze.

"Really?" I arched an eyebrow at her.

She sighed. "I have no right to comment on anything that you do in the shop, Angie. This is your property, and you are my boss. After I have lied to you, I have no right to criticize anyone." Her face turned bright red.

"Don't lie to me again. We're good."

She clasped her hands over her apron. "Oh, *danki,* Angie. *Danki.*"

"You don't have to thank me," I said, smiling.

"In that case, why did you have to bring that rascal to the quilting class?" She smiled.

I laughed. "That's more like it."

As usual, Shirley, one of our longtime class members, was the first to arrive. "Good morning!" she said cheerfully after setting her quilting basket by her favorite spot in the class and making a beeline for the goodie table. This morning, Mattie had stocked the table with doughnuts and muffins from her family's bakery. I'd tried to pay Rachel and Aaron countless times for the food they supplied for all the events at Running Stitch. As of yet, I had been unsuccessful in that campaign. To compensate, I'd printed a large sign that stated ALL REFRESHMENTS PROVIDED BY MILLER'S AMISH BAKERY and made sure to put out some of the bakery's business cards. I liked to think that the free samples translated into sales. Having watched many of the quilting class attendants make their way over to the bakery after each class, I had to assume that the tactic worked.

At the table, Shirley ignored the muffins and selected two doughnuts with sprinkles. I always made the same decision when faced with the choice between doughnuts and muffins. And when there were sprinkles involved, was there really a choice?

Oliver plopped himself down at her feet with his most pitiful expression plastered on his wrinkled face.

I clicked my tongue. "Oliver, give Shirley some space."

Shirley chuckled. "Oh, he's fine." When she thought I wasn't looking, she dropped a piece of doughnut on the pine plank floor for Oliver. He swallowed it whole.

I pretended not to notice.

Soon all the ladies were settled into their spots. Mattie began the class. "Welcome, everyone," she said in a clear and confident voice.

Behind the sales counter, I couldn't help but beam with pride. When Mattie had started working at Running Stitch, she had been a quiet and shy Amish girl, too frightened to speak in front of a room of *Englischers*. Now, she took on the task with ease.

The women praised the colors of the pot holder pieces cut to resemble tulip petals, and everyone, for once, seemed to be pleased with the fabric that they had been given. The women settled into the work, and as the stitches began, so did the gossip.

Shirley threaded her needle. "Angie, I heard about the tragedy at your mom and dad's home yesterday morning."

"Oh, yes." Another class member, Lois, adjusted her green plastic-framed glasses. "What a horrible thing to have happened to your parents after moving here."

I nodded. "Mom and Dad are both upset about it."

"Griffin Bright, the electrician, was the man who died—isn't that right?" Shirley asked. "It's all over the county that he was electrocuted." She clicked her tongue. "Real shame."

"What an unfortunate way to go," Alice, a new member to the class and a round woman with rosy cheeks, said. "To be killed by your own profession seems so cruel."

"Did he make a mistake?" Lois asked as she peered up from her stitches.

I wouldn't say that I encouraged the gossip, but I certainly didn't put a stop to it. Since the quilting classes had begun just months after I took over the shop, I had learned some very interesting tidbits from the ladies that later led me to a murderer. However, this was the first time that they knew I was directly involved because of where the dead body had been discovered.

"What do you know about his death? Was it really murder?" Shirley asked with a glint in her eye. It was the same hungry-for-information look that I had seen on Sarah's face countless times.

"I'm afraid so," I said.

Alice covered her mouth, and a few of the other women in the room stifled gasps.

"How terrible," Lois murmured.

"I would have given them the name of a better electrician, one that no one would have wanted to kill," Alice said.

"What's the name of your electrician?" I asked as I moved around the room, keeping an eye out for anyone who needed help with their stitches.

"Rex Flagg," Alice said.

Rex Flagg? That was the name of the rival electrician who started the wiring job at the mercantile and then suddenly quit. If he was such a great electrician, why then did he leave that job if it had been his choice to be there in the first place? I thought back to my conversation with Liam the day before. As I recalled, Liam hadn't said why Rex gave up the job at the mercantile. In fact, Liam had given me the impression that he had no idea why Rex hadn't shown up for work.

"What can you tell me about Rex?" I asked.

Alice frowned. "He's good at his job." She pursed her lips. "When he shows up. The man has some demons."

Shirley snorted. "She's trying to tell you that he's a drunk."

Alice's frowned deepened. "He is trying to better himself."

"How do you know him?" I asked.

"He did some work on my husband's office. My husband is a dentist. He did a really wonderful job." She narrowed her eyes at Shirley.

Shirley ignored the look. "Must have been one of those rare times that he was sober."

Alice pursed her lips. "I had heard that he relapsed," she finally admitted.

If Rex had gone on a bender, that would explain why he had abandoned Liam's job at the mercantile. "Do you know where I can find him?" I asked.

Alice shook her head. "No, I'd recently tried to call him to have some work done on my house, but the number that I had from when he worked in my husband's office had been disconnected."

Lois shifted in her seat. "The murder is one thing, but there is an even bigger rumor circulating the county than the murder."

I inwardly groaned. I knew where this was going.

Shirley leaned forward over her quilted tulip pot holder. "That's right! There are a bunch of Bigfoot hunters running loose in the county." She laughed so hard it came out as a cackle.

"A bunch?" I squeaked. Other than Willow I knew about only three.

"What are you talking about?" an elderly member asked.

Shirley sat back in her seat now that she had her audience. "Someone saw Bigfoot in the county."

"Bigfoot isn't real." Alice tsked.

"That may be true," Shirley said. "But don't tell that to these men running around through the woods looking for him. They'll never believe you. Nor will Willow Moon for that matter." She chuckled and smoothed the two pieces of fabric she was stitching together over her lap.

"Is anyone really surprised in anything Willow Moon believes?" Alice asked. "With all her interesting ideas, how she ended up opening a tea shop in the middle of Ohio's Amish Country will be forever baffling to me."

"I heard there is supposed to be a meeting of Bigfooters later this morning," Lois said.

"When is the meeting supposed to be held?" I asked with more than a little bit of anxiety.

She threaded her needle. "Ten fifteen, I believe."

If Shirley believed that it was ten fifteen, it was ten fifteen. She was as good at gathering information as Sarah Leham.

From across the room, I could feel Mattie watching me. I knew my assistant would advise me not to go to the meeting. But how could I do that when it could be somehow related to Griffin's murder?

Shirley shook her head. "It would be Bigfoot that would be the only thing to bring Raymond Sacks back to Holmes County."

My brows shot up in surprise. "He's from the county?" It seemed strange that he or Willow hadn't mentioned that the night before. I wondered if Willow even knew.

She nodded. "Oh, yes, he grew up in Millersburg."

"Why did he leave?" I asked.

"His wife died in a fire. He swore he would never set foot back in the county after that."

"What started the fire?" I squeaked out.

"If I recall correctly, it was an electrical fire," Shirley said.

My mouth went dry. That was what I was afraid she was going to say.

Chapter Twenty-four

"I'm just having the worst time matching up these pieces, Mattie," Shirley complained, shaking two cloth petals in frustration.

Mattie smiled. "Let me help you."

With that, the conversation moved back to the pot holders, but I couldn't return to the task at hand as easily. Jonah's cousin, Kamon, died in an electrical accident caused, at least in Jonah's mind, by Griffin's negligence. Was Griffin somehow responsible for Raymond's wife's death too?

"Shirley," I asked, "do you know what caused that electrical fire?" I tried to keep the excitement out of my voice.

She wrinkled her nose. "I believe it was in a century-old farmhouse. The wiring in the basement was bad and caught fire while his wife was asleep. Raymond wasn't there during the fire. It was rumored that he moved away out of guilt."

"When was this? When did the fire happen?" I asked.

Shirley thought for a moment. "It was before my daughter was born. I would say nearly thirty years ago."

Thirty years? That was even longer ago than Kamon's death.

Through Running Stitch's large display window I saw Raymond Sacks standing outside of the Dutchman's Tea Shop. He was alone.

"Mattie, I'm just going across the street for a moment," I said. "I should check in with Willow about this Bigfoot business."

My assistant arched her brow at me and nodded. I opened the front door and Oliver wriggled out around my feet. Maybe he thought I would need backup. The ladies' noisy chatter followed us out of the shop.

Outside on the sidewalk, Oliver and I waited for an Amish buggy to pass before we crossed the street. Through the large front window of Miller's Amish Bakery, I saw Rachel behind the counter. It was a Friday morning, and business appeared to be brisk.

Raymond waved at me with his cigarette as I approached. "Glad to see you. We thought you weren't going to make it."

I raised my eyebrows. "You've been expecting me?"

"Willow suggested that you might drop by to tell us more about your Sasquatch encounter."

Oh, she did, did she?

"We've been waiting for you," he said eagerly.

I cleared my throat. "Actually, I would like to talk to you too. When did you arrive in Rolling Brook?"

"Late yesterday afternoon."

I hid a grimace. "So you weren't here yesterday morning."

He studied me. "No."

"What about your two friends?" I asked.

"No, we came together." He frowned.

Oliver leaned against my leg.

"Have you been to the township before?" I asked, half expecting him to lie to me.

He took a drag of his cigarette. "I grew up here." His eyes narrowed. "But why do I think you already knew that?"

"A member of my quilting class mentioned that she recognized you."

He dropped his cigarette. "I knew I should never have come back here. Even if there was a promising Bigfoot sighting."

"Why did you leave?" I asked.

"Why don't you tell me since you know so much about me?"

"Your wife died in an electrical fire."

His eyes narrowed. "I was away on business when my wife died. I'll never forgive myself for that." He pulled a pack of cigarettes from the breast pocket on his jacket and lit another one. "This is about Griff, isn't it? You know that he was the electrician I hired to work in my house here."

I blinked. I hadn't *known* Griffin had been the one. I only suspected. "Yes," I fibbed, "and you blame him for your wife's death."

"Of course I blame him!" he bellowed so loudly that

a buggy horse parked on the street jumped. "If it hadn't been for him, she'd still be alive."

He was so angry that it was easy for me to believe Raymond could hold a grudge against Griffin for thirty years. I held my arms loosely at my sides. "What happened? Did Griffin do something wrong that caused the fire?"

"He didn't do anything; that was the problem." His hands shook at his lifted the cigarette to his lips. When he lowered it again, he said, "We had just moved into the house. We knew there were issues with the wiring in the basement. The inspector told us that, but we were so eager to move into our new home, we didn't want to wait for all the work to be done. Griff and I were friends. I asked him to take a look at it. He said that the electrical would be fine until he finished another large job. He said there was no reason to push back our move-in date." He took another drag from his cigarette. "Stupidly, I believed him because Griff was my friend."

"Why didn't you just find someone else to do the job sooner?" I asked.

"I trusted him, and I thought I was doing him a favor by giving him the work. I should never have done that. He's the reason my wife is dead."

"And you're back and now he's dead."

His lip curled. "I had nothing to do with it. I can't say that I'm sorry the man is dead. He ruined my life. Something you might not know was my wife was two months pregnant when she died in that fire."

I shivered. "I—I'm so sorry."

"Not as sorry as I am." He stared up the street in the direction of the pie factory. "It wasn't until after I was already here that I heard about Griff's murder. Had I known that the Bigfoot sighting had any connection to Griffin Bright, I would never have come. I found out about it last night outside of your parents' home. I had no idea a crime had been committed until that moment."

Willow popped out of the tea shop. "Ray, we're ready—" She stopped talking when she saw me standing on the sidewalk a few feet away from the tea shop door. "Angie, you made it!"

Raymond continued to glare at me.

I cleared my throat. "I made it."

She clasped her hand over the purple crystal that hung from her neck. "Does that mean you're a believer?"

"Ummm . . ." I trailed off.

Raymond stubbed out his second cigarette on the sidewalk. "I'll go inside and prepare the crowd for you, Angie."

Crowd? There was a crowd?

The door closed behind Raymond but not before I caught a peek of the inside and saw that the place was packed. "How many people are in there?"

She scrunched up her nose. "Can't say for sure. Maybe thirty."

"Thirty? Are you kidding?" I squeaked.

"I would never kid about Bigfoot, Angie." She sounded offended by the very idea.

I looked heavenward. The sun was bright and handfuls of clouds were suspended in the blue sky. For the first time since the beginning of the month, it didn't look as though it might rain at any moment.

She sighed. "Just come inside and see for yourself."

I sighed. "Fine."

She beamed. Then she pointed down to Oliver. "You might want to carry him. I'd hate one of the Bigfooters to step on his paw."

I scooped Oliver up off the sidewalk and followed Willow into the tea shop.

Once inside, I gasped. The place was packed. There were mostly men, but I spotted at least four women. The only people I recognized were the three men I met the day before. The trio stood at the far end of the shop on a small stage that Willow sometimes used for live music or poetry readings that she hosted in the tea shop. Raymond pointed to a topographical map spread across a table.

Willow beamed. "It's impressive, isn't it?"

I wasn't sure that "impressive" was the word that I would use.

She walked over to a sideboard where scones, tea, and other refreshments had been set out. She removed a quilted tea cozy from one of the many teapots.

"All of these people are here with the hope of seeing Bigfoot?" I asked.

She nodded and held a full teacup of the inky black liquid to me. It smelled suspicious, almost swamplike. Willow prided herself in making up her own tea recipes. The only problem was she wasn't very good at it. In fact, her teas were terrible. Her worst offering was her October tea, Witch's Bite. The memory of tasting that still brought tears to my eyes.

"This is a new recipe of mine," she said. "I'm calling it Bigfoot Brew."

If there was any tea on planet Earth that sounded worse that Witch's Bite, it just might be Bigfoot Brew. I wasn't dumb enough to take a sip to see if that prediction rang true.

I shook my head. "I can't drink it while holding Oliver."

She set it on the table closest to me. "I'll just put it right here until you are ready for it."

I'd never be ready for it.

"What are all these people going to do all day?" I asked. "They can't go thrashing through the woods searching for the Sasquatch."

Willow sighed. "Not everyone here is actively searching. Ray and his companions plan to give a presentation about the history of Bigfoot. Many of the people here are interested in that and are just here to learn more. They aren't serious members of the society," she said as if she found that to be a shame.

Raymond scowled at me before turning back to his map.

The door to the tea shop swung opened, and Head Township Trustee Caroline Cramer stomped inside followed by a smiling Farley Jung. "Willow!" our fearless leader bellowed. "I hope that you can explain this."

Chapter Twenty-five

Some of the Bigfooters looked up from their notes and plates of scones. When Caroline shot them her death glare, they averted their eyes. They weren't afraid of coming face-to-face with a mythical creature, but Caroline scared them to death. That sounded about right.

"Caroline." Willow clasped her hands and her gauzy blouse billowed around her. "What a surprise to see you here this morning. Did we have a trustees' meeting that I didn't know about?" Willow smiled. "Can I pour you a cup of tea? It's my new recipe called Bigfoot Brew."

I inwardly groaned.

Caroline wrinkled her nose. "No, thank you." Her blond hair was pulled back in a perfect chignon and she wore a suit as if she'd just come from a business meeting. Caroline took her elected position as head township trustee as seriously as the queen of England took her post, and she made sure to dress the part.

"It seems I'm the one unaware of some type of

gathering." Caroline gestured around the room. "What is going on here?"

Willow forced a laugh. "It seems that the word has gotten out that we had a little Bigfoot sighting in the township."

"A little Bigfoot sighting?" Caroline glowered. "So this Bigfoot business is true?"

In my attempt to escape, I bumped my hip into a table where two Bigfooters were working on a grid of some sort.

Behind Caroline, Farley stepped in my path as if he knew I was trying to flee. As always, his black hair was slicked back *Grease*-style. He smirked. I scowled in return.

Caroline took a deep breath. "And how did all these people find out about our little sighting here in the county?"

Willow played with her crystal. "I thought it would bring some business if I shared the news with the local chapter of the Bigfooter Society. I never imagined that there would be so much interest."

I winced. *Oh, Willow, don't admit it to Caroline right off.*

"You did what?" the head trustee asked through clenched teeth.

Willow spun her crystal at double speed.

Caroline's dark eyes narrowed. "Do you not realize that we are the laughingstock of the county? My counterparts in Berlin and Charm are already calling me, making Bigfoot cracks. Is *this* what we want Rolling Brook to be known for?"

"Caroline," I said in my most reasonable voice,

"Willow never intended to hurt Rolling Brook's reputation."

"And you!" She pointed at me. "All of this is your fault."

I held Oliver protectively to my chest. "What? Me? What did I do?"

"Don't play dumb with me, Angela Braddock." Her glossy lip curled in disdain. "Everyone knows the supposed sighting of the *thing* was at your parents' house. What do you think you're doing by spreading rumors like this?"

"The Bigfoot thing didn't come from me," I said. "The first I had heard of this Bigfoot theory was from . . ." I stopped myself from saying Deputy Anderson's name. The poor guy had enough problems without my offering him as a sacrificial lamb to Caroline.

She didn't miss a beat. "From whom did you hear it?"

I shifted Oliver in my arms. He snuffled and turned his face away from the conversation. He didn't care for Caroline. She wasn't an animal person, clearly a character flaw. "It doesn't matter who I heard it from," I said.

"It's not Angie's fault. It's mine," Willow said. "I was the one who posted the news about the sighting on the chapter's message board. I did it without Angie's knowledge." She continued to twirl the purple crystal as she spoke.

"Of course you would be interested in this ridiculous myth," Caroline said accusatorily.

"Now, Caroline," Farley said in his most condescending voice. "You can't blame Willow or Angie for what happened. We can only move forward and deal with it. When I was head trustee . . ."

"Farley," Caroline snapped, "if I have to hear another anecdote of when you were head trustee, I swear I'm going to scream."

He only smiled.

Before Caroline could actually let loose a screech that would bring a banshee to tears, I interrupted. . "This is not the time to discuss this." I nodded at the Bigfooters, who were watching us. "Don't you think it would do better to have a private meeting where we can speak more freely?"

Caroline scowled at the eavesdroppers, who turned away. "You're right," she said as if she hated to admit that could be true. "We need to have an emergency trustees' meeting tonight to go over how to deal with this latest crisis."

"The tea shop shouldn't be as crowded later when the Bigfooters start their search," Willow said.

I winced. That wasn't the right thing to say to Caroline.

The head trustee pursed her lips. "We can't have it here with your *friends* coming and going at all hours." She glared at another Bigfooter, who hid his face.

"We can meet in my shop tonight," I jumped in. "How does seven work for all of you?"

"I suppose that will have to do since Jason doesn't seem to make meetings that are right after he leaves his office for the day," she said with thinly veiled disgust.

Caroline constantly complained about Jason Rustle's schedule. Of the five trustees, he was the only one who had a true nine to five job. Willow and I owned our own businesses. Other than her trustee position, Caroline's work was mostly volunteering, and who knew what Farley did all day. It was probably for the best that I was clueless about his whereabouts most of the time.

"We'll meet at Running Stitch at seven sharp." Caroline pointed at Willow. "I expect that you will have a plan as to how to deal with this crisis."

Caroline and Farley left the tea shop.

Willow's shoulders dropped. "They didn't even stay for a cup of my tea."

Against my better judgment I asked, "What's in it?" My cup was still on the table.

Willow brightened. "Anise. I think it gives it a zing."

I bet.

"I need to head out," I said, making no move to pick up the cup of tea from the table. "Please try to have a plan for the trustee's meeting tonight. You're going to need it."

She nodded. "Don't you worry, Angie. I will have a plan."

Why did that comment make me worry?

She picked up my tea mug and poured it into a to-go cup, handing it to me. I thought it was easier to take the cup than to argue with her about it.

When I crossed the street, I sniffed the concoction. I caught a whiff of spices, but there was something else there reminiscent of freshly mowed grass. Against my better judgment, I took a tentative sip. "Ahh!" I spurted and gagged. It tasted like spiced mud.

Oliver circled me and whined.

Still spurting, I poured the contents from the travel cup into a large potted plant along the sidewalk. "If that plant dies after a dose of Bigfoot Brew," I croaked, "we don't know anything about it."

My trusty Frenchie barked in solidarity.

After I had mostly recovered from my tasting of Willow's tea, a large tour bus rolled down the street in the direction of the mercantile. I should return to Running Stitch. I hadn't told Mattie how long I would be gone, but I knew she had the quilting class well in hand. It wouldn't hurt to make one more stop. I pointed my cowboy boots in the direction the tour bus had gone.

Just like the day before, a CLOSED sign hung in the mercantile's window, and just like the day before, I ignored it. I set Oliver on the sidewalk beside me and tried the doorknob. The door opened inward. I stepped inside the mercantile. The store was in the same state of disarray that I found it in the day before.

As we entered the store, the noise of Oliver's toenails clicking on the hardwood floor was the only sound.

I peered into a long aisle when a handheld camcorder was shoved in my face.

Chapter Twenty-six

"Hey!" I cried, and jumped backward.

Oliver braced his paws on the floor as if trying to decide to protect me from the camera or to make a break for the door.

The person holding the camera lowered it from his face, which was beet red. "You're not Sam."

"Umm . . . no, I'm not. Who's Sam?" I asked, taking a good look at the teenager in front of me. He had messy dark hair worn a little too long to keep under control, and he wore jeans and a video game T-shirt. He was most certainly not Amish.

"Cameron!" A voice called from somewhere deep in the store. "Put that blasted camera away and help me feed this wire."

The teenager spun around and headed toward the voice. After a beat, I followed him. In the middle of the canned-vegetables aisle, one of the tiles from the drop ceiling had been removed, and I saw a pair of legs standing on the second-to-top rung of the ladder under the opening. The rest of the man's body was somewhere inside the hole.

The man in the hole dropped his hand. "Give me the wire."

Cameron was fiddling with a setting on his camera.

"Cameron!" the headless legs barked again.

After carefully setting his camera on a shelf next to a stack of canned beets, Cameron jumped into action. He unwound a spool of wire and placed the end of the wire in the man's hand. As the man pulled more of the wire into the hole, Cameron allowed the spool in his hands to unwind.

I watched this for a moment. Cameron seemed to have forgotten I was there. I was about to announce myself when legs started coming down the ladder. After a few steps I saw the face and had to stifle a gasp, because I knew I was looking at Blane Bright, Griffin's younger brother. Blane was the spitting image of his older brother, and the men looked enough alike to be twins. In fact, their features were so similar that I almost felt as though I was staring into the face of a dead man.

Blane rested his arm on the top of the ladder and stared at me. "The store's closed."

I cleared my throat. "I know that."

His eyes narrowed. "Then can I help you?"

His question shook me out of my stupor. "I hope so. I'm Angie Braddock."

"You're the sheriff's girlfriend. I've heard about you." He continued the rest of the way down the ladder.

Immediately, I bristled. Yes, I was Mitchell's girlfriend, but that wasn't my defining characteristic and certainly not the one I wanted to be known for the most. "I'm also the owner of Running Stitch and a Rolling Brook township trustee."

He waved that statement away as if my other titles were of little consequence as he stepped from the ladder onto the floor. "Liam told me you'd be stopping by to ask me about my brother. He said you were something of a sleuth and wanted to know about Griff's death."

Thanks, Liam.

I refused to be put on the defensive by this man. "I wouldn't call myself a sleuth, but yes, I would like to talk to you about Griffin. He died in my parents' backyard and, of course, they are concerned."

"That's a tough break for them, but I can't tell you anything. I wasn't with my brother when he died. I wasn't included on that job." His last statement held a hint of bitterness.

"Maybe you—"

"You might as well be on your way. I told you I have nothing to say. I have this big job here, and I need to get back to it so that Liam can open the store tomorrow." He walked over to the toolbox that was set in the middle of a rolling cart in the aisle and began to sort through the tools in the box.

"But—"

He held up a flathead screwdriver and examined it. Apparently dissatisfied with the tool, he dropped it back into the box and continued to sift through the tools. "Here's what I know. Nothing. I'm sorry he's dead. I really am. Griff and I didn't always see eye to eye, but he was my blood. That's all I have to say about it." He snapped his fingers at the teen. "Cam, I need another length of wire."

The boy was texting on his phone, and Blane had to call his name twice more.

"Sorry, Dad." Cameron shoved the phone in the back pocket of his jeans.

His use of "Dad" got my attention. So this was Blane's son. That also meant he was Griffin's nephew. Now that I knew that, I could see the resemblance between father and son. Because of Blane's close resemblance to his older brother, I should have seen the same similarities between Cameron and Griffin too.

Blane appeared pleased with the next screwdriver that he found and climbed back up the ladder. "Cam, I need that wire."

Cameron handed his father the end of the wire to be fed up through the ceiling.

"Son," Blane said, "how many times do I have to tell you to pay attention? You have to pay attention on a job like this. If you don't, that's how you're going to get hurt."

I took the last statement as an opening. "Do you think your brother forgot to pay attention the morning that he died?"

He scowled at me from halfway up the ladder. "Of course he did. If he'd minded his surroundings, he would have seen the wire, however small, and never stepped on that step. It was a stupid mistake that cost him his life."

"Was it his first mistake?" I asked.

His black eyebrows knit together. "What do you mean?"

"I heard that one of his former employees, Kamon Graber, died in a similar accident."

He frowned. "That was twenty years ago."

"I know, but there are similarities."

"They were both electrocuted, but Kamon wasn't murdered. His death was a careless accident."

"What do you mean?" I asked.

He sighed. "The circuit breaker was mislabeled in the factory were Kamon was doing the work. He turned off the wrong one before starting the job and was electrocuted as a result. As I said, stupid accident. A good electrician doesn't trust the breaker labels, especially in an older building with bad wiring. They should all be tested before any work begins."

"So you blame Kamon?" I asked.

"Yes, and my brother. He should have been more thorough in his instructions to Kamon. He never made that mistake again." He climbed up another step. "Now, I have work to do."

"Linda told me to talk to you about Griffin," I said.

He stiffened. "How do you know Linda?"

"I eat at the Double Dime a couple of times a week. We're friends."

He frowned, and seemed to be considering me for the first time. Being Mitchell's girlfriend wasn't impressive, but being Linda's friend was. "I assume that she told you that Griff and I were her foster kids."

"She did," I said, looking up at him. "She's heart-broken over Griffin's death."

He snorted. "She would be. Did she send you here? Is that what this is about?"

"She wants me to find out who killed your brother."

He climbed back down the ladder, leaving the piece of wire dangling over the platform at the top. "Good luck with that."

"You can help me," I said.

"I can't," he snapped. "I couldn't even if I wanted to help you, which I don't."

"Not even for Linda?"

"Why do I care what she wants? She's not my real mother."

I glared back at him. "She raised you."

He shrugged.

I balled my hands into fists at my sides. Blane was going to tell me what he knew whether he liked it or not. "Who might have wanted to murder your brother?" I thought I would just jump to the heart of the matter.

He eyed me. "You mean other than me."

My mouth fell open.

He laughed. "I'm not stupid. I know people are talking, and my brother and I just divided our business not long before he died. I got the bad end of the bargain. Sure, I got a nice chunk of money when he bought me out, but he kept on the contracts and clients. I was going to have to rebuild my new electrical repair company from scratch. Now I don't have to."

"Because your brother is dead."

"That's right," he said with no emotion. "I get the business in a survivorship deed. He never changed it when the business broke up. He probably thought he would have plenty of time for that later. He was wrong."

I shivered. Griffin had wanted to leave his business to Linda, but he was murdered before he could make that happen. Blane came out the victor. Did he force that victory by murdering his brother?

"There's really no reason for me to talk to you about this. The police have already spoken to me twice."

I frowned. It was something else Mitchell didn't tell me. I had to remind myself he was a cop and wasn't able to talk to me about his ongoing investigation, but knowing that didn't irritate me any less. "Do you have an alibi for the time that Griffin was murdered?"

He frowned. "No. Believe me when I say that I wish that I did."

"Where were you?" I asked.

He didn't answer, so I tried a different question. "What can you tell me about Griffin's girlfriend, Mallory?"

His face darkened. "Let's just say that she enjoys the finer things in life, much finer than an electrician living in this county can afford. I wouldn't be surprised if he couldn't get her something she wanted and she retaliated."

I frowned. That sounded as if she would hit him or yell at him, but Griffin's death had been methodical and planned out to the last detail. "Would she know how to connect a circuit like the one that killed your brother?"

He balanced his screwdriver in his hand. "It wasn't a complicated setup. She may have picked up a thing or two from Griff, and everyone knows that water and electricity is a recipe for disaster."

"Where can I find Mallory?" I asked.

He frowned. "Her family owns one of those large furniture warehouses that sell overpriced Amish furniture to tourists out on Route Thirty-nine between Millersburg and Sugar Creek."

"Which one is it?" I asked. There were several furniture warehouses on the same stretch of road.

"Zeff Oak Emporium." He grunted. "Even the name is pretentious." He placed his left foot on the bottom rung of the ladder.

"One more question," I said before he could disappear back into the hole in the ceiling again.

He sighed. "What?"

"Were you working with your brother when Kamon Graber was killed?"

He gave a sharp intake of breath. "No, I wasn't." He stared over my head. "I was in manufacturing. Griff went into the trade right after school, but I dabbled in several jobs before settling in on this one. Linda probably told you Griff and I didn't always see eye to eye." His voice caught, revealing just a tiny bit of emotion for the first time during our conversation. "He was still my brother, and I'm sorry he's dead." With that, he made his way up the ladder.

Out of the corner of my eye, I saw that Cameron had picked up his video camera again and was recording me.

I yelped. "What are you doing?"

"Cam, cut that out." Blane peered out of the hole in the ceiling at his son. "The kid is obsessed with that toy."

"It's not a toy," Cameron said defensively. "I'm studying cinematography in college. I'm going to be a director. I have to practice if I want to make it."

His father pressed his lips together in a thin line. "It's his mother that lets him get away with outlandish dreams like that. I would much rather the boy came back down to reality and helped me with this job."

I glanced back at Cameron, and the teen seemed to shrink at his father's words.

"Movies are a good career," I said.

"Not if you live in Ohio," Blane replied from his post on the ladder.

"Who says I'm going to stay in Ohio after college?" Cameron fired back.

"We'll discuss this later." His father's tone left no room for argument.

Chapter Twenty-seven

By the time I returned to Running Stitch, the quilting class had ended. Mattie said good-bye to the members of the class as she packed up the leftover cookies. There weren't many.

I held the door open for Shirley as she left the shop. "I saw you run over and talk to Raymond Sacks." Her eyes twinkled. "It seems I gave you what could be called a clue into this murder."

"You might have." I couldn't help but smile.

She chuckled, enjoying herself just as much as Miss Marple would have, and headed for her car.

Oliver ran inside the shop to check on Dodger. I followed more slowly. Dodger, who had slept in Oliver's dog bed through most of the class, stood up. Oliver bumped the cat with his nose. Dodger stretched and gave an enormous yawn. He scanned the shop. When he saw Mattie, his lips curved into a smile. That was a bad sign. I thought it was best not to bring it to Mattie's attention.

Mattie grabbed a broom from the back corner of the

shop and began to sweep up the thread and tiny pieces of fabric the ladies dropped while in class. "Where did you run off to all of a sudden?"

I told her about seeing Raymond through the window and my conversation with Blane at the mercantile.

She gripped the broom a little more tightly. "Did you talk to Liam too?"

I shook my head. "He wasn't there."

She relaxed and began sweeping again.

"Can you mind the shop for a few hours? There are a couple of people that I need to talk to."

"I wish you wouldn't be involved with this, Angie. It sounds like that Griffin had a lot of enemies, some of them for good reason."

"Which is all the more reason to talk to them," I said.

She shook her head. "Just be careful."

I promised her that I would.

I knew that Mallory would be relatively easy—or at least I hoped—to track down through her family's furniture business. Rex Flagg was a different story. I didn't even know where to begin in finding him. Blane might know where Rex might be because he's a fellow electrician, but I didn't think he'd tell me anything more, and I didn't want to have another conversation with him, as he so clearly disregarded Linda.

Besides Blane—and Mitchell, whom I most definitely didn't want to ask—the only other person in Holmes County that I knew who might know where to find Rex was Linda, and I had promised to drop in the Double Dime Diner for lunch anyway.

"Oliver, are you okay with eating a little bit early?" I asked the Frenchie at my feet.

He wiggled his stubby tail. I didn't have to ask him twice.

I grabbed my bag, called for Oliver, and headed out of the door.

"What about Dodger?" Mattie called after me.

"You guys will be fine," I reassured her.

She groaned, and I smiled as the door closed behind me.

I parked in a spot right in front of the diner. It was a good time for me to catch up with Linda between the breakfast and lunch rushes. Once noon hit, she would be on her feet until at least three.

I opened the glass door that led into the diner, and Oliver pranced up to Linda with his tongue hanging out in anticipation of the bacon to come.

She beamed at my little dog. "There's my boy!"

Oliver dropped the front of his body into a bow. Linda beamed at his antics, and I shook my head. To Oliver, Linda was the source of bacon. Therefore, a respectful bow when he was in her presence was always warranted.

Linda studied Oliver's face. "You look famished. Do you need a double order of bacon?"

He twirled in a tight circle.

Show-off.

"Linda, Oliver doesn't need a double order of any-thing," I protested. "The vet has already told me that if he puts on any more weight, I'll have to put him on a diet."

Oliver whimpered. He and my father had the same feelings toward diets.

"Pish," was her response. "He's perfectly healthy. Your vet doesn't know what he's talking about. Put sweet, lovable Oliver on a diet? It's cruel, I tell you. Cruel."

Oliver barked agreement. It was two against one.

I sighed. It was pointless to argue with the two of them when they ganged up on me like that. "Okay," I said. "It has been a trying couple of days. Maybe one extra piece of bacon won't hurt him."

Linda grinned and yelled through the pass-through to the kitchen. "Hurry up on that double of bacon!"

The cook waved his spatula to acknowledge he'd heard her. The cook didn't talk much, but he loved to spoil my Frenchie just as much as Linda did.

I shook my head. They were all hopeless.

Linda pointed at me with her pencil. "You go take your regular booth, and I'll be over as soon as I get Oliver settled."

I shuffled to the booth by the front window. It was my favorite spot in the diner. I could see all the way up and down Jackson Street. A semi rolled up the road past the county courthouse followed by an Amish courting buggy. A young couple sat in the buggy closer together than they would've dared if their parents had been nearby.

Before I knew it, a plate stacked high with pancakes, eggs, and bacon—because Linda thought everyone needed bacon—appeared in front of me.

"You look like you need breakfast for lunch." Linda glanced at the antique cat clock with the roving eyes on the wall. "And since it's too early for lunch, we'll call it brunch."

"Works for me," I said as I unwrapped my flatware from a white paper napkin.

"Be back in a jiff," Linda said. She returned before I could even wrestle my fork free from the napkin and set a full mug of coffee next to my plate. "I already put the cream and sugar in there how you like it." She stepped away from the table to see to another diner patron and left me with the enormous breakfast.

My mouth watered. There were more calories on the plate than my diet—if I ever got around to sticking to one—would allow for a week. I should stick to the small portion of the eggs and the coffee.

Instead, I picked up my fork. I was in the middle of a murder investigation, so I needed my strength. I cut into one of the buttery pancakes and took a bite. I suppressed a moan. The pancakes didn't even need maple syrup. They were that good. Of course I doused them with syrup anyway, because it was sugar, and sugar helped me think.

Linda returned as I was halfway through the stack of pancakes. Apparently, I ate pancakes by inhalation. I wasn't proud of it. She had a full mug of black coffee in one hand and a coffeepot in the other. She sat across from me in the booth.

Behind her, I spotted Oliver crouched by the rotating pie case with his paws on either side of a plate of bacon. He held the plate in place with his paws so that it didn't have the chance to run away. I ignored how many pieces of bacon were on that plate. The vet was going to send me to bad dog–parent school. Oliver would be on tasteless dry kibble for the rest of the month.

Linda wrapped her hands around the white mug. Her fingernails were painted a bright pink that seemed to go well with her powder blue waitress outfit and beehive hairdo. Linda was a throwback. She lived a retro life before retro was a thing.

She cleared her throat. "I know you haven't had much time to snoop, but have you learned anything yet about what may have happened to Griffin?"

I set down my fork. "I've spoken to a couple of people. Just this morning I spoke with Blane, and I met his son."

Her expression softened. "Cameron. He's a sweet boy, even if his head's in the clouds."

I added just a drop more syrup to my plate. "When I met him, he had a video camera in his hand. He said he was making a movie."

She touched the handle of her coffee mug but made no move to pick it up. "He's wanted to be in the movie business since he was a child."

"Ohio might not be the best place for that," I said, picking up my own mug.

"It's not. I wouldn't be a bit surprised if he ran off to Hollywood after college. He wanted to go to school in California as it was, but his father refused to help pay his tuition if he didn't live at home."

"There are loans and things he could have applied for if he really wanted to leave Ohio," I said.

She shook her head. "His father was dead set against it. Blane is hard on the boy."

From what I gathered during my brief conversation with him, Blane was hard on just about everyone, but I didn't say that.

Linda went on. "You shouldn't squash a child's dreams while he has them or he'll stop dreaming as an adult, and that will be a true tragedy. You should see some of the movies that he's made; they are so creative. I would hate for a child like Cameron to stop dreaming, wouldn't you?"

I nodded.

Her tone turned thoughtful. "If you don't have dreams when you're young, what are you going to live up to when you are older? I never had grand dreams like Cameron does, of going to Hollywood, but I always wanted to own my own diner." She held her arms wide as if to encompass the entire room. "And here I am, living the dream over fifty years later. Every penny I have I put back into this diner and into a nice nest egg for when I retire. No idea when that will be, since I'm over retirement age and can't seem to walk away from here just yet. In any case, I would say that I did all right."

I smiled. "You did just fine."

She dropped her arms. "I just wish I had done better by Griff and Blane."

My heart went out to her.

"Linda, I could use a warm-up." One of the older men in the back of the diner held up his mug.

"Hold on to your pants, Sal. I'm talking to Angie here," she shouted back.

The man grunted and lowered his mug. Everyone

knew that Linda ruled the Double Dime Diner, and the patrons there would receive their food and coffee when she was ready to serve it.

"I also learned that Griffin had replaced another electrician for the large job at the Eby Mercantile in Rolling Brook," I said, bringing the conversation back to the investigation. "I was wondering if you knew anyone by the name of Rex Flagg."

"Rex Flagg?" she asked. "I don't know much of anything about his work ethic, but I can tell you that the man has a sour disposition. Whenever he comes into the diner, which isn't often, he's in a foul mood." She pursed her lips. "He's not a great tipper either."

That was interesting.

"Do you know where I can find him?" I sipped from my coffee mug.

She frowned. "No, I can't say that I do. I know who he is, of course, as he's come in here from time to time, but he's not a regular."

My face fell. I had been counting on Linda knowing where I could find Rex. If I had to go to Mitchell about it, that would only mean trouble for me. I supposed that I could always go back to the mercantile and ask Blane. I would much rather do that than ask Mitchell.

Linda turned toward the man who'd wanted his coffee warmed up and yelled across the room, "Sal, do you know where Rex Flagg would be between jobs?"

The man looked up from the book he was reading. "What do you want with that old drunk? He's a mean drunk too," he said in an ominous tone.

"Angie here is looking for him," Linda said.

Sal turned his watery eyes toward me. "If you are looking for an electrician, sweetheart, I can tell you names of half a dozen that have a better bedside manner than Rex Flagg. Ones that are better at their job too and won't drink away your time."

I picked up my nearly full coffee mug and slipped out of the booth. When I reached Sal's table, I asked, "May I?"

"Sure, have a seat," he grunted. "It's not often I have the company of a pretty girl."

Linda walked toward the table with the coffeepot in hand. She filled Sal's mug with a practiced motion. "You don't pay any attention to Sal's flirting," she advised.

I smiled. "I don't mind."

Sal grinned. "See, Linda, not every woman ignores me. I'm quite a catch. I'm glad Angie here sees that."

Linda snorted. "Angie is Sheriff Mitchell's girl."

Sal appraised me. "You don't say. I had heard that he'd taken up with someone new since his divorce. You couldn't be more different from his first wife, could you?"

I shifted uncomfortably in my seat.

Linda smacked him lightly on the back of the head. "You quit that and answer sweet Angie's questions about Rex." She moved to the next table with her coffeepot.

Sal poured cream from a small pitcher into his coffee. "I still don't know what you want with him. He's a drunk, and a mean one at that."

I thought it was best if I didn't mention the murder

unless Sal brought it up. The fewer people who knew about my investigation, the better.

I cleared my throat. "He did some work at my friend's store, and really made a mess of things." This wasn't technically a lie, although I didn't know if Liam would consider me a friend. "I was hoping I could track him down so that I could talk to him about it."

Sal nodded. "Your friend should look elsewhere for help."

"He already has." I paused. "But I still want to talk to Rex about it."

Sal squinted. I could tell he didn't buy my story. To be honest, I wouldn't have either.

He held his mug up to me as if in a toast. "I like your spunk. It's about time someone told Rex a thing or two about how to work and how to treat a lady. If you are looking for him, look no further than Eight Lanes."

I frowned. "Eight Lanes? What's that?"

"It's a bowling alley in Millersburg," Linda said as she walked effortlessly carrying two full trays of food. The food was meant for the men sitting in the corner of the room.

"Rex hangs out in a bowling alley?" I asked.

Sal shook his head. "He doesn't hang out there. He lives there. There's an apartment above the bowling alley. From what I heard, he gets a break on rent to keep up the maintenance of the place, which he needs since he can't seem to hold down a job."

I winced. "It must be hard to sleep." I imagined bowling balls crashing into pins in the middle of the night. I certainly wouldn't be able to sleep in such a place. I frowned.

"Rex could sleep through a hurricane. A few balls crashing into bowling pins aren't going to bother him."

"Where is Eight Lanes located?" I asked.

"A couple of miles from here on the way to Berlin." He rattled off the address.

I stood. "I had better get over there then and see what I can find out."

I found Linda standing behind me, free of her trays and again holding her coffeepot. "I wish I could go with you, Angie. I really do, but it's best for me to leave the sleuthing to you." She smiled. "You're the professional."

I laughed. "Don't let the sheriff hear you say that."

Oliver and I walked out of the diner. We were only a few steps from my car when Oliver flattened low to the ground and growled.

"What's gotten into you?" I asked. Oliver wasn't a growler.

"Did you send the police after me?" a gravelly voice asked.

Chapter Twenty-eight

I spun around to find Nahum Shetler sitting on a park bench just south of my car. I couldn't believe I hadn't spotted him there before. Perhaps I was a little too focused on my mission to talk to Rex Flagg.

"Excuse me?" I asked.

Nahum braced a hand to his side and winced as if in pain as he stood up. His grizzled beard that hung down to the middle button of his coat appeared more tangled than usual, and that was saying something. He wore a wool winter coat. It was early May, so it was most definitely not summer in Holmes County, but the temperature now that the line of rain had passed through held steady at sixty degrees. It certainly wasn't winter-coat weather. Sixty might have been cold in Texas, but since I moved to Ohio, I noticed that people wore shorts and flip-flops when it reached that temperature.

I took a step toward him. "Are you all right?"

He scowled at me as he maneuvered around the bench. "I'm fine."

It took everything that I had not to run around the

bench and lend him an arm. I knew he never would forgive me if I did.

"What's wrong with you?" I asked. The question wasn't all that polite, but Nahum and I didn't base our relationship—if you could even call it a relationship—on pleasantries.

"It's none of your concern. Why won't you answer my question? Did you send the police after me?"

Oliver slunk behind my legs.

"No," I said. "Why would you ask me that?"

"Because the sheriff came to my cabin early this morning wanting to talk to me," he said with a grunt.

Cabin was an exaggeration. Nahum lived in the woods in what could only be called a glorified shack, and that was pushing it.

"The only time," he went on, "that the police want to talk to me is when you tell them to."

"I didn't ask the police to speak to you," I said honestly. "What did the sheriff want to know?"

Nahum frowned and leaned on the mailbox as if he needed the support. Now, I really was becoming worried for him. I guessed Nahum was somewhere in his sixties, but he had always, despite his gray beard, carried himself like someone half his age. Now, he looked as stiff as a ninety-year-old. His face was drawn, and his eyes appeared to be more deeply sunken in too. I bit my tongue to stop myself from asking him if he was okay again.

"The sheriff wanted to know if I had seen anyone suspicious in the woods in and around the county."

"You mean besides you?" I blurted out.

Nahum narrowed his eyes.

Okay, that had been the wrong thing to say. "What did you tell him?"

"I said I hadn't," he answered after a long moment of glaring at me. "I always see hunters and teens looking for trouble in the woods, but I couldn't say any of those people were suspicious in the way he meant."

"What way was that?" I asked.

"He wanted to know if I had seen anyone in the woods wearing a costume like a gorilla suit. I said *nee*. I would have remembered that."

Ah, I thought, Mitchell was following up on the Bigfoot angle. The sheriff left no stone, however ridiculous, unturned when working on a case.

"That says to me that the police aren't after you. Sheriff Mitchell was just seeing if you were an eyewitness who he could consult about a case."

Nahum held his side. "About a gorilla?"

From the way he answered, I had a feeling Mitchell didn't tell Nahum about the Bigfoot sightings in the county.

"Any involvement with the *Englisch* police is too much for me." With care, he pushed off the mailbox. He grimaced as his body made its way to an upright position.

"Maybe you should see a doctor," I said.

The older Amish man glared at me. "I have no need for English doctors."

That I knew to be true. Nahum believed that his wife, Rachel's mother, had been killed by English medicine. His wife had complications with Rachel's birth. Nahum asked his bishop what he should do. The bishop had told him to go see an English doctor for help. Nahum did as he was told, and although Rachel was saved, her mother died. Nahum couldn't or wouldn't care for his baby girl, so he sent her away to be raised by her mother's family.

Nahum blamed both the English doctor and his Amish bishop for his beloved wife's death. That was why he left his Amish district. Now, he was what I called a rogue Amish. To be truly Amish, a person had to be a member of an Amish district. The culture and religion was all about community, but Nahum didn't live in any Amish district. In most cases, when an Amish person was angry with an Amish community, he left and joined another or became English. Not Nahum. He dressed and acted Amish, but followed his own set of rules of what it meant to be Amish. He didn't answer to any church elders or bishops and lived alone in the woods.

"Why would the sheriff want to know about a man in a gorilla suit?" Nahum asked.

Mitchell most likely didn't tell Nahum about the Bigfoot sightings for a reason, but I thought Nahum had a right to know, especially since I knew that Bigfoot fans would be or might already be descending on his woods in search of the Sasquatch. It would probably be best for everyone if Nahum knew that they were coming. I didn't want any visitors to meet the business end of Nahum's pitchfork.

"Some people think they saw a creature in the woods," I said, and went on to describe what Bigfoot was to the best of my ability.

"You mean a Sasquatch," Nahum sniffed. "*Englischers* aren't the only ones with that story in their folklore."

"Oh," I said, taken aback. I had not expected Nahum to know what I was talking about. "Have you seen anything like that?"

"*Nee.* Crazy *Englisch*," he snapped. "I live in those woods and have for over twenty years. I see everything that comes and goes through those trees. If there was such a creature, don't you think I would have seen it?"

"Yes, I do," I said.

He squinted at me as if I hadn't given him the answer that he expected to hear.

"I don't believe there is a Bigfoot in the woods either. I think someone is pulling a practical joke on the community. The sheriff is worried about it because the person who is doing this was near a murder."

"The murder of the *Englischer* at your parents' home." He tugged on his beard.

"Yes." I nodded, not the least bit surprised Nahum knew about Griffin's death.

"I know what happens in this county," he said.

I didn't doubt that Nahum knew more about what happened in Holmes County than I did.

"I know," I said. "Which is why you can help. No one knows these woods as well as you do. You can find out who is playing this trick and prove that it's just a man wearing a suit."

"Why would I want to help?" he asked.

"Because there are about thirty Bigfoot enthusiasts stomping through the woods looking for the creature.

The sooner it's proven that it's all a hoax, the sooner they'll leave."

His lip curled as if he smelled something bad. Probably the thought of tourists in his woods made him sick to his stomach. "There are *Englischers* in my woods?"

They weren't technically Nahum's woods, but I thought it was best not to correct him when I was in need of his help.

His eyes narrowed. "I will find who's playing this prank."

"Great. And when you do, tell me or the police. The sheriff and his men will take care of him," I said.

"Oh no," he said. "I will take care of him myself."

I grimaced. Okay, so telling Nahum about the Bigfoot issue might not have been the best idea in the world. I hated it when Mitchell was right.

I watched Nahum limp away. All the time, he had a hand braced over where his right kidney would be. If Nahum was sick, I had to tell Rachel, whether or not she was ready to deal with the emotions that came with speaking to her father. She might not have much time left to make amends.

Chapter Twenty-nine

I couldn't remember the last time I had gone bowling. It might have been in elementary school with bumpers. Even with the bumpers to guide my ball down the lane, I hadn't been very good at the sport. If I remembered correctly, I let the ball go on the backswing and hit my friend's father in the stomach with it. I hadn't been invited to go bowling since.

Not that I was invited to go bowling today either, I thought as I stepped into Eight Lanes Bowling Alley. The business was aptly named because there were eight lanes. Other than the lanes, there was a small snack bar and a Ping-Pong table that looked as if it dated back to the Cold War. That was it. Eight Lanes wasn't fancy.

A set of Amish teenagers was at one of the lanes. They laughed and teased one another in Pennsylvania Dutch when one of them threw a blue bowling ball into the gutter of a neighboring lane.

The rest of the lanes were empty, which was a good thing, considering how well the boys played. Other than the young Amish men, there was an older man sitting at the snack bar, nursing what I hoped was a root beer for this early in the day. There wasn't a soul behind the counter.

To be honest, I would have much rather approached the teens with my questions than that rough-looking man and his root beer.

When I got closer, I noticed the man wasn't drinking root beer as I first thought. It was birch beer, which was the Amish version of the drink. The soda inside was red and was just a bit smoother than most root beer. It came in a bright yellow can and I had only ever seen the drink in Holmes County.

"What do you want?" the man asked, taking a swig from his can.

I didn't answer right away, and he said, "You're not here to bowl. I can tell when people come to bowl, and you're not one of them. So I'll ask you again. What do you want?"

"I'm looking for Rex Flagg," I said.

He held up his birch beer to me. "You found him. What can I do for you?"

"My name is Angie Braddock, and I—"

"Braddock!" he bellowed. "You wouldn't be any relationship to Daphne Braddock, would you?"

"She's my mother."

The scowl on his wrinkled face deepened. "In that case, I have nothing to say to you."

"But—"

"That heartless woman wouldn't give me a job."

I put my hands on my hips. "What do you mean?"

"I bid on the electrical job at her house, and she went with another electrician. My guess is you're here because the electrician she hired bought the farm, and I'm the runner-up. Sorry, miss. I don't take sloppy seconds. Your mother will just have to find someone else to take over for Griff."

I grimaced at his crude language. I hadn't known that my mother got multiple bids on the electrical work in the kitchen. I should have expected it though. Mom took every aspect of interior design seriously and would have hired only who she thought were the best people for the job. No wonder she was so terrified when Dad said that he was going to demolish the kitchen himself. Mom didn't believe in doing any work that you could hire someone else to do, especially if that someone could to it better. I thought it was best if I let Rex believe he was right about my reason for visiting Eight Lanes. Maybe I would catch him off guard, and he would reveal what he knew about Griffin's death, if anything.

"So you're not interested in any of the work Griffin Bright left unfinished. Not even the job at the Eby Mercantile?"

He set his can on the bar and sat up straight. "Is that job back up for grabs? I hadn't heard anything. The arrogant owner won't return my calls."

I folded my arms. "Why would he after you didn't show up for work with no explanation?"

He grunted. "I'd had a rough night before. I needed to sleep it off. Amish don't know what it's like to fall off the wagon." He sipped from his can and some of the red liquid ran down his chin. He wiped it off with the back of his hand. "If Mr. Holier Than Thou would just return my calls, I could have explained what happened. I missed one day, and he went out and hired the Bright brothers. Those two are the bane of my existence. I used to work with Griffin, you know, before he cast me aside to work with his little brother." His speech was slightly slurred, and I wondered if he spiked his birch beer with something a bit stronger.

"You did?" I didn't even bother to hide my surprise.

Rex shook his head. "It was a good thing. Being dropped by Griffin spurred me on to starting my own business, and I've done all right for myself when I can avoid the drink."

I tried not to glance around the bowling alley. I wouldn't count living over a bowling alley as all right, but what did I know?

Rex picked up his can again and jiggled the contents inside. "I never liked working with Griff. He was a stickler. I obey the rules to finish the job, but Griff was a fanatic about it. Every 'I' had to be dotted and every 'T' crossed twice. It was maddening. I shouldn't be surprised that your mother chose him over me. She seemed to be an 'I'-dotter and 'T'-crosser to me."

She was that.

He held up his can to me. "The problem with Griffin was he wasn't a team player. Guys in our line of work need to look out for one another. Griffin wasn't like that. If he saw anyone cutting corners, be it a contractor or a plumber, he called them out on it, not only to the plumber or contractor but to the home owner or the business owner, depending on the job. He made a lot of enemies that way."

I think my suspect list just increased tenfold. How would I find every contractor and serviceman that Griffin had blown the whistle on?

"Including you?" I asked the man in front of me.

"No. I do good work"—he lifted his can—"when I'm sober."

"Do you know why Griffin was so strict?"

"It was the boy he got killed all those years ago. Shoot, it must be over twenty years ago that happened, but if you spoke to Griffin, you'd think it was yesterday. It affected him that much."

I froze. "Do you mean Kamon Graber?"

He shrugged. "I can't remember the name. That's an Amish name, isn't it? That must be right because the kid that died was Amish."

I swallowed. "He spoke about Kamon?"

"Never spoke his name that I recalled, but he talked about mistakes that he made that cost a life. What else could it be?"

It surprised me that Griffin had still been tortured by Kamon's death after so many years, decades really, had passed. When I met him with Jonah the day before he died, he seemed not to have a care in the world. I wondered if Jonah would have had more compassion toward the man if he'd known how tortured Griffin had been by Kamon's death.

"Where were you early yesterday morning around five?" I asked.

His face flushed. "It's time for you to leave." He

shook his drink at me. As he did, I got a strong whiff of the contents. There was a lot more than birch beer in that can. "I don't have to tell you anything."

I took a step back, remembering Sal's warnings back at the diner. The Amish teens on the lanes weren't paying the least bit of attention to us, but I was grateful that there was someone else in the room that would hear me if I had cause to scream. "Is there a reason you won't answer the question?"

"Because it's none of your business," he slurred.

"You lost two jobs to Griffin recently. The mercantile and the job at my mother's."

"If I was going to off Griffin for every time he took a job away from me, he would have been dead ten years ago." He took a swig from his can. "Who are you really? Are you really Daphne Braddock's daughter?"

I nodded. "I am."

"Then why are you asking all these questions about Griffin that have nothing to do with the job at your mother's house?" His eyes narrowed to dark lines on his face. "Haven't I seen you out and about with the sheriff before? Are you some kind of cop?"

"The sheriff and I have a working relationship," I said vaguely, "when it comes to certain investigations."

He banged his can on the counter. "I knew it. You're a cop. You think I was the one who offed Griffin. Well, I'm here to tell you that it wasn't me. No, ma'am."

"If it wasn't you, then who?" I asked, not correcting him with my real identity.

"How should I know? I only knew him from jobs

that we worked on together and then competed for. That doesn't make me an expert on his life."

"You can't think of anyone who might have wanted to kill him?" I did my best to sound official like Mitchell did when he questioned someone.

"No one except his brother."

"Blane?"

He nodded. "That guy has an anger problem, if you ask me. Griff and I were there giving your mother our bids for the electrical work at the same time. We hadn't planned to be there together, but it had just worked out that way. When we left the house Blane was waiting for his brother beside Griff's truck. If I ever saw anyone who I would describe as mad enough to kill, it would be Blane Bright."

I frowned. Blane had told me that he hadn't known about the job at my mother's. He had lied.

"Did my mother see this?"

He shrugged. "Doubt it. We had parked well up the street and out of view of the house at your mom's request. She said a construction trailer was to be delivered around the same time, and our cars needed to be out of the way."

That would explain why my mother hadn't mentioned the arguments between the two Bright brothers. She didn't know about it.

"What did Blane say to Griffin?" I asked.

Rex rubbed his chin. "Something about how Griffin was more loyal to some woman named Linda than he was to flesh and blood." He settled back onto his stool and shook his can at me. It sounded as if there wasn't much left inside. "I didn't stick around to see what happened. I don't borrow trouble unless you count the liquid variety."

Blane must have known that Griffin planned to change his will and leave his business to Linda, not to him.

The man in front of me looked so bedraggled that I immediately felt sorry for him. He was down on his luck even if that downward spiral appeared to be self-inflicted. At the same time, I was surprised that my mother had even allowed him into her house. She was not one to take on a charity case.

He finished what was left of his drink. "If you really want to know where I was, you should ask the Amish man who stopped to give me a lift back to town."

I leaned forward. "When was this?"

"Can't remember exactly. Before the sun came out. I had had another rough night."

"Where did he find you?"

"On the side of the road somewhere." He shrugged. "It happens."

"Who was the Amish man?"

"Don't know. I can't tell them apart with all those plain clothes and beard, but unless I was hallucinating, I do remember seeing a goat in the back of the buggy. Don't see that every day." He laughed mirthlessly.

Jonah?

Chapter Thirty

I stumbled out of the bowling alley. Rex had to have meant Jonah. What other Amish man would have a goat ride along in his buggy? And Jonah wouldn't think twice about helping an inebriated man back to town. Then why had he refused to share this alibi with the police or with me? He hadn't been doing anything wrong. In fact, he was being a Good Samaritan. Why keep that a secret?

Had Jonah had a cell phone, I would have called him that very second and demanded some answers. Sometimes it was a real pain that most of my friends were Amish.

Before I backed out of my space in Eight Lanes's parking lot, my cell phone rang. My mother's face appeared on the screen. Usually, I would ignore her calls if it was in the middle of a workday, but that was before someone was murdered in her backyard.

"Angie!" she shouted when I picked up. "You need to come over here and talk some sense into your father.

He says he's not going back to physical therapy because the therapist tried to kill him!"

I sighed. I didn't doubt that my father said he wasn't going back to the physical therapist. I knew it was going to be a battle to convince him to commit to it.

"Are you coming?"

I suppressed a second sigh. "I'll be there as soon as I can."

"Good." She ended the call.

I patted Oliver on the head before putting the car in reverse. "It seems we have another nine-one-one call from Grandma."

He placed his paws on the dash as if he was ready to go and drive into danger. Then again, he knew Grandma's house meant beef jerky from my father.

I arrived at my parents' home exactly twenty minutes later. As I let Oliver out of the car, I surveyed the county road and was happy to see no sign of Willow or any of her Bigfoot compatriots.

My mom threw open the front door. "Don't just stand there—get in here. Your father is in the living room." Without waiting for me to reply, she spun around and marched away, leaving the front door wide-open.

"Tread softly," I whispered to Oliver. "Grandma appears to be a little bit on edge."

He licked his nose as if in preparation.

I found Mom and Dad in the living room. Dad was in his favorite chair, still wearing the blueberry sweat suit and looking downcast. I went over to him and kissed him on the forehead. "Hey, Dad, how are you?"

"Terrible," he said. "It was so much more horrible than I imagined it would be. I'm not ever going back."

My mother hovered in the doorway. "Talk some sense into him. He can't use a walker for the rest of his life."

"Mom," I said as gently as possible, "why don't you go check on Jonah and Eban and see how the kitchen is progressing? I bet a lot has changed since you and Dad left this morning."

"Don't you want me to stay and help you talk to your father?" She frowned at her husband.

I gave her my brightest smile. "We'll be fine."

She glanced in the direction of the kitchen. I knew she was itching to see what had been done while she and Dad were out. "All right," she said, and left the room.

I felt mildly sorry to sic Mom on Jonah, but it would be much easier to talk to my father without her nearby contributing her two cents every two seconds. My mother was one of those people who actually liked exercise. She jogged three miles on her treadmill every morning. I loathed exercise just like my father. He and I could speak on a kindred-spirit level about an issue that she would never understand.

He shivered. "They put me on a table and bent me back like my spine was a fold in the Sunday newspaper."

"Dad, they're trying to help you."

"AngieBear." He took my hand. "I'm telling you, the woman had glee in her eyes as she watched me be twisted into a pretzel. Do you hear me? Glee!"

"Maybe she's just a happy person," I said.

"She's a masochist," Dad said with feeling.

I sighed. "How does your back feel now?"

He thought about it for a moment. "Sore, but in a different way. The whole thing is sore like someone used it for a punching bag. That's the therapist's doing."

"That's because the therapist worked on strengthening the muscles in your back so that the disc will have support. I've done a little research on your injury, and it sounds to me that she put you on a flex extension table."

He grunted.

"Did you like anything about it? There has to be one good part," I said.

He frowned. "I did like the end when she put this massive damp heating pad on my back."

"See, it's not all bad," I said in my most upbeat voice.

He folded his arms. "It was fine for the last ten minutes. The other fifty she turned me into a contortionist."

I folded my arms too. "You promised that you would give therapy a chance."

"I did." Like a toddler, he wouldn't meet my eyes.

"You didn't give it enough of a chance." I perched on an ottoman a few feet from him. "You promised that you'd do this for me."

His face softened. "You're right. I did. I suppose one visit isn't much of a fair shake." He gave the loudest sigh I'd ever heard. I wouldn't be surprised if Mattie heard it miles away at the Running Stitch. "I suppose I can give it another shot for you."

"Good." I stood up.

His eyes sparkled. "Don't tell your mother just yet that I agreed to go back. I like it when she's all riled up."

I shook my head. "You're terrible. I'll let you tell her when you're ready, but don't put it off too long. She's really wound up."

"Just for another half hour," he said with a wink.

I kissed him on the top of the head. "I'll go check on the kitchen and Jonah before I head back out."

Oliver and I went to the kitchen. I was surprised to see that the new floor was almost complete. Eban, who wore kneepads over his trousers, kneeled at the far edge of the huge kitchen, installing the last few floorboards. Jonah and my mother stood on the opposite side of the room, surveying the work. Other than the new floor, everything was out of the room, even the light fixtures in the ceiling.

The new French doors were opened wide and there was a makeshift workshop of sawhorses and power tools on the back patio.

"Wow, you guys work fast," I said.

Mom nodded. "I was just telling Eban how impressed I was with their work."

Eban removed a bandanna from the back pocket of his trousers and wiped his brow. "*Danki*. The cabinetry was delivered while you were gone. It's in the garage. We'll paint tomorrow and install the cabinets on Monday."

"Where's Jonah?" I asked.

"He had to return to his farm about an hour ago."

I bit the inside of my lip. "Is everything okay?"

Eban shrugged. "I suppose so."

This meant I would have to wait to talk to Jonah about the alibi Rex Flagg gave him. I tried to hide my disappointment. "And the doors are fixed," I said.

Eban nodded. "And they lock too."

I gave my mother a sideways look. "If that's the case, I'll sleep at my own house tonight, Mom." I didn't think I would survive another night with the accusatory giraffe.

"Yes, that's fine," she said absentmindedly. "Is your father going to return to physical therapy?"

"He's thinking about it," I said, keeping my promise to my father to let him tell her.

"Thinking about it?" my mother exclaimed. "You were supposed to talk him into it. I ask you to do one thing . . ." She stomped out of the kitchen.

I watched her go. I had a feeling that I was going to get the blame for my father's desire to see my mother riled up.

"Angie," Eban said.

I jumped. I hadn't realized he stood only a few feet from me.

"May I talk to you for a moment?"

I stepped back. "Sure, Eban. I'm on my way out, if you want to follow me outside to talk."

He nodded. "I could use a break anyway."

Eban and Oliver followed me through the house. As we passed the living room, I heard my mother lecturing my father as to why he needed to keep doing physical therapy. I shook my head. I hoped Dad told her about his decision to go back soon or I would never hear the end of it.

In the front yard, Oliver snuffled one of the tulips that Petunia had decapitated the day before. I supposed I should be happy that Mom was too caught up in Dad's physical therapy drama to notice the number Petunia had done on her front garden. She would eventually and I would never hear the end of that either.

I turned to Eban. "What did you want to talk about? Is something wrong with the kitchen job?"

"Nee." He shook his head. "I'm very grateful to have the work. I am grateful to both Jonah and your mother for it. It pays well, which will allow me to send money back to my mother for her and my younger brothers and sisters."

"No father?" I asked. Immediately, I regretted it. It was too personal a question to ask someone who I'd just met, especially if that person was Amish.

He shook his head. "My father died when I was younger."

"I'm so sorry."

He gave his head a hard shake, causing his glossy bowl haircut to bounce in place. "It was a long time ago. The reason I wanted to talk to you is because of this Bigfoot creature." He whispered the last part.

"Oh?" That was the last thing I expected Eban to want to talk to me about. "What about it?"

"I saw it with my own eyes in the forest this morning. Jonah was inside taking measurements to cut the flooring, and I was carrying the uncut pieces from the garage to the back patio. The creature startled me so much that I dropped the stack of wood. When I did that, it must have scared the animal, and it ran off." Eban was breathing heavily by the end of his tale.

"What did it look like?"

"Sort of like a cross between a gorilla and a bear. It was much taller than me," he said. He held his hand about a foot above his own head to demonstrate the creature's height. "The odd part is I could have sworn the animal was wearing shoes. I know I caught sight of white tennis shoes as it was running away."

Ahh, I thought, Bigfoot was busted.

Chapter Thirty-one

I was still mulling over how I was going to break the news to Willow that her Bigfoot was an impostor when I parked my car outside of Zeff Oak Emporium. I wasn't sure how this was going to go. It was very likely Mallory would recognize me from my parents' house the morning before. My hair was hard to miss. If she recognized me, I knew she wouldn't answer my questions.

"Ollie, we need a disguise," I said.

He whimpered. Oliver wasn't much for clothing.

"Okay, I need a disguise." I unbuckled my seat belt and peeked in the backseat.

A navy blue ball cap peeked out from under the passenger seat. I grabbed it. HOLMES COUNTY SHERIFF DEPARTMENT was emblazoned across the front. Mitchell must have left it in my car.

"This could work."

Oliver whimpered again.

Staring in the mirror attached to my window visor, I tucked my blond curls the best I could up under the hat. Some of my hair sneaked out, but for the most part my hair was covered. "Ollie, this is between you and me, okay?"

He hid his face in his paws.

I knew why he was so anxious. If it got back to Mitchell that I was impersonating an officer, I was dead meat.

I made sure the hat was firmly in place and got out of the car. Oliver reluctantly followed, jumping to the gravel parking lot.

I pushed open the door to Zeff Oak Emporium. As the door swung inward, the scent of vinegar and lemon oil washed over me. It was a familiar scent that I always associated with an Amish home because the Amish used the mixture as an all-purpose cleaner, especially on furniture, which was why the fragrance was so pungent in the emporium. At my feet, Oliver sniffed the ground. Maybe he caught another scent of something other than lemon and vinegar with that pushed-in nose of his. I certainly couldn't.

Mallory Zeff, with her dark braid coiled on the top of her head, polished a dining room table in the middle of the room. As she worked, the bangles around her wrist clattered together. A spray bottle of vinegar water sat next to her on the impossibly long table that looked as if it could seat fifteen or more. A table of that size was not unusual to find in an Amish home. A large Amish family could easily fill fifteen spots at one Sunday dinner.

She picked up her spray bottle and rag and walked around the table. "I'll be with you in a minute."

I nodded and flipped the sales tag over that was attached to a dresser while I waited. I whistled under my breath. Amish-made furniture wasn't cheap anywhere, but this store's prices were double what I'd seen at other places throughout the county. The craftsmanship was slightly different too. It wasn't as simple. The wooden furniture in this store held intricate engraving and embellishments on almost every piece. Clearly this was an attempt to appeal to the English shopper of means.

"Sorry about that." She forced a smile after stowing her cleaning supplies. She wiped her hands off on her khaki pants. "I thought I would get some dusting in while the store was empty. You wouldn't believe the amount of dust we collect in here, and that's just in the front sales room. Out back where the Amish craftsmen work, the sawdust is so much worse . . ." She trailed off when she saw my hat. "You're from the police?" Her voice is sharp. "Is this about Griff?"

"I would like to talk to you about Griffin Bright," I said as officially as possible.

Her frown deepened. "And is he a police dog?"

"Umm," I said. "He's in training."

Oliver made a snuffling sound that, if it had been translated from dog to English, would have been "Oh, brother."

She folded her arms. "I don't know what more I can tell you. I've already spoken to the sheriff and I've even been fingerprinted."

That was interesting.

"Do you know how humiliating that is?" she asked. Tears gathered in her eyes.

Actually I did, but I didn't tell her that.

"You and Griffin were engaged?"

She glared at me, but then her shoulders drooped. "I might as well dust while I answer your questions." She collected her spray bottle and rag and walked to the back corner of the store where the bedroom furniture was.

In the corner of the display area, an ornately carved nightstand caught my eye. It consisted of three drawers and each drawer had a different quilt pattern carved into the front of it. I spotted a Rolling Block, a Goosefoot, and a Wedding Ring. I gravitated toward it and ran my hand over the smooth top. "This is a beautiful piece."

Mallory smiled. "You have a good eye. That must make you a good cop."

"Observation is important in police work," I said, praying Mitchell never found out about this conversation.

She sprayed the top of the nightstand and began to polish it. "That one has always been my favorite. I think that's why I have it hidden back in the corner here because I don't want anyone to buy it."

I stepped out of the way of the spray bottle. "The craftsmanship is amazing."

"The man who made it said he was inspired by his wife's quilts."

"I can see that. It's beautiful. I would love to see the quilts that inspired it. They must be breathtaking. I own a—" I stopped myself just in time. I almost told her about Running Stitch.

She looked up at me as she moved to the next nightstand with her spray bottle. "You own a what?"

"Oh, I was just going to say that I own a few Amish quilts, is all."

"Most people in this county do." She opened the drawer of the second nightstand and wiped the inside. Her bracelets made a terrible racket as they knocked against the sides of the drawer.

"Tell me about Griffin," I said.

Mallory sniffed and tears gathered into her eyes as she straightened up. "I hate that man."

My eyes went wide. "Why's that?"

She removed a tissue from her pocket and dabbed at her eyes. "Because he died and left me. Now, I don't know what to do . . ." Her breath caught.

"Weren't you broken up?"

"Yes," she snapped. "But that doesn't mean we wouldn't reconcile. That didn't mean that he wouldn't finally come around and we would get married."

"I am sorry for your loss," I said sincerely.

"I still don't think I've accepted he's gone. I keep feeling irritated he hasn't called or texted me today, and then I remember he's gone. Isn't that awful I feel angry at him like that?"

"I'd think it was perfectly normal when you lost someone," I said.

She put the tissue back in her pocket. "I shouldn't have come to work today. My brother, who is also my boss, tried to send me home earlier, but what good would that do? Griff isn't there and being at home will only remind me of his absence."

"How long were you engaged?"

She flashed me her left hand. "I don't have a ring.

He never asked me to marry him even though he promised that he would. Someday. We were together for ten years, and I never got a proposal. Now that he's dead, I have nothing to show for that relationship, just a wasted decade of my life." She sat on the double bed next to the quilt-carved nightstand as if her legs no longer had the strength to hold her up.

"You have your memories," I said. It didn't sound like much of a consolation even to my own ears.

"Whatever good those will do me. I wish I had never given him that ultimatum. Then, at least, he wouldn't be angry with me when he died. That's something I will have to live with," she said bitterly.

"What ultimatum was that?"

She sighed. "It was my fortieth birthday, and I was staring middle age right in the face. I wanted to be married and have children. I wanted a real life that mattered. I didn't want to keep limping along, waiting for Griff to make up his mind about our future. What right does he have to make all the decisions?" She sighed. "So at my birthday dinner, I gave him an ultimatum. I said he had to either marry me in the next year or we were over. Well, since we broke up, I suppose you can guess what option he chose."

"Did he ever say why he didn't want to get married?"

She frowned.

Maybe I pushed too hard. "I'm only asking because I was in a similar situation. I was with the same man for seven years. He ultimately didn't want to get married because he was afraid of commitment."

"Men!" She removed the tissue from her pocket a

second time and pressed it to her face. "You would have thought seven years with one person would qualify as commitment. Or in my case, ten years."

"You'd think," I agreed.

She nodded. "Then you've been through it too. Griff said that he didn't have any use for marriage the day we broke up. Honestly, I knew that when we started dating over a decade ago. At the time, I never thought it would bother me. Years later, it did more than I ever expected it to."

"On the day Griffin died, you told the police that you hadn't seen Griffin for a couple of days."

"What's your point?" she asked.

"We have an eyewitness that saw you in his truck the day before he died outside the Braddocks' home."

"That's the rich lady's house where he died, right?"

Internally wincing, I nodded.

She glared at me. "So what if I was there? I was trying to talk some sense into him. He was overloaded with work. The only time I could talk to him was when he drove from job to job. A lot of good that did."

"Why didn't you tell the police that when you arrived at the crime scene?"

"I don't know. I just found out that he was murdered. Haven't you ever fibbed to the cops?"

I didn't answer that.

"I guess being a cop, you wouldn't have done that," she said as if she found it disappointing.

If she only knew . . .

She rubbed the wad of tissues across her nose. "I'm sorry. It's just so hard to believe he's dead. I still love him, you know. I left him because we didn't want the same things, but I did love him. I had since the day that I met him."

"How did the two of you meet?" I asked.

Her face softened as she recalled the memory. "At the county fair. I was there with my girlfriends, determined to win a teddy bear for myself from one of those silly games where you throw a softball at a stack of milk bottles. I had three balls and missed my first two throws. Griff came up behind me and took the third ball from my hand just when I was about to throw it. He tossed it at the milk bottles and won me the bear."

I hid a frown. If a man I didn't know came up to me like that and won me a teddy bear, I would tell him to keep the bear.

"It was love at first sight for me." Her face crumbled, and she set her rag and spray bottle next to her on the edge of the bed. "I'm sorry. Maybe I should have gone home when my brother told me to. My sister keeps texting me, trying to convince me to take the rest of the week off."

"Maybe you should go see your sister. Being around family might help," I said.

She shook her head. "She lives in Michigan."

"Maybe you should take a few days off and go and visit her," I suggested even though I knew Mitchell would be annoyed with my suggesting that a murder suspect leave the county.

"She wants me to. She wanted me to drive to Michigan today, but I can't go yet. I have to know what will happen to Griff. If there is a funeral or any kind of service, I want to be there." Her mouth turned down. "I hope I will be told."

"Have you spoken to his family about the funeral arrangements?" I asked.

She laughed. "He only had a brother, Blane, and no, I haven't. Blane and I don't get along."

"Maybe you should talk to Linda from Double Dime then," I suggested.

Her blue eyes narrowed as if seeing me for the first time. "How do you know Griff's connection with Linda?"

I recovered quickly. "The police know about Linda being Griffin and Blane's foster mother."

"Oh, right." She eyed me suspiciously. "But why are you suggesting that I go see my sister in Michigan? The sheriff told me that I couldn't leave town."

Her rag slid off the edge of the bed and floated to the carpet. Automatically, I bent over and picked up the rag. As I did so, my hat fell to the floor and my curls tumbled into my face. I snatched up the rag and hat, but it was too late.

"Hey!" Mallory yelled, jumping up from the bed. "I've seen you before. You're not a cop."

"I never said that I was." That was *technically* true.

"I saw you at the house where Griff was killed!"

"I'm Angie Braddock and own Running Stitch in Rolling Bro—"

"Braddock!" she gasped. "Didn't Griff die in your home?"

I shook my head. "It isn't my home. It's my mother's," I said, as if that would make a difference to her. I knew it wouldn't.

"So you are here about Griff's death? You're pumping me for information, and you're not even a cop." She glared at me. "I think it's time for you to leave."

"Please, let me explain." I held up my hands as if in surrender.

"Why should I?"

I bit the inside of my lip. "I'm a friend of Linda's. She asked me to look into her son's death."

"Her son?" Mallory scoffed. "She wasn't Griff's mother."

"She was his foster mother," I said, going on the defensive myself.

"That's not the same thing." Her face was almost purple.

I took a big step back from her. "It is to Linda. She's heartbroken over his death."

"She can't be as heartbroken as I am," she snapped. "She has no right to be."

Before I could ask her what she meant by that last comment, the store's front door opened, and a tall, lanky man strode in wearing a polo shirt with the store's logo embroidered over the pocket. He marched toward us. I was trapped between the two of them, clutching Mitchell's hat in my hands.

Chapter Thirty-two

"I said it's time for you to go," Mallory said to me again, this time through gritted teeth.

"Everything okay, Mal?" the man asked, appraising me while he spoke.

"Yes," she said. "Everything's fine. This customer was just leaving. We didn't have what she needed."

I was relieved that she hadn't said my true purpose for coming to the store or the fact that I sort of misled her into believing I was a police officer.

I gave the lovely little nightstand a mournful look, and Oliver and I headed for the door.

I turned as I reached the door. "You should speak to Linda. I know she'd love to hear from someone who cared about Griff as much as she did."

Mallory folded her arms and glared at me.

I sighed and walked out into the sunlight.

Giving Oliver a boost into my car, I said, "Maybe the hat was a bad idea."

He gave me a look that said, "I told you so."

By the time Oliver and I returned to Running Stitch,

it was only a half hour before the shop closed. Sugar-tree Street was quieting down, and I felt it was late enough in the day to take one of the diagonal parking spots in front of my quilt shop. Typically, I left those for the tourists.

Mattie must have seen me coming down the street because she opened the door for Oliver and me. "That cat of yours has been a complete terror."

Oliver ran into the shop to check on his charge. Dodger was curled up in Oliver's dog bed, sound asleep. It looked like the contented slumber of the victorious to me.

Mattie waved a pot holder at me. "Look what he did to this!"

I slung my bag on the sales counter and took the pot holder that Mattie offered. The front of the pot holder had been slashed. I flipped it over. The back wasn't much better.

"When I saw he had it, I tried to get it away from him, and the little monster took off with it. It took quite a battle to get it back."

I winced. I didn't doubt it, but at the same time I hid a smile. I would have loved to see Mattie in her Amish lavender dress chasing Dodger all over the shop with the pot holder in his mouth.

Dodger opened one eye and the corner of his mouth turned up in a smile. The faker wasn't even sleeping.

"You can't keep bringing him here if he's going to destroy the merchandise." Mattie folded her arms.

She had a point, but before I could answer, the little

bell on the shop's door jingled and Zander bounded inside. "Angie!" he cried.

His mother, Hillary, came in after him. She was breathtakingly beautiful with long, straight raven-colored hair, which I'd envied since the moment I had met her. Zander had his mother's hair and his father's eyes. Anyone could see he was a gorgeous child and would be a devastatingly handsome man someday.

Hillary carried Zander's *Thor* backpack. "Hello, Angie." Her greeting, although friendly, wasn't nearly as enthusiastic as her son's had been.

I wouldn't exactly say that Hillary and I were friends, but we were cordial, and if she didn't happen to be my boyfriend's ex-wife, I probably would have liked her a lot more.

"This is a surprise," I said. "You need quilting sup-plies?"

"Didn't James tell you that I'd be dropping Zander by? I have a charity event this evening in Canton for my job, and I can't take him with me. Since this was supposed to be James's week with Zander as it was, he said I could leave Z with you until he got off work."

I removed my phone from my pocket and looked at the screen. Sure enough, there were six text mes-sages and one call from Mitchell warning me about Hillary's arrival. I had turned the phone onto silent before going into the Zeff Oak Emporium because I hadn't wanted to be interrupted by my mother's ranting about my father's physical therapy.

I waved the phone. "He sure did. I just missed the message. Of course Zander can hang with me."

"Good." Her brow smoothed. "James said he'll pick him up around eight."

"Sounds good," I said.

She paused at the door. "You must be excited about James's parents coming up for a visit for a few days. It will be the first time you will meet them in person— isn't that right?"

I felt the color drain from my face. What? What was she talking about? Mitchell's parents were coming to Rolling Brook? I knew the couple moved to Florida and had lived there for years. Mitchell and Zander went to see them at least twice per year. I had never gone, and I had never met them. Mitchell had asked me to go their last trip, which had been over Zander's spring break in March. I had made up some excuse about not being able to leave the shop. I just hadn't been ready to meet Mitchell's parents yet.

I plastered a smile on my face. "I'm really excited to meet them."

Mattie knew about the trip last March. Her face clearly said, "Liar!"

I widened my eyes at her, and she turned away but not before I saw her shoulders move up and down in suppressed laughter.

I realized this must have been what Mitchell wanted to tell me the day before. He hadn't been about to pro-pose marriage at all. To my surprise, I felt a slight pang in my chest. A blush crept up the back of my neck.

Hillary smiled at me. "I love James's mother. She and I have always been close. Do you know she still sends me Christmas and birthday cards? And we talk on the phone at least twice a month. She's such a dear."

"That's great," I squeaked. "I'm glad that you're still close to Mitchell's family. That makes it easier for Zander."

She smiled. "It most certainly does." She opened the door. "Don't worry, Angie. James's mother will warm up to you. Eventually." She flounced out of the shop.

What was that supposed to mean?

Mattie left not long after Hillary's dramatic exit. She didn't say if she was headed to the mercantile to visit Liam, and I didn't ask. That left me with a cat, a dog, and a boy.

I texted Mitchell back and told him that I had Zander with me at Running Stitch and he could pick his son up at the shop because I planned to work late. I didn't say a word about the trustees' meeting. I hoped that it would be over by the time Mitchell arrived. I didn't think he wanted to hear another word about Bigfoot or the central Ohio chapter of the Bigfooter Society.

"You've got homework?" I asked Zander, who was rolling around on the shop floor with Oliver and Dodger.

He rolled onto his back with Oliver on his stomach. "Yep."

"Do you want to do it?" I asked.

He rolled his eyes. "It's Friday night."

"I'll take that as a no. Do you want pizza?"

"Yes!" He sat up with a jolt.

The cat and dog meowed and barked respectively. Pizza was something we could all agree on.

"Should I order brownies too?" I asked.

The pizza place also made killer brownies.

"Yes!" Zander pumped his fist. "You always get the best junk food, Angie." His voice held true respect.

I was going to be a stellar parent.

The four of us were polishing off what was left of the pizza, and Zander and I were moving onto the brownies, when a rapid knock at the Running Stitch's locked front door interrupted us.

"Who's that?" Zander asked with a mouth full of brownie.

"It might be one of the township trustees. We're having a meeting here tonight."

He swallowed. "That sounds boring."

Because I was the grown-up, I didn't agree with him. Out loud. The meetings usually were boring, but considering this meeting's subject matter was Bigfoot, I thought it had the potential to be a little more animated than usual.

I brushed the crumbs from the brownie off the front of my shirt and opened the door.

Willow trundled in carrying an easel. "Zander! Hello! So glad to see you."

Zander shoved a brownie into his mouth and said, "Hi" with a mouth full of chocolate.

"What's with the easel?" I asked with some concern. I knew it was trouble when Willow used props.

She set up the easel in front of the wall of fabric. "Caroline asked me to come to this meeting with a plan for the Bigfooters, and I have."

I inched toward the easel. "Can I see?"

She moved in front of it and held out her arms. "No, it would ruin the surprise."

I had a sinking feeling. The only surprises I'd experienced from Willow involved her teas. I couldn't see this one being much better.

A little before seven, the rest of the trustees entered the shop. Caroline frowned when she saw Zander there, playing on his iPod, but she made no comment.

She settled into one of the folding chairs I'd set up in front of Willow's easel.

"What's with the easel?" Jason Rustle asked. He was still wearing the business suit that he must have worn to his office that morning.

Willow clapped her hands in front of herself. "I have a plan for the Bigfooters, just like you requested, Caroline." She beamed.

Farley rubbed his hands together. "We are all here; let's get this meeting started. I, for one, can't wait to see what Willow has in store for us."

Caroline scowled. "*I* will be the one who decides when the meeting will begin." She took a dramatic pause. "Willow, will you begin your presentation?"

Jason Rustle stared longingly at the door. I knew he'd give anything to bolt. I sort of felt the same way, but since the meeting was in my shop, I was trapped.

"Thank you, Caroline," Willow said formally. "As all of you know, there are a number of Bigfoot believers in Rolling Brook because of the recent sightings around the home of Angie's parents." She nodded to me. "The Bigfooters are here and don't plan to leave until they see Bigfoot or it is proven that it was all a hoax—"

"Because you told them about the supposed sighting," Jason grumbled.

"Be that as it may," Willow said evenly, "I believe we can use their presence for the good of the town." She stepped back and flipped around a large piece of poster board sitting on the easel. In giant block letters in the middle of the poster board, it read, "Bigfoot Day! Join us in Rolling Brook this Saturday to learn about the myth and legend!"

The rest of the trustees, including myself, just stared.

"Cool!" Zander said. "I love Bigfoot."

Willow grinned. "Me too!"

"You have a nine-year-old on board," Jason said. "A resounding endorsement indeed."

"Not cool," Caroline said, standing up. "Not cool at all. We're already the laughingstock of the county. Don't you see that this will only make it worse?"

"Saturday is tomorrow," Jason said. "How can we plan it in time?"

Willow grinned. "That's the beauty of it. There's nothing to plan. My friend Ray, the president of the local chapter of the Bigfooter Society has T-shirts and other merchandise to sell, and the society has ready-made presentations. All we need to provide is a location right here on Sugartree Street."

"There is no way this is happening," Caroline protested. "I don't give my time to manage this township in order to be mocked!"

"I really thought you would like it." Willow's face fell. "I know it's a little outside of the box . . ."

Caroline closed her eyes as if she couldn't stand to look at Willow.

Jason leaned close to me and whispered, "She's gonna blow in three . . . two . . . one—"

"Willow, how can you do this without consulting with the trustees? This is not the first time you've gone off on your own to plan an event. We can't just throw something together. A street fair takes planning. Not to mention, we don't want to do anything to tarnish Rolling Brook's reputation."

"Actually," Farley said, speaking up for the first time since Willow's big reveal, "I think Willow's plan is the best we have to go on. These Bigfooters aren't going away, and it seems that more are coming each day. With the weekend coming, I'm afraid that the numbers will rise. Why not take advantage of it?"

Caroline gaped at him. "You can't be serious."

"I'm very serious," he said. "If we fight it, the other communities in the county will only get more enjoyment about poking fun at us. It's best to embrace it and show that we can laugh at ourselves."

I found myself nodding. Farley had a point. I could tell by the look on Jason's face he was considering it too.

"Farley!" Caroline cried.

He smiled at her. "We can't run these people out of the township with shovels and pitchforks, so we might as well make some tax dollars off their time here."

"Yeah, it makes sense when it is presented that way," Jason said. "I think it's the best course of action."

Willow grinned. "Should we put it to a vote?"

"I say yea," Farley said.

Jason and I agreed.

"But!" Caroline stared at us openmouthed.

Jason stood. "Now that we have decided about the Bigfooters, is the meeting over? I have some real work for my real job this evening."

Farley, Willow, and I stood too.

Caroline fell into her seat. "You're all in agreement that this is a good idea? That we should cater to these—these people?"

"They won't be here much longer," I said. "If no one sees a Bigfoot this weekend, they will leave of their own accord, and I have it on good authority that it's a practical joke. Someone saw Bigfoot's sneakers."

"Really?" Willow asked, sounding disappointed, but she quickly recovered. "Don't worry. None of you will have to do a thing for Bigfoot Day other than stop by Sugartree Street to join in the fun."

Caroline groaned, covering her face with her hands.

As the trustees were leaving at the end of the meeting, Jason stopped me. "I heard about Griffin dying at your parents' house. Bad break."

"Did you know him?" I asked.

He shook his head. "No, but one of my old business partners used to be an insurance investigator. He knew Griffin from that. I guess he had to adjust a job where an Amish man got killed on one of Griffin's jobsites."

"When was this?"

"Years ago. Not really sure."

"Thirty years ago?" I asked.

He rolled his eyes. "No way that long ago, Angie. How old do you think I am?"

So that ruled out the fire that killed Raymond's wife.

"Was the Amish man named Kamon Graber?" I asked.

He shook his head. "No, that's not it. It was an Amish name, but not one as unusual as Kamon. I would have remembered one so unusual. I do remember that it wasn't even in Holmes County."

Another person had died because of Griffin's business and outside of the county? If I counted Raymond's wife, that was the third death attributed to Griffin in some way.

"Can I talk to your friend?" I asked.

He shook his head. "I don't know where he is now. He got another job in Arizona or New Mexico—somewhere hot at least—and we lost touch. Sorry—I'd stick around and chat but . . ." Jason looked down at his watch. He'd already said he had a lot of work to do tonight.

While I stood in the doorway of Running Stitch and watched Jason drive away, Martha Yoder stepped out of Authentic Amish Quilts next door and locked the door. She glared at me, and I smiled back. It was a typical exchange between Martha and me. The atypical part was when she marched over to me. "I heard that you were bothering my cousin today."

My brow knit together. "Your cousin?"

"Mallory Zeff." She said this as if it was something I should have already known.

"Mallory is your cousin?" Clearly, it was taking me a minute to catch up on this new information.

She sniffed. "Distant cousin. On the side of the family that turned *Englisch* over fifty years ago. I can't hold that against Mallory."

"That's nice of you," I deadpanned.

"She said that you came sniffing around pretending to be a police officer and wanted to know if she killed Griffin Bright."

"I never said that I was a police officer." I never said it outright, I added silently to myself.

She put her hands on her hips. "Well, I'm here to tell you to leave her alone. She was with me the morning Griffin died. She was so upset about her breakup with Griffin that she spent the night at my house. She just needed to get away from everything for a little while. My Amish home was the best place to escape to."

"Oh," I said, slightly disappointed that I had just lost a promising suspect. "Did you tell the police that?"

"Mallory did, and I confirmed her story when a deputy stopped by this afternoon to ask me about it."

Mitchell's department SUV parked in the spot next to my car.

Martha glanced at the car and said, "Stop sticking your nose in places where it doesn't belong. You wouldn't want the sheriff to know what you're up to, would you?" With that, she stomped down the street in the direction of the community parking lot where her horse and buggy waited.

As Mitchell got out of the car, Zander flew through Running Stitch's open front door and threw his arms around his father's waist. Mitchell gave him a huge bear hug and kissed the top of head. My heart filled up watching father and son together. An unwanted image of that darn giraffe from the nursery in my mother's house entered my mind again. I swallowed.

Mitchell walked over to me and nodded in the direction that Martha had just gone. "Do I want to know about what was going on here?"

I shook my head. "Probably not."

"Dad!" Zander cried. "Bigfoot is real, and tomorrow will be Bigfoot Day in Rolling Brook. Can we go? I've never been to a Bigfoot Day before."

Mitchell smiled at me with those aquamarine eyes over his son's head. "Neither have I."

All I could think was "stupid giraffe."

"Dad, did you tell her yet?" Zander asked.

I looked from one to the other. "Tell me what?"

"Grandma and Grandpa are coming up from Florida for a visit," the boy shouted at the top of his voice.

Mitchell gave me a half smile.

"Ahh," I said. "Hillary might have hinted about that to me."

"I thought she might have," Mitchell said, studying my face. "Don't look so worried."

"Worried? Why would I be worried?" I squeaked.

"Before we can move forward with what comes next"—Mitchell gave me a meaningful look—"I need you to meet my parents." He laughed. "I've certainly gotten to know yours over the last couple of years."

A lump caught in my throat. My brain spun with ideas as to what *next* might be. "When will they be here?"

"Within a few days," Mitchell said. "They are driving up from Florida, and they like to take their time and visit friends on their northward trek. It's hard to predict."

Great. That wasn't exactly the precise time of arrival I was hoping for.

"Grandma and Grandpa will love you, Angie," Zander said confidently. "Just like Dad and I do."

My heart felt as if it would burst out of my chest at Zander's sweet words. I silently prayed his prediction was right.

Chapter Thirty-three

Between the murder and looming arrival of Mitchell's parents, I had a fitful night's sleep even though Dodger, Oliver, and I were safely tucked back into our little rental house in Millersburg.

I wasn't feeling chipper when my alarm went off the next morning, and I was feeling even less so while driving to Rolling Brook. Both situations were maddening, but I decided to focus on the murder because that had the greatest chance of being resolved.

Something Jason Rustle said the night before nagged at the back of my mind. He said that he'd heard that an Amish man had died in an accident years ago, but he was almost certain that the man's name wasn't Kamon. That could only mean that there was another accident in Griffin's past. Perhaps Blane would know what that accident was, but I was tired of evasive answers from Griffin's friends and family. I needed hard facts. Before going to sleep the night before, I had searched the Internet for any mention of another death years ago associated with Griffin Bright that wasn't

Kamon's. I came up with nothing. Not even Kamon's. It had been twenty years ago, but that was just at the very beginning of the Internet. The county papers that would have reported the death might not have been online yet. It was clear I needed professional help.

I pulled to the side of the county road between home in Millersburg and Running Stitch in Rolling Brook and dug my phone out of my hobo bag. I scrolled through the contacts until I found the right number, and then called.

"Hello," a groggy voice answered on the other end of the line.

"Good morning, Sunshine," I said brightly.

"Angie, it's like nine in the morning." Amber Rustle yawned in my ear. "On a Saturday."

"Don't you have to be at the library this morning?" I asked. Amber was Jason's college-age daughter who worked at the main county library. In the past, I had helped Amber find her best friend's killer. Ever since then, she had sort of become my personal librarian-in-training-on-call. Everyone should have a librarian on speed dial in my opinion.

"I don't have to be there until nine forty-five."

"And you are still in bed?"

"Yeah, it will take me like two minutes to get ready."

Ahh, the ease of youth. "I have an assignment for you when you get to the library."

"Is it about Bigfoot Day?" she asked. "Dad told us all about it when he got home from the trustees' meeting last night. He said Caroline's face turned purple when you all voted for the Bigfoot Day."

Bigfoot Day. I had forgotten. I rubbed the spot between my eyes where the headache was starting to form. "It did indeed."

She giggled, sounding more awake. "I wish I could've seen it. We have a few books on Bigfoot. Do you want me to hold them for you?"

"No, this isn't about Bigfoot. It's about the murder."

"You mean that guy who got electrocuted. What a way to go."

I grimaced. "I know. I think something from his past was the reason he was killed. I want you to do some digging in the newspaper archives at the library."

"Are you investigating his death?" Before I could answer, she went on. "Why am I even asking? Of course you are. What do you need?"

I smiled. I knew Amber would be up for the challenge. I told her about the accident from twenty years ago that had killed Kamon. "I think that there was a second accident where a second man died. At least your father thought so. He couldn't remember the man who died's name."

"When did it happen?"

"That's the problem," I said. "I have no idea."

"You want me to pour over twenty years of newspapers to find a suspicious death that you're not even sure happened."

"Is that too hard of a task?" I asked cheerfully.

She snorted with a superiority that only a future librarian could manage. "Maybe for the average person, but not for me."

"I knew I could count on you."

On the street an Amish buggy rolled by.

"It might take me a few hours. Those older records wouldn't have been digitized, but I will find it."

"Take all the time that you need. I would rather you be thorough than fast," I said.

"I'd better get a move on then," she said, sounding excited. "I'll call you when I have news."

I started the car again, feeling much better about the day. I patted Oliver on the top of the head before I pulled the SUV out onto the road. "We have a plan now, Ollie. I always feel better when I have plan. Don't you?"

He licked my hand, and we continued on our way to Rolling Brook.

On Sugartree Street, I parked in the community lot and froze the moment my feet hit the sidewalk. Willow hadn't been kidding when she said that the trustees wouldn't have to do anything for Bigfoot Day. Up and down the street, street vendors were selling T-shirts, mugs, umbrellas, and just about anything you could slap a Bigfoot silhouette on, and there were numerous placards telling what time the Bigfoot talks would be in the Dutchman's Tea Shop.

Mattie stood in the doorway to Running Stitch, gripped the sides of her apron as if she needed its support. "Angie, what on Earth is going on?"

I sighed and told her about the trustees' meeting the night before.

She shook her head. "Many of the Amish aren't going to like this."

That's what I was afraid she might say.

Two men sold Bigfoot key chains in front of

Running Stitch. Their display blocked the view of the shop's door from the street. Mattie went inside to prepare the shop for opening, and I walked over to them. "I'm going to have to ask you to move. You're blocking access to my store."

One of the men, with a goatee and who I guessed was in his late twenties, stared at me as if he had seen a ghost. "It's you." He pointed at me.

I stepped back. "Excuse me?"

A second man, who was clean-shaven and larger than the first, took a step up to me. "It is her. You're right. We found her. I can't believe it. We've been looking for you everywhere!"

I took a bigger step back. "What are you talking about?"

"You're the girl," Goatee said. "You're the one in the video. You saw him."

"What video?" I asked, starting to become annoyed.

"What was it like?" the second man asked. "Could you smell him? I know it was kind of far away from you, but I have always wondered what a Sasquatch smelled like. Experts say it's kind of musky."

"Yeah," his friend agreed. "Like wet fur."

Now there was a small crowd gathering around us.

"What on Earth are you talking about?" I shouted.

"Bigfoot. You saw him." He waved his smartphone at me. "I have it right here on video. It was just posted early this morning, but it's already all over the Internet. You're famous in the Bigfoot world. If we can get more proof of the Sasquatch's existence for the nonbelievers, you might be famous in, like, the entire world."

"Let me see that." I held out my hand, and he placed the smartphone in my palm. The screen showed a You-Tube video. I tapped to play.

The video was from two days ago and showed me standing in my parents' front yard with Petunia. Yikes, my blond curls were wild; it was clear that I had dashed out of the house after Jonah's urgent call. I was talking to Petunia. Suddenly, I look up and stared across the street at the large tree. My mouth falls open as if in shock. The shot widened out and showed me and the furry figure across the street. On the video, the thing looked even more like Bigfoot than I remembered. The camera doesn't zoom in on the creature, instead it stays on me. Eban arrives in his cart and I talk to him pointing at the tree. He shakes his head and leaves the shot. Officer Anderson comes out of the house and it shows me accosting him and pointing across the street. Clearly, I'm telling him to go check it out. Mitchell appears and Anderson takes off toward the tree after a direct order, but the creature is gone by then. The last scene is Mitchell touching my cheek.

"Lady, I know it's none of my business, but I think that cop has a thing for you," Goatee said. "He seemed a little too familiar if you ask me."

"Yeah," the second one agreed. "He was using your fear to get fresh."

I looked heavenward. I could see no good coming of me telling these men that Mitchell was my boyfriend and therefore not getting fresh, whatever "fresh" might mean.

"The shot on the creature isn't as good as we would

like to see," Goatee said. "But all the evidence points to a Bigfoot."

"Definitely," his friend agreed. "I don't have any doubt in my mind that's a Bigfoot."

"Who posted this?" I scrolled down and found the screen name: AmishInsider. Interesting screen name.

"See, the guy who posted this is Amish. It must be authentic. Amish don't lie."

"That is impossible," I said. "The Amish don't use YouTube."

There was a tiny image of the AmishInsider next to his name. I pinched the screen for a better look. Blown up, the picture was fuzzy, but I immediately recognized the face. I handed the man his phone. "I have to go." I hurried away.

"Wait? What? You didn't tell us about your sighting."

I ignored him and popped my head into the quilt shop. Mattie was counting out the cash drawer. "I have to run an errand," I told her. "I don't know how long I'll be gone."

She looked up from the drawer with concern. "Did something happen?"

"I'm an Internet star, but I may have solved at least part of the mystery."

"An Internet star?" she asked, confused.

"I have to go. I'll explain everything when I return."

"But—"

I stepped back onto the sidewalk in front of the shop before she could finish her question.

"There she is!" Goatee shouted. "She's the one from the video!"

I gave a sharp intake of breath as I saw a crowd twenty strong of Bigfooters surrounding me.

"Tell us what you know," another voice said. I couldn't make out who in the crowd.

I had to get out of there. Scooping up Oliver, I pointed across the street to Willow's shop. "There he is. It's Bigfoot!"

There was a collective gasp as the crowd turned in the direction in unison.

I slipped around a woman to my left and dashed down the alley between my and Martha's shops.

"Where'd she go?" I heard someone cry.

"Down the alley," another voice called.

I didn't wait to hear any more and ran for all I was worth through the back gardens of the shops toward the community parking lot across from the mercantile. I glanced back to see them racing down the alley. I doubled my pace, holding Oliver to my chest and my heavy hobo bag thumping against my thigh hard enough to leave a bruise.

Chapter Thirty-four

Feeling like an escaped convict on the run, I darted behind an RV in the middle of the parking lot, still clutching Oliver to my chest. "Shhh," I whispered to the Frenchie.

A moment later, I heard the Bigfooters' thundering feet hit the pavement.

"Where did she go?" one cried.

"She couldn't have disappeared into thin air!"

There was more grumbling, and then someone called over the others. "Let's head back to the tea shop or we are going to miss Raymond's presentation. We'll find her later."

The sound of their thundering feet receded. I slid to my knees behind the camper on the asphalt.

The camper door opened, and an overweight man stepped out. "You all right, miss?" He peered at me.

I straightened up in my kneeling position.

"Are you praying or something over that dog? Is he sick?"

I realized that it might appear that I was praying

from how I knelt with Oliver in my arms. My face flushed, and I scrambled to my feet. "No, I'm not, and the dog is fine."

He rubbed the stubble on his chin. "Do I know you from somewhere?"

That's when I saw the Bigfoot T-shirt stretched across his belly.

"Gotta go!" I cried, and hurried through the small parking lot and across the street to the mercantile.

The mercantile front door opened just as I was reaching out to open it, and Liam Coblentz stopped me from plowing into him by grabbing me by the shoulders. "Whoa, careful there." He let me go.

Out of breath, I asked, "Where's Cameron? Is he here?"

Liam stared at me as if I had asked him if aliens had touched down in the middle of the mercantile. Considering there were a good number of people wandering around Rolling Brook that morning who thought Bigfoot was real, I wouldn't be surprised if my pursuers would accept an alien invasion too. "Why don't you come inside?" he asked. "You look like you're about to pass out."

I stumbled after him into the store, feeling a tad shaky. I hadn't run this much in, well, ever. Maybe I should take up exercise just like my father. I followed Liam to the back of the store. I glanced around. "Are you open?"

He shook his head. "Not yet." He sighed. "Monday should be the day. I do have a sidewalk sale going on out front just to take advantage of Bigfoot Day." His eyes twinkled when he said Bigfoot Day. I was glad he found it amusing. After being chased up and down Sugartree Street, I could no longer see the humor in the situation.

A frown formed on his lips. "Angie, I'm glad you stopped by. I've been wanting to talk to you." He paused. "About Mattie."

I set Oliver on the floor. "What about Mattie?"

He swallowed. "I just want you to know that I care about her, and I will court her properly. I plan to talk to her brother later today and ask his permission. I know that she hasn't had an easy time in the past with suitors. I need you to know that I won't be like her last beau."

"I'm glad to hear it." I paused. "Because if you break her heart, you will have to deal with me."

He grinned. "She already told me that I would." He chuckled. "I think I'm more afraid of you than I am of her brother Aaron."

"You should be." My smile took the bite out of my words. "Mattie deserves a happily ever after."

"I mean to give her that."

"Now that that's settled, is Cameron here?" I repeated my original question.

"Blane's son? What do you want with him?"

"I discovered he's the one behind the Bigfoot prank, and I have to talk to him. It might be the only way to put all of this Bigfoot hysteria to rest."

"Who's looking for my son?" Blane appeared in the middle of the aisle behind Liam, holding a pair of wire cutters.

"I am," I said. "I'm sure you've seen all the excitement in Rolling Brook over Bigfoot, and I think the thing that eyewitnesses were actually seeing was part of a movie Cameron was making."

Blane shook his head. "I knew he was working on a movie, but I didn't know it was that."

"Can I talk to him?"

"He's not here," Cameron's father said.

"Do you know where I can find him?" I asked.

Blane considered my question. "He said that he had to film today to finish the project he's working on for class. He and his friend Sam are working on the assignment together. Out in the backwoods near Yoder Road."

"Yoder Road?" I asked. I swallowed. I didn't want to alarm Blane, but that was the street closest to Nahum's shack. This wasn't good. I backed out of the store, picking Oliver up as I went. "Can you text or call him to see where he is?"

Blane scowled. "I've been trying all morning, and he doesn't text me back. He's either ignoring me or out of range. If you find him, you tell him he is grounded for the entire summer. I don't care if he's over eighteen."

That was more confirmation to me that Cameron might be in Nahum's woods. The cell reception there was terrible.

"One more question," I said to Blane.

He lowered his wire cutters to his side as if in resignation. "What?"

"Was there a second electrical accident in Griffin's past, other than the one that killed Kamon Graber?"

He glowered at me. "You are still on that."

"Can you just answer the question?"

"There was. In the second accident, a barn burned down."

My hands began to tingle when he said that. I knew it was important. I took a deep breath. Before I could track down the barn fire, I had to save Cameron from Nahum's pitchfork. I put my hand on the doorknob. "I'll track Cameron down. Don't worry."

Outside, I ran around the back side of the mercantile, all the while on the lookout for Bigfooters. I waited for a buggy to cross my path and dashed across the street. At least my car was parked in the community lot across from the mercantile. I wouldn't have to go back to Running Stitch and risk being seen by the mob that thought I was an Internet celebrity.

"Angie!" Willow called. "I saw the video. I can't believe that we have evidence that Bigfoot is real and you're on the tape!" Her purple crystal twirled in the sun as she hurried toward me.

"It's evidence, but not in the way you think." I unlocked my car with the fob.

She frowned. "What do you mean?"

"Cameron, the teenager who posted that video, is a film student. He must be making a Bigfoot, or some type of creature, movie. I'm going to confront him now about it. Then, maybe these Bigfooters will leave the county."

Willow's face fell. "You mean the video's not real."

I put Oliver in my car. I hated to be the one to burst her bubble, but I had to be honest. "It's not. It was a teenage boy playing a joke. Now, I have to go find him." *Before Nahum finds him first.*

Behind Willow, someone shouted. "There she is!"

The next thing I knew, the mob was headed straight for us.

Willow jumped into my car. "I'm coming too."

Out of the corner of my eye, I saw the Bigfooters coming for me. I didn't have time to argue with her. "Buckle up," I ordered.

Chapter Thirty-five

I had been to Nahum's shack one time before, over a year ago in the middle of winter. This time there weren't feet of snow to contend with, but the woods were soggy from the frequent rains. I would have to take care where to step in order to protect my cowboy boots from permanent damage.

If I thought my footwear was impractical for a trek into the woods, Willow's was downright ridiculous. She wore pointy-toed granny boots with a two-inch heel.

"You're going to get stuck in the mud with those," I warned.

She waved away my concern. "I'm a pro at walking in these. You'll see."

After his first step in the forest, Oliver held up his paw to me and whimpered. He might live in the country now, but Oliver was born in Dallas and was still very much a city pooch.

"We'll wash your paws when we get back to Running Stitch," I said.

He sighed and set his paw on the muddy ground.

I glanced back at Willow as I made my way through the woods. "Nahum's cabin is about a quarter mile in. Keep an eye out for him, Cameron, or Bigfoot."

"You got it," she said cheerfully.

At least one of us was enjoying herself.

I heard Cameron long before I saw him.

"Help! Help!" the teenager's voice broke through the trees.

I scooped Oliver up and took off at a run, following the sound. I broke through the trees into the clearing where Nahum's shack stood. Nahum's yard was like a minefield with pieces of twisted metal and wood sticking out all over the place. Some were alone and others were attached to cast-aside appliances. The first time I had seen it, it had been buried under snow. Now, I could see the metal objects and they made the yard look far worse. I wondered if Nahum decorated his yard with them to serve as a barrier around his property. The sparse tufts of grass completed the horrendous landscaping.

"It's a project for school. I didn't mean any harm!" Cameron cried.

I couldn't see Cameron yet, so I followed the voice. As I came around the side of the shack, I found Nahum holding Cameron and Bigfoot at pitchfork point.

Bigfoot wore white sneakers just like Eban had described. He was clearly an impostor.

Cameron saw me. "Hey, we need help! This Amish dude is going to skewer us!"

"Yeah," Bigfoot agreed. "I'm too young to die!"

"Nahum!" I shouted at the older man. "What are you doing?"

"I found these boys sneaking around my land, taking moving pictures of my property." He jerked the pitchfork in their direction.

Bigfoot jerked back.

Cameron looked at me pleadingly. "I didn't know anyone lived here, honest! I thought it was an old abandoned shack. We were only here to shoot a scene for my movie. I wouldn't have come here if I knew *he* was living here. Honest!"

Nahum thrust the business end of the pitchfork forward, stopping just short of Cameron's chest. "This is my home!"

Cameron's hands went up. "I know that now, and I'm sorry. I'm really sorry. I was just making a movie for my class."

"Bigfoot, remove your mask," I said.

The creature didn't move.

Nahum waved the pitchfork at him. "Do what the lady says or prepare to meet your Maker."

Bigfoot removed his mask, and what appeared was the sweaty and pimply face of a teenage boy Cameron's age.

"What your name?" I asked the teen.

"S-Sam Bauer," he stammered, watching Nahum with wide eyes.

I folded my arms across my chest. "Well, Sam and Cameron, do you know the township of Rolling Brook has been overrun by people who believe that Bigfoot is here because of your little movie?"

Cameron, whose hands were still suspended in the air, said, "I was just doing a school project. I didn't mean anything by it. I never thought all these people would come."

"When you saw the rumors about Bigfoot in the county growing larger and larger, why didn't you come forward and tell someone what was really going on?" I asked.

He scowled. "I didn't want anyone to steal my idea."

"Yeah," Sam agreed. "We wanted to win the film award at school, and the best way to do that would be to keep the content of our project secret. Last year, someone in the same class let his idea be known, and he was totally sabotaged by another kid in the class."

"Are you going to tell him to let us go?" Cameron asked, sounding winded. "My arms are getting tired."

I arched my brow at him. "I will after you answer my questions."

The boys groaned.

"Why would you film where your uncle was working?" I asked.

"I didn't know Uncle Griff was working there. Honest. I just wanted to film on a remote road that might have a house or two of added drama." Beads of sweat gathered on Cameron's forehead. "I would have never filmed there if I knew Uncle Griff was working there. My dad would kill me. He and Uncle Griff don't get along."

I rocked back on my heels. "You do know that you need the landowner's permission to film on private property like that. My parents have a right to sue you if they wanted to."

Cameron turned a light shade of green. "It was for school."

Willow emerged out of the wood. "What did I miss?" She took in the scene. "Bigfoot is a pimply teenager?" she whispered to me. "My heart is broken."

I ignored her and continued with my questioning. "What did you see the morning your uncle was killed?" I nodded to Sam. "I want to know what you saw too."

"Nothing," Sam said. "I can barely see where I'm going in this gorilla suit."

Cameron's answer didn't come as quickly. It seemed that he was considering what to say.

I glared at him. "Cameron. Tell me or I will let Nahum at you."

He opened his mouth as if he was about to tell, but suddenly Nahum dropped his pitchfork and stumbled toward the boys. With the pitchfork no longer holding them at bay, they both jumped away from the Amish man.

For a moment, Nahum regained control of himself.

"Let's get out of here," Sam said.

"Stay!" Willow ordered in such a commanding voice, I had to make sure it was coming from her.

Oliver must have thought she was talking to him because he plopped his back end in the mud. He was so going to need a bath later.

Nahum leaned his pitchfork against the shack and staggered.

I took a step forward. "Nahum, are you all right?"

He waved me away, opened his mouth as if to say something, but collapsed onto the muddy ground before he could utter a word.

Chapter Thirty-six

I knelt in the mud next to the prostrate man. "Nahum? Nahum?"

He groaned and squinted at me. He was conscious. That was something. I had to take him to a hospital. There was no telling how long he had been sick or what was wrong with him.

Willow stood over me. "What should we do?"

Nahum stared at me with glassy eyes.

"Can you stand up?" I asked.

He tried to sit up and cried out in pain.

I pushed him back down by the shoulder. "New plan. Don't get up. We'll carry you out."

"Angie, he has to weigh a hundred and eighty pounds. How are we going to carry him?" Willow asked.

"The boys will do it as a favor in return for me not suing them for the video." I never had any intention of suing Sam and Cameron for the Bigfoot video, but they didn't know that.

They both swallowed and nodded. No one liked the threat of a lawsuit.

I jumped to my feet and ran into Nahum's one-room shack that was surprisingly neat and tidy. I knew I was tracking mud on Nahum's clean floors, but that couldn't be helped.

I pulled the quilt from his bed and ran outside with it.

"Shouldn't we call an ambulance and let the EMTs take him?" Sam asked.

"Shh," I said. "He'll refuse to go with the EMTs, and he needs to see a doctor."

As much as it pained me to see the beautiful Log Cabin quilt get covered in dirt, I laid it in the mud and then waved the boys over to help me.

We rolled Nahum as carefully as possible onto the quilt and lifted him up. The quilt made a perfect cocoon for the ill man.

Sam, still wearing his gorilla suit with the mask tucked under his arm, Cameron, and I carried Nahum out of the woods in the quilt. Nahum groaned with every bump, but I was happy he didn't fight us. Willow and Oliver led the way out of the woods.

We put Nahum in the backseat of my car. The boys said they would meet us at the hospital. I wasn't sure if they were lying, but I didn't care. Nahum was my primary concern at the moment.

There was a small private hospital on Route Eighty-three. They would be able to perform only some of the care but would know if Nahum would need to be transported to one of the larger hospitals in Canton or even farther away in Akron.

The ride to the hospital was tense. Nahum groaned

with every tiny bump in the road. As I drove, I asked Willow to call Mitchell and tell him what was going on.

I could hear him firing questions at her through her end of the conversation. I gripped the steering wheel, wondering if I should call the bakery and tell Rachel to meet us at the hospital. It would take her some time to reach the hospital by horse and buggy.

We arrived at the hospital before I made my decision. Willow hopped out of the car and ran inside to find help. Three people came out in scrubs and carefully placed Nahum, still wrapped in the mud-covered quilt, on a gurney.

After I parked the car and cracked the windows for Oliver, who I would have to leave inside while in the hospital, I walked into the lobby. Willow handed a pen and chart attached to a clipboard to me. "They want you to fill this out."

The first question that popped out at me was "emergency contact." That should be Rachel. Rachel should be filling out this form. But she wouldn't know any of the answers any more than I did.

I was about to take the clipboard back to the woman at the desk and explain when the automatic hospital doors slid open again, and Mitchell strode inside followed by Rachel.

I jumped out of my seat.

Rachel ran into my arms. She pressed the side of her face into my shoulder. "Where is he?"

"They're examining him right now." I guided her to the desk. "The man I brought in a little while ago. This is his daughter," I told the nurse at the desk.

"I want to see my fa . . . I want to see my father," Rachel said, finally managing to say the words.

The nurse came around the side of the desk. "You can go back, dear, but no one else." She wrapped her arm around Rachel and led her down the hallway.

I turned to Mitchell with tears in my eyes. "Thank you for bringing Rachel. I didn't know what to do."

He smiled. "I thought you might want her here."

I threw my arms around his neck and kissed the Holmes County sheriff right on the mouth in the middle of the busy waiting room. When I pulled back, Mitchell was bright red, but he was grinning. "If I'd have known the reunion of Rachel and her father would give you that reaction, I would have done it a long time ago." His tone turned serious, and he led me to a corner of the waiting room. "Tell me what happened."

I recited my story, including being chased through Sugartree Street by the mob of Bigfooters. At the end of it, I looked around the waiting room. "Cameron and Sam said they would meet us at the hospital."

Mitchell shook his head. "They probably ran off, but it sounds like it was a good thing that you were there when Nahum collapsed."

"If he recovers, he's going to be furious with me. He didn't want to come to the hospital." My forehead creased.

Mitchell nodded. "I know." His cell phone rang and he held up his index finger to me. Stepping away, he answered the call, "Mitchell." He turned his back to me so I couldn't eavesdrop. He knew me well.

Less than a minute later, he spun around. "Angie, I

have to go. There's been a serious semi versus Amish buggy accident on a county road."

My stomach dropped. "Is everyone okay?" I asked.

He grimaced. "I don't know yet."

He brushed my lips with his. Was this a new thing that Mitchell would allow kissing in public? Because that was fine with me.

"I'll call you later," he said, and strode out through the automatic doors.

It wasn't until he was gone that I realized that I'd forgotten to tell him what Blane had told me about the barn fire. It could wait, I thought.

Willow sidled up to me. "You know, I've been thinking." Willow shook her head. "Just because that boy was dressed up in costume doesn't mean there isn't a Bigfoot in the county. He's still out there."

I sighed and went to the desk to ask after Nahum. The nurse told me that he was undergoing tests, so it might be another hour before I could see him. I relayed this information to Willow.

She sighed. "Do you want me to stay?"

I shook my head. "Go back to Sugartree Street. Bigfoot Day needs you."

Willow called one of her Bigfoot friends and got a ride back to Rolling Brook. I asked her to take Oliver with her and drop him off at Running Stitch with Mattie. She agreed. I wanted to stay so I could be there when Rachel needed a ride home.

An hour later, I was considering leaving and coming back when a nurse came up to me with a room number for Nahum. He was on the second floor, and I took the elevator up.

The door to Nahum's room was ajar, and I peeked into the hospital room. Rachel sat at Nahum's side and held his hand. She murmured to him in Pennsylvania Dutch. She was crying. He was crying too.

I backed out of the room and bumped into someone in the hallway. I was shocked to find Cameron Bright behind me. I'd never expected to see the teen again.

He nervously licked his lips. "Will he be all right?"

"I think so," I said. "I thought you took off."

He shoved his hands into his jeans pockets. "I did. I wasn't going to come back. Sam told me not to but I had to know . . ." He trailed off.

"Know what?" I studied his face. Standing under the hospital's fluorescent lights, he looked so much younger than nineteen.

"Did I make him have a heart attack or something by trespassing in his wood?" The teen's brow crinkled in worry.

I patted his shoulder. "No. Nahum is sick. Very sick. There's something wrong with his kidney. It's not working right."

He gave a sigh of relief. "Oh, but will he be okay? Don't you need your kidneys?"

I patted the boy's arm. "He will be all right if he concedes to the surgery to remove one of his kidneys. You only need one."

"He won't concede because he's Amish?" Cameron asked.

I glanced through the open door at Rachel's bent head. "I don't know. He might now if he has something to live for."

"I'd better head home then."

I grabbed his wrist. "Not so fast." I dragged him to a couple of chairs at the end of the hallway.

"What are you doing?" He tried to pull away, but I outweighed him by a good twenty pounds. He wasn't leaving until I was ready to let him go.

I sat him in one of the two chairs. "All right. You are going to tell me what you saw outside my parents' the morning your uncle died."

He frowned.

"I know you saw something. I could see it on your face when we were in the woods. Who or what did you see?"

His frown deepened. "No one that wasn't supposed to be there."

"What does that mean?" I asked.

"The only person I saw there that early was an Amish guy, but I knew he was supposed to be there because I saw Amish working at the house the day before."

"What Amish guy? Jonah Graber?"

"I don't know. They all kind of look the same to me."

I clenched my fists. "What color was his hair?"

He shrugged. "I don't know that either. It was dark. I mean it was really early in the morning. The sun wasn't up yet."

"If you couldn't see him, how do you know he was Amish?"

"He was walking around the trailer holding a lantern. Only an Amish person would use a lantern."

I bit the inside of my lip. Could it have been Jonah? He didn't have an alibi for that morning and refused to tell anyone where he had gone when he left his farm at four a.m. But then Rex gave him an alibi in a way, but was it a real alibi when Rex didn't even know from where or at what time Jonah picked him up from the side of the road? If Jonah left his farm at four, he could have picked up Rex, dropped him somewhere, and still gotten to my parents' house in time for the murder. I rejected the idea. Jonah would never hurt anyone. It was impossible. And Eban was Amish too. Could it have been Eban who Cameron saw? But Eban wasn't there when I arrived at my parents' house. He came later after the police were already on the scene.

I had to talk to Jonah. I jumped out of my chair as if I had been electrocuted. "The woman in the room with Nahum," I said to Cameron, "is his daughter, Rachel. Can you tell her that I had to go?" I ran to the elevator before he could say another word.

Chapter Thirty-seven

Outside in the hospital's parking lot, I called my mother's cell phone. She answered on the first ring. "Mom," I said with so much relief as I stumbled into my car.

"Angie, what's gotten in to you?" she asked.

"There's no time for that. Are Jonah and Eban there working on the house?"

"No," she said slowly. "They left for the day. They finished painting the kitchen, and it has to dry before they can do anything else."

"Oh," I said.

"Are you all right?" my mother asked.

"Yes," I said. "I'm fine. I just need to make another call. I'll talk to you later." I hung up. Hanging up on my mother would come back to haunt me later, but I needed to think. I considered calling Mitchell, but I knew that he would be dealing with that semi accident somewhere else in the county.

What I wouldn't give for Jonah to have a cell phone! If I wanted to talk to Jonah, I would have to find him.

So the first place I would look was his farm, whether Miriam liked my arrival or not.

As I pulled into the Grabers' long gravel driveway, Petunia raced to my car before it came to a complete stop. Her tan-colored ears were flopping on the sides of her head. I got out of the car, but when Oliver didn't follow me, Petunia pulled up short.

The screen door banged against the house as Jonah came out. I recognized Miriam's silhouette in the doorway as Jonah walked toward me. I waited for Jonah to reach me.

"What?" Jonah asked, peering into the car. "No Oliver?"

I gave him a half smile. "He's at the shop with Mattie."

Jonah's brow knit together. I didn't have time to answer the unspoken question about Oliver's whereabouts and why he wasn't with me. I cut right to the heart of the matter. "Is Eban here?" I asked.

Jonah frowned. "He went home."

"Oh," I said. "Where's he staying?"

"Not home in Holmes County, but *home* back to his family's farm in Wayne County."

"He left Holmes County?" I asked. Suspicion started to tickle the back of my brain. "Why would he leave before you finished the remodel of my mother's kitchen?"

Jonah nodded and still appeared to be confused over my questions about Eban. "He said he had to go back home to his mother and sisters. Did you come here looking for Eban?"

I shook my head. "Jonah, I need to know where you were the morning Griffin died. It's important, really important."

His jaw clenched. "I told you that I wasn't going to speak of it."

"I know, but—"

"Angie, please," his voice was as sharp as I'd ever heard it.

"Rex Flagg saw you that morning," I blurted out.

He stepped back with confusion written all over his face. "Who?"

"Rex Flagg," I said. "He was the drunk you picked up in the wee hours and drove into town."

His mouth hung open. "How could you know about that?"

"It doesn't matter how I know. Why didn't you tell the police?"

"Why would I do that and shame a man who was clearly in trouble? It wouldn't have made any difference for me and could have caused much trouble for him."

I admired Jonah for his compassion, but this was no time to be chivalrous. "But you're wrong. It does matter. It gives you at least part of an alibi. That's a good start. Where were you the rest of that morning before you found Griffin's body?" I was shouting now. I couldn't help it.

Jonah glared at me. "Angie, you are going too far this time."

"I'm asking because I want to help you." I threw up my hands. "Cameron Bright, Griffin's nephew, saw an

Amish man around the trailer the morning right before his uncle was killed."

"He saw *me*?" Jonah asked in disbelief.

"He couldn't identify you personally, but he said an Amish man. You are the only Amish male suspect. Don't you see how serious this is?"

Hurt filled his eyes. "Are you asking me if I killed Griffin Bright, Angie? Is that what this is? Do you think I killed him?"

I stepped back. "No. Of course I don't think that, but it looks bad."

He turned away from me and faced his house. I wrapped my arms around my waist.

Miriam opened the screen door and stood on the top step that led into their house. I had overstayed my welcome.

I spoke to Jonah's back. "Believe me when I say that I know you didn't kill anyone, and I'm only trying to protect you."

His shoulders sagged, but still he didn't turn around.

"Don't worry, Jonah. I'll prove it with or without your alibi." I glanced around him at Miriam, who had her arms folded across her chest. "And if it will be easier for you, I won't come to your farm any longer."

"Angie," Jonah said as he turned around, "I don't want that."

I met his eyes, and I could feel tears forming in mine. "You might not, but it's what Miriam wants. I don't want my presence to cause any pain in your marriage."

"Angie—" Jonah began, but before he could say more, I climbed back into my car and drove away.

I was turning out of the Grabers' county road toward Rolling Brook when my cell phone rang. I fished it out of my bag and checked the readout. The call was from Amber. She must be calling in to report on the research project I'd given her that morning.

I held the phone to my ear. "Tell me what you learned," I told Amber on the other end of the call.

"A lot, actually," she said, seemingly unoffended at my lack of greeting. "You were right. There was another accident involving Griffin Bright. Sixteen years ago to be exact, four years after Kamon's death, so it didn't take me as long to find as I thought it might."

"A barn fire?" I asked.

"How did you know?" she asked, sounding miffed that I beat her to the punch.

"I don't know any more than that, so please go on," I said.

"Griffin was working on installing electricity to a former Amish barn for a new English owner. There was an electrical fire during the job at night. One of the Amish farmhands ran into the building to save the horses. He was able to free the animals, but he died in the fire."

I had a tingly feeling again. "What was his name?"

"Hold on—let me check."

I heard rustling paper on the other end of the call. It was torture waiting for her answer.

"Peter Hoch. This was in Wayne County, so there wasn't much talk about it here in Holmes, which may be why people don't remember it as well as Kamon's death twenty years ago."

Peter Hoch. Eban's last name was Hoch. Eban said his father had died.

"After Peter died," Amber said, warming up to her subject, "Griffin dissolved his electrician business. He seems to have disappeared for a couple of years. Then ten years ago, he came back and opened Double Bright Electric with his brother, Blane. There have been no incidents since Peter's death. The Bright brothers' business has gotten superb ratings for every year they've been in business. Griffin was even given some type of statewide safety award last year because he is such a stickler for rules. I guess he learned his lesson about safety the hard way."

Eban. The Amish man Cameron had seen that morning hadn't been Jonah. It had been Eban.

Amber went on to tell me more of what she learned about Griffin's business, but I was only half listening at that point. Eban? Could friendly and kind Eban really be the killer? I needed to talk to Mitchell.

"Thank you, Amber," I cut into her recitation of Griffin's history. "This is just what I needed to know. I have to go."

"But, I have more . . ."

"Can you send it to me in an e-mail? I really have to go."

"Oh-kay," she said.

"You did an awesome job," I said. "Really."

"I did?" She sounded pleased.

After I ended the conversation with Amber, I tried to

call Mitchell, but it went straight to voice mail. He must still be caught up in that accident. This wasn't a conversation for voice mail. I stopped myself from calling the emergency number. I wasn't in danger. I would just keep calling Mitchell until he answered.

Back in Rolling Brook, I parked in the community lot and nervously glanced around when I stepped out onto the sidewalk on the way to Running Stitch. Much to my relief, no Bigfooters jumped out of the alleys, calling my name.

There was only a handful of Bigfoot merchandise vendors still on Sugartree Street, and the ones that were there were in the process of packing up their wares. It was only two in the afternoon. There were at least two more hours of shopping to be had. I stopped one of the vendors and asked him why he was packing up.

"Didn't you hear?" the man asked. "It was a hoax. Some kid was making a movie for school. Everyone is packing it in."

"Too bad," I said, feeling relieved. At least the Bigfoot mania was over, and I no longer had to fear for my life. I continued on my way to the shop. There were still plenty of people on the street. I'd try to reach Mitchell again from inside the shop where no one would overhear.

In front of Running Stitch, I stopped. Something was wrong. The CLOSED sign was flipped around on the door. Did Mattie leave the shop? Had she gone to the mercantile to visit Liam? Why wouldn't she tell me?

I put my key into the lock and turned. The door swung inward. The interior was dark, but at first glance everything seemed to be in order. "Mattie," I called, taking a few tentative steps inside.

Where was Mattie? Where was Oliver? Something was very off. I was about to turn around and go back outside when the door slammed behind me.

I spun around and found Eban Hoch standing between me and the closed front door, holding a knife as long as my arm.

And then I heard Mattie crying.

Chapter Thirty-eight

"Eban," I cried when I regained my voice. "What are you doing?"

Barks came from the stockroom. I almost wilted with relief. Oliver was all right. He was trapped, but all right. My eyes adjusted to the dimness of the shop, and I spotted Mattie tied to a chair next to the giant quilt frame. Her eyes were the size of dinner plates, but she appeared otherwise unharmed.

Eban shook the knife at me. "Give me your purse."

"No," I said. My phone was in my hobo bag, and I wasn't giving that up. "Eban, we can talk about this. I'm sure it's not as bad as it seems to you."

Without a word, Eban ran around me to the back of the shop and placed the giant knife at Mattie's throat.

"Angie, please." Tears rolled down Mattie's cheeks.

I dropped the bag on the floor without a word and kicked it to him.

Eban picked up the bag and began rooting through the contents. He dropped my wallet, a stapler—I didn't remember putting that in there—and a packet of tissues on the floor. Finally, he came up with my phone, which he shoved into his trouser pocket.

If I wanted to, I had a clean getaway out the front door, but that would mean leaving Mattie and Oliver with Eban and his knife. That wasn't going to happen. I started talking. "You should have kept going home to Wayne County, Eban. You would have been home by now."

He laughed. "So that you could send the police for me there? Don't pretend that you wouldn't have done that. In the last two days working with Jonah, I have heard all about Angie Braddock, the sleuth, and her determination to find a killer. I knew that I would never get away with Griffin's murder."

I was right. Eban had killed Griffin. I wish that I had been wrong, but I was right. I closed my eyes for the briefest second, wishing that Jonah hadn't bragged about me.

"You came here for me, right? Then let Mattie go. She has nothing to do with Griffin's death."

"She's not going anywhere. Neither of you are."

"You can't keep us here forever," I said as reasonably as my shaky voice would allow.

He seemed to consider this. "If I let her go, she'll go to the police."

I shook my head. "No, she won't. Will you, Mattie?"

"I—I won't." Mattie trembled.

"I want to help you, Eban," I said. "But I'm not going to do that as long as Mattie is in danger."

"Stop trying to confuse me," he shouted, and moved the knife closer to Mattie's throat.

I held up my hands. "Okay, okay. We'll stay."

He pointed to a folding chair in the middle of the room. "Sit there."

I sat. I glanced back through the display window. There were only a few tourists left walking up the street, and none of them even glanced at Running Stitch to see the drama unfolding inside. There wouldn't be any help coming from that quarter. I had to think of a way to free Mattie, Oliver, and me from this situation.

"Stop looking at the window," Eban shouted.

I turned back to him. "I'm sorry." I gave him my full attention. As the man had a huge knife, he deserved it. "What did you want to talk to me about, Eban?"

He glared at me.

I licked my lips, which were impossibly dry. "Why did you wait so long to avenge your father's death?"

To my relief, he lowered the knife and stepped away from Mattie. He came toward me with the knife, but I'd much rather have him do that than have the knife at Mattie's throat.

"I knew you knew I did it. That's why I came here." He waved the knife erratically. "When the Amish girl said you weren't here, I knew you were out talking to people and collecting proof. I knew you would figure it out."

"Tell me about your father," I said.

He glared at me. "I never got to know my father, not really. Griffin robbed me of that when he killed him."

Behind Eban's back, Mattie wiggled quietly in her seat, inching the chair backward. Then, I saw what she was trying to reach. There was a small pair of thread scissors sitting on the edge of the quilt frame. One of the ladies must have forgotten them during the last quilting circle meeting.

"In the barn fire," I said. "How old were you then?"

"Five! I was only five." He narrowed his eyes, taking another step toward me. "You do know about the fire. You do know everything."

"Not everything." I braced my hands on my knees. "But I do know the fire was an accident," I said. "One that Griffin regretted the rest of his life."

"What do you know of it?" he snapped.

I held up my hands. "Everyone I talked to said how careful Griffin was. They said that he regretted an accident in his past. I thought it was Kamon Graber's death—and maybe that was part of it—but I think it was what happened to your family too. After that happened, he really started to take protocols more seriously."

Behind him, Mattie reached the scissors and began cutting away at the duct tape that tethered her to the chair.

Eban began to pace. Mattie made eye contact with me. I gestured with my eyes to the back room. I hoped that she would get the hint to take Oliver and run when she broke loose. I would get out of the shop another way.

"Because of Griffin, I had to become the man in my family at age five, and my mother had to take my sisters and me back to her community. It is not a *gut* place. The Amish there were strict. The bishop is cruel. I saw him whip a man for the length of his hair. I was on the receiving end of his punishments as well. My mother thought that by marrying my father she had escaped that harsh district, but with my father's death, she had to return to it with her children. Over the years, I saw the bright and happy mother I knew as a child pull into herself and away from my sisters and me. And it was all because of all the loss she had suffered."

"Eban, I'm sorry your bishop is cruel, but Griffin didn't cause that."

"Yes, he did," he bellowed, taking two steps toward me with the knife outstretched. "If he hadn't murdered my father, I would have grown up in a loving district, and I would have had both of my parents. My mother might as well be dead and my father most certainly is."

Mattie, now free from the duct tape, stood up. I took care not to look at her as she stepped around the chair. But as she turned, she bumped the edge of the quilt frame with her hip and it made a screeching sound across the wooden floor.

Eban spun around at the noise. "Stop!" he bellowed.

I jumped out of the chair and picked it up and whacked Eban in the side with it. He staggered across the room into the wall of fabric. Half a dozen bolts of cloth from the shelving fell onto his head. The knife flew from his hand and skittered across the room in front of the display window.

"Mattie, get Oliver and go out the back!" I cried, and ran for the knife below the window.

Mattie hesitated for a second, and then ran to the stockroom door. She threw it open and Oliver raced to me.

I grabbed the knife. "Oliver, no," I cried. "Go with Mattie!"

The little Frenchie pulled up short, obviously confused by my command. It was long enough for Mattie to grab him and run out the back door. I was weak with relief.

Eban struggled to his feet while I was distracted by Oliver and charged at me. I didn't notice until he was almost upon me. I jumped to the side, and Eban crashed through the front window of Running Stitch.

Eban's body hung halfway out of the window. He was badly cut. Gingerly, I picked my way to him. He was lying on his stomach and was still breathing. Thank God. I removed my phone from his pocket and called 911. And related what happened as quickly as possible.

The street was filling up as shopkeepers, customers, and the remaining Bigfooters came out of the shops up and down the street to see what all the commotion was about. Mattie ran into view around the side of Running Stitch still holding Oliver.

The sirens approached and I let out a breath because I knew Mitchell was coming.

Epilogue

The day after Eban held Mattie and me hostage in Running Stitch was a Sunday, so at least the shop was already closed regardless of whether or not I had a front window. Early that morning, Oliver and I went into the shop to clean up. I sighed as I unlocked the door, turned on the lights, and surveyed the mess. I left the front door wide-open. In the morning light, I was relieved to see that nothing was seriously broken other than the front window, of course.

Before we left the night before, Mattie and I had swept up most of the glass, and Old Ben had come down the street from his woodshop with a large piece of wood to cover the worst of the broken window.

I grabbed a broom and began to sweep just in case there was a speck of glass that we might have missed.

Jonah walked through the open door, holding a casserole dish in his hands.

"Jonah?" I asked. "What are you doing here? It's Sunday. Shouldn't you be in church?"

"Oh, Angie," he smiled. "Do you not remember the

passage in Luke when Jesus was in the home of a
Pharisee on the Sabbath and cured an ill man? The
Pharisees thought Jesus should not heal on the Sabbath
Day, but Jesus told them it was like rescuing an ox that
had fallen into a pit on the holy day. Some work must
be completed on the Sabbath out of necessity."

"I must have missed that one," I said.

He chuckled. "To *Gott*, I think fixing your window
would qualify as an ox in the pit."

I smiled, and nodded at the dish in his hand. "And
what would God say about that?"

"Oh, this? It's breakfast casserole. Miriam asked me
to bring it to you."

"Miriam did?" I whispered.

"*Ya.*" His smile widened. "She and I are both so
grateful for what you did. You put your life at risk to
prove my innocence."

I took the casserole from his hands and set it on the
cutting table. "Please thank Miriam for me."

"Miriam says you are welcome in our home anytime."

I blinked back tears. "I'm glad. How is Eban?" I asked.

"The doctors say he will be all right. Most of his
cuts were minor. It could have been much worse for
him. When he's released from the hospital, the deputies will take him straight to the county jail."

"I'm glad that he's going to be all right. I still sort
of like him. If his life had gone differently, I truly
believe he would have been a different person."

He broke eye contact. "I need to ask your forgive-
ness, Angie. If it hadn't been for me, none of this would
have happened. I was the one who brought Eban Hoch

into our lives. If it had not been for me, he would not have come at all."

I shook my head. "If it had not been through you, Jonah, Eban would have found another way to kill Griffin. He was so bitter over what happened to his family."

Jonah looked down. "I am ashamed to say that I understand how he felt. You know I idolized Kamon because he was brave. He saw the world not as a litany of rules passed down by our church leaders but as an opportunity. For Kamon, anything was possible. I think that was why I was so affected by his death. When he died, those possibilities for me died with him and were buried along with him in his grave." He took a breath. "That's where I was the morning Griffin died, after I dropped the drunken man off in Millersburg and before I went to your parents' home."

"Where?" I asked.

"Kamon's grave. I just had the yearning to visit it again after seeing Griffin. I know Kamon isn't there. I know he's not on this Earth, but I felt I needed to be there. I had to tell my cousin that it was time to let my anger over his death go. Seeing Griffin showed me that."

"Why didn't you tell Mitchell this?" I asked, barely above a whisper.

He shook his head. "No one was there. No one saw me, so it didn't matter if I told the police where I was or was not. It was too private. I didn't want it to become some part of English law and record, to be recorded and be asked about over and over again."

I tightened my grip on the casserole dish. "Thank you for telling me now."

He nodded. "I know Miriam has been unkind to you. That is my fault. When Kamon was alive, I had once thought—"

I shook my head. "Jonah, that's all in the past. Don't say whatever it is because it's no longer true. We're both different people now who are happy with our lives." I paused. "I'm happy and grateful to be your friend. That's more than enough."

He smiled. "I am glad, my friend, so very glad." He cleared his throat. "I should get to work replacing that window. I have a pane of glass in my wagon."

As Jonah replaced the window and I cleaned up more broken glass, there was a knock on the door. I set my broom against the fabric shelves and opened the door to find Linda standing there with an enormous roaster in her hands.

"This is for you," she said.

I took it from her and set it on the cutting table. "Thank you."

She nodded at the roaster. "There's a full chicken in there, roasted with lemon, rosemary, and other herbs. It will make a nice Sunday meal for you."

"I'm sure it will. Jonah's wife sent over a casserole, so I'm all set. I'm just not sure I'll be able to eat it all."

The chicken smelled heavenly. Oliver was already circling the cutting table as if he was in a remake of *Jaws* and he was the shark.

"I assumed that you would share it with Zander and the sheriff."

"I will," I promised.

She smiled. "I'm glad. I can't stay," she said quickly.

"The cook is holding down the diner while I'm gone. He can only take pouring coffee for so long before he wants to run back to the kitchen."

I laughed.

"I just want to say thank you for all you've done." She patted her beehive as if to make sure it was still intact. "The chicken was the least I could do. I spoke with Blane last night, and we're planning a small memorial service for Griffin next week. I would like you to be there and bring the sheriff."

"We'll both be there," I said. "And you and Blane will be seeing more of each other?"

"I'm hopeful." She gave a small smile. "Cameron starts working in the diner as a busboy next week. He wants to save up money to go out to Hollywood."

"Blane is okay with that?" I asked.

"He didn't forbid it." She smoothed the sleeve of her waitressing uniform. "It's a start."

"A good start." I gave her a hug.

After Jonah and Linda left, it didn't take me long to put the shop back in order. I stood in the middle of Running Stitch, happy to see there was no indication of the violence that had happened there the day before.

Oliver woofed and waddled to the front door just in time to meet Tux there. Mitchell and Zander followed their dog inside. The two dogs and boy bound through the shop and out the back door into the garden.

Mitchell stood in front of me. "I thought we'd come by and help you clean up, but it looks like you have the job well in hand."

"Jonah was here earlier. He fixed the window. I should be open tomorrow."

"I have no doubt that you will." He cleared his throat. "I can't believe I wasn't here for you yesterday." His jaw twitched.

I touched his cheek. "You were saving lives on the other side of the county. That's important."

He covered my hand with his. "You're more important to me, and there's something I have to tell you."

"What is it?" I dropped my hand.

Before he could answer, the shop door opened again and a fit-looking and very tan older couple walked inside.

"What a charming shop you have," the woman said. Her eyes were the same unique blue-green color as Mitchell's.

Mitchell gave me a half smile. "My parents are here. They wanted to meet you as soon as possible." He lowered his voice. "I put them off as long as I could."

"Oh," I said, and then I remembered my manners. "Hello, Mr. and Mrs. Mitchell. It's so nice to finally meet you."

Mitchell's mother smiled. "You too, dear, but we aren't much for formality. Please call me Ivy."

"And call me Luke," her husband said in a booming voice.

"All right," I said, unsure I would be able to do it.

Mitchell's mother walked up to me and gave me a tight hug. "You have made my James happier than I have ever seen him." She placed a hand on my cheek. "I'm so grateful for that."

"As am I," Mitchell's father said.

"He has made me happier than I have ever been too," I managed to say.

Over his mother's head, I saw Mitchell watching us with a silly grin on his face.

"Then it is a perfect match." She beamed.

"Grandma! Grandpa!" Zander called through the open back door. "Come see the backyard!"

Mitchell's mother smiled. "I hate to leave you so soon, Angie, but I can never say no to that boy. We'll have plenty of time to get to know each other over the next few days. I'm looking forward to meeting your parents and your friends in the quilting circle too. James has told us so much about all of them."

I nodded dumbly, and Oliver toddled into the shop through the back door as the elder Mitchells were heading out. Mitchell's father leaned over and patted Oliver on the head. "This must be the famous Oliver that we have heard so much about. My, you are a fine-looking chap."

Oliver licked his hand.

I found myself grinning as Mitchell's father followed his wife outside to join their grandson.

Oliver ran over to me and leaned against my leg.

"That wasn't so bad, was it?" Mitchell asked.

I met his aquamarine eyes, the eyes that I had fallen in love with the first time I'd seen them, even if I didn't know it then. "No, it wasn't." I smiled.

"I'm glad. I told you I wanted you to meet my parents before we moved forward."

My pulse quickened.

"And now that you have, I can't wait any longer." He removed a small square box from his jacket pocket. Even before he opened it, I knew there was a diamond ring inside.

And in the Amish quilt shop I'd inherited from my beloved aunt, I said "Yes" with Oliver at my side.

Quilted Tulip Pot Holder

By Angela Braddock, Owner of Running Stitch

Spring is in the air, and the many tulips that are popping in the Amish and English gardens all over Holmes County are my favorite signs of the season. To celebrate the arrival of spring, my quilt shop assistant at Running Stitch, Mattie Miller, created this adorable quilted tulip pot holder and asked me to share it with my readers. You can use the steps below to make the pot holder at home or feel free to stop by Running Stitch, located in picturesque Rolling Brook, and join one of our many quilting classes, where we will give you one-on-one instruction. You will see this pot holder is just the practical decoration to brighten your kitchen this spring.

Supplies

Fabric
Scissors
Thread
Needle
Cotton batting

Step One

Cut six petals from a fabric of your choice. The petals should be at least nine inches long and four inches wide. Take care to make the petals uniform in size and shape.

Step Two

Take three of the petals and sew them together in a tulip blossom shape. This is one side of your tulip pot holder. Repeat this step with the other three petals. Match it to the same pattern as the first side.

Step Three

Cut a piece of cotton batting to the shape of the tulip.

Step Four

Place the two fabric petals together with the "good" sides touching and sew around the edges. Leave a hole large enough in the seam for the batting and then turn the tulip inside out so that the "good" sides are now on the outside.

Step Five

Tuck the batting into the tulip through the hole you left in the seam and sew closed.

Step Six

Quilt a waves pattern across your pot holder to hold the batting and two pieces of fabric together. You're done!

Read on for a sneak peek of

PROSE AND CONS,

a Magical Bookshop Mystery
written by Isabella Alan
writing as Amanda Flower.
Coming in December 2016.

The petite teenage girl stood in front of the display of sports biographies that was tucked away in a small corner of the bookshop Charming Books, which I co-owned with my grandma Daisy in the village of Cascade Springs, New York. The girl chewed on her lip.

I set down the stack of fall-themed picture books, decorated with smiling pumpkins and mischievous squirrels, and held on to the top of one of the lower bookshelves a few feet from her. "Can I help you?" I asked in my most polite bookseller voice. The trick was to sound friendly and helpful, not too eager for a sale.

The girl turned to me, and tears glistened in her big green eyes. "I don't know. I'm supposed to pick up a birthday present for my boyfriend's father. It's his birthday, and the party starts in a half hour. I'm doomed!"

"I'm sure he would love any book that you give him," I said encouragingly. "It's the thought that counts, right?"

She shook her head, and her brown hair covered her face. "You don't know his parents. They're horrible.

Nothing I do is right. I just want them to like me or at least pretend to."

I straightened a row of books that sat unevenly on the shelf. I wouldn't be the least bit surprised if Grandma Daisy had moved the books just a little to drive me crazy. She and I had different ideas on the proper way to keep the books organized. I wanted everything in its place, preferably in alphabetical order. Grandma Daisy was satisfied if the books were on the correct floor of the shop. She always said the books would find the person who needed them most, no matter where they were shelved in the shop, so precision didn't matter. That might be literally true in Charming Books, but still, the alphabetizer in me couldn't handle the lackadaisical shelving method. After the books' spines were all sitting precisely at the edge, I said, "That sounds familiar."

She wrinkled her nose. "What does that mean?"

I gave her a half smile. "My high school boyfriend's parents didn't like me either."

"What would they have bad to say about you?" She blinked at me. "You're so tall and pretty."

I chuckled. "Being tall isn't everything. Neither is being pretty. That's sweet of you to say that I am, though. You're a beautiful girl, so if that argument doesn't work for you, it most certainly wouldn't work for me."

She blushed at the compliment and said, "If your boyfriend's parents didn't like you, I really am in trouble. Maybe I should just go to his birthday party empty-handed. Why waste my money when it's not going to do any good?"

"Maybe you just need to let your subconscious pick the book," I said.

She wrinkled her smooth brow. "What do you mean?"

"Close your eyes and reach for the books. I think the right book will find you."

She gave me a dubious look.

I shrugged. "It's just a hunch. What do you have to lose?"

"Oh-kay." Her voice was still heavy with doubt.

While the girl's eyes were closed, I watched as a book flew across the shop from the history section and later appeared in her hand.

Her eyes snapped open, and she stared at a tome with Abraham Lincoln on the cover. "How did this get in the sports section?"

"Oh," I said unconcernedly, "it must have been misplaced. Would you prefer a sports-related title?" I moved to take the book from her.

"No!" She jerked the book away from me and held it to her chest. "No, this is perfect. His father is a history buff, and I've seen a picture of Lincoln in his office. I'm only afraid he might have already read this one."

I fought to hide a smile. "I'm pretty sure he hasn't read it."

"How do you know?" She stared up at me with those big green eyes again.

"Call it bookseller intuition." I smiled.

She hugged the book more tightly to her chest. "This is the right book. I just know it. Thank you so much . . ." She trailed off.

"Violet," I said.

"Thank you, Violet. You really saved my life with this."

"Happy to help. Let's ring you up then, so you can make that party." I led her across the room to the sales counter.

Faulkner, the shop crow, walked across the counter. His talons made a clicking sound on the aged wood. I clapped my hands at him, and he flew over the girl's head, cawing, "Four score and seven years ago!"

The girl ducked, and her eyes went round. "Was the crow quoting the Gettysburg Address? Does he know about this book?"

I forced a laugh. "We've been playing a lot of historical audiobooks in the shop lately. He must have picked it up from there."

While she reached in her purse for her wallet, I glared at Faulkner, who landed on one of the low branches of the birch tree. The crow smoothed his silky black feathers with his sharp beak and ignored me. I wondered where my tuxedo cat, Emerson, had gone off to. He usually was able to keep the crow in line. Also it was never a good sign when Emerson wandered off. The cat was up to something or wandering around the neighborhood. I hadn't yet figured out how to keep him in the shop. His previous owner had taken him all around town.

She swiped her credit card through the machine.

"Would you like me to gift wrap the book for you?"

"Can you? That would be great and would save me so much time. I'm already running late as it is."

"Of course." I cut off a piece of brown paper stamped

with orange and red leaves from the roll behind the counter.

After the girl took the newly wrapped biography out of the store, I locked the door behind her and winked at the birch tree that grew in the middle of the bookshop. A spiral staircase led up to the second floor of Charming Books, where the children's fairy-book loft and my one-room apartment were. My ancestress Rosalee had built the original house, which had been remodeled and expanded a number of times over the last two centuries by other relatives, around the birch tree when she had bought the land after the War of 1812. "Nice work." I gave the tree a thumbs-up.

My seventy-something grandmother, who with her trim figure could easily pass for a woman of half her age if it weren't for the sleek silver bob that fell to her chin, came around the side of the tree, shaking her head. "Violet, my dear, you are becoming a little showy with helping customers choose books. What if another customer was in here when you pulled that stunt? It would not do for them to see books flying across the shop." As usual, she wore jeans and a Charming Books sweatshirt, which was orange that day in celebration of the nearness of Halloween. To complete the outfit, she had added a gauzy infinity scarf decorated with cheerful jack-o'-lanterns.

"Grandma Daisy, it's after seven. The shop was supposed to close fifteen minutes ago. There was no one else here."

"Still, you need to be careful." She tucked a lock of silver hair behind her ear. "Remember, the most important job of the Caretaker is to keep the shop's secret. No one outside of the family can know."

"Four months ago you were arguing with me because I didn't believe in the shop's essence. Now I'm in trouble because I do and make use of it." I couldn't keep the whine out of my voice. I knew I sounded like a stubborn four-year-old, and I knew it wasn't attractive on a woman nearing her thirtieth birthday.

Grandma Daisy adjusted her cat's-eye glasses on her nose. "You're not in trouble. I just want you to remember your duty as the Caretaker." She turned and headed in the direction of the kitchen, which was separated from the shop by a thick swinging door.

Like I could forget? Being the Caretaker of the huge Queen Anne Victorian house and the birch tree that grew in the middle of it had been a duty of the women in my family for the last two hundred years. Ever since Rosalee watered the tree with the mystical and healing waters from the local natural springs. After a time, the water manifested itself in the shop and the books, and now the essence of the water was able to communicate with the Caretaker through cryptic messages sent through the books themselves. Trust me. I know how unbelievable that sounds. I hadn't believed it myself when my grandmother tricked me by pretending to be sick into returning to the village to take over being the Caretaker. Considering the stunt she had pulled over the summer, she should really be glad that I have embraced what she called my "duty."

My mother should have been the Caretaker after my grandmother was relieved of her post, but fate had other plans. My mother died tragically when I was only thirteen. As a result, the Caretakership skipped a generation and landed directly on my shoulders. Since I had no children, female or otherwise, it was unknown what would happen to the shop when it was time for me to pass it on to the next generation. I would love to have a child . . . someday, but no woman in my family line had been able to keep a long-lasting relationship. Raising a child without a father wasn't what I wanted for me or my fictitious child. It's how I grew up, how all the women in the Waverly family had grown up. I pushed those melancholy thoughts aside and rolled my eyes at Grandma Daisy's receding back.

"I saw you roll your eyes at me," Grandma Daisy called over her shoulder.

"The essence doesn't give you the ability to see out of the back of your head," I countered.

She glanced over her shoulder. "How do you know? You've only been the Caretaker for a few months. How do you know everything the essence can and cannot do?" Before I could think of a smart remark, she said, "Don't you have some cookies to be picked up from La Crêpe Jolie for the Poe-try Reading tomorrow?"

I smacked myself on the forehead. "Oh, right, I forgot. I'll go collect them now."

She nodded. "The Red Inkers should be here by the time you return. Be careful. The traffic will be horrid on River Road with the start of the Food and Wine Festival tomorrow."

"I'll be careful," I promised. The Cascade Springs Food and Wine Festival was the biggest event for the small village, which depended on tourism for its survival. The festival was held annually the third week of October. This year, at my urging, Charming Books was participating in the festivities by hosting a Poe-try Reading, highlighting the work and life of master of the macabre, Edgar Allan Poe. I couldn't think of a more perfect author to showcase this close to Halloween. Thankfully, Grandma Daisy seemed to welcome the idea, especially since I was able to recruit the help of the Red Inkers, a local writers' group whose members regularly met in Charming Books after shop hours to discuss their work.

I grabbed my coat from the coat tree by the kitchen door. "I should be going, then."

"Don't be too long. I know *everyone* in the group is looking forward to seeing you," she said in a teasing voice.

This time I rolled my eyes to her face so there was no mistaking it. Grandma Daisy's bell-chime laugh rang through the empty shop, and Faulkner joined in on the chuckle fest. Her comment about the group wanting to see me was much more pointed than it sounded. She'd implied—not so subtlety, might I add—Chief of Village Police David Rainwater wanted to see me.

The truth was, I was looking forward to seeing him too.